CYBER BOMB

BY

Jim Jackson

Published by
Goodness Me Publishing Limited

http://www.goodnessmepublishing.co.uk

CONTENTS

Page

Prologue

It was more than an almost new automatic pistol to him. It was his father's pistol. A little used, Bersa 40 which he had brought back as a souvenir from his service in the Falklands conflict. Growing up he had often seen it in a drawer of his father's desk. Against all instructions not to pry, there was not a corner of that small house he had not explored. He had known, for some time where the magazine and ammunition were hidden, but he could never find the nerve to introduce one to the other.

Perhaps his father had been correct in his secret disappointment in him. Both father and son were propense to keep their emotions under wraps.

But having said that, if he had had any desire to earn his parents' love and respect, he did nothing to earn them. In spite of his practised and polished feigned indifference there were, in those early days clues and signs of an emotional concoction which once brought near to boiling, simmered and festered, never far below the surface of his mind, but never at that critical temperature at which the pressure might have at first fractured his grasp upon reality and then exploded. A prescient observer, however, might have noted that such an eruption would not have been too far distant.

With the passing of long slow adolescent years, the beneficent touch of friend or lover might have soothed and calloused over the hurt, which is almost universal amongst the bright but alienated yet he had neither. He looked deeply inside but seldom, for to do so exposed to his mind's eye the full extent of his social ineptitude and selfish inadequacy, which, had he had the courage to probe, painful as it might be, a little deeper he might have discovered himself to be just another lost and tormented human being .

CYBER BOMB

Long service professional soldiers live in a different world from the rest of us. Frequently, they marry young and spend a lot of time away from home. Their mates, the unit, the battalion becomes their family. A soldier had to sublimate his notions of rank and discipline whilst at home. Home was an alien regiment where unwritten rules take time to assimilate. So it was that what his father regarded as a laid back, calm tolerance was received as thinly veiled contempt for him, his weak son.

On a dull grey afternoon in late November after his father's funeral he went home to his untidy flat and sat on his bed and drank Red Bull and vodka. Things would be different now. A raw naked power seemed to flow from his father's souvenir automatic pistol which spread like St Elmo's fire over his entire body.

Where celibacy and solitude might make one man a poet and a philosopher it may just as easily drive another man mad until at one and the same time, he might wish to control the world and yet destroy everything. But all that was for another day.

The world which he ruled now was a room five metres by four. To move from bed to door involved an assault course around dirty dishes of half eaten meals, beer cans, pornographic magazines, odd shoes, and trainers. Amid all this stench and squalor were pile upon pile of books. Textbooks which rose like stalagmites upon diverse subjects which included computer science, telecommunications, electronics, internet fraud and banking, principles, and practice. Global economics and the finance of emerging nations. On top of one such pile, nearest the bed, his latest acquisition. Paul Messervy's encyclopaedic *Soviet Decline, Disintegration, and the Birth of the Oligarchy.* A wooden coffee stirrer marked the page containing a brief biography of Andrei Vostok – Brevet KGB Colonel now living in comfortable exile in London.

He caressed his father's pistol with a sensuous gentleness approaching reverence. In another time and place it might have been called a fetish. Superficially masculine, but assuredly feminine – all powerful, a goddess of distinction - like the Indian Blood Goddess Kali crying out to be satiated. But that would be too simple, too manifestly human.

He pulled back the slide and let it snap forward with an evocative metallic thud and placed the muzzle to his pursed lips. The smell of the Parker Hale gun oil an erotic invitation to embrace his destiny. He squeezed the trigger and the hammer crashed down the firing pin disappointed by an empty chamber.

He laughed at the fragility, stupidity, waste, and impermanence of existence.

Tomorrow it would start.

With the pistol in the waistband of his trousers he caught a bus, then a train and finally the underground. The tube train carriage was crowded and at Green Park Station there was a great tightly packed shuffling towards the doors. With his arms pinned to his side in the crush he felt the pistol move. Just a little at first, a little more. Then with a rush it went all the way down his left trouser leg to slip silently upon the floor of the carriage. When the shuffle of feet had passed several men moved to retrieve it. It was swiftly picked up and after a momentary inspection was dropped with a clunk into a bag of builders' tools.

Some of the men who had seen the gun thought to move but thought again when the gaze of builder Sean Jones fell upon them. He was huge and he was ugly. Moreover, he had a bag full of heavy and sharp instruments. In addition, he now had a gun. A gun he was years later to use in the intimidation, abduction, rape, and murder of a young and highly talented young violinist.

Out on the platform the man who dropped the gun turned in panic to see someone pick it up and was still looking at it intensely as the doors closed and the train pulled away.

It was not an auspicious start to a project that was destined to change the world forever.

In fact, his talisman brought to him no more luck than it brought to the Argentinian who first owned it.

Andrei Vostok sat quietly at a window table in the Ritz as he did every Thursday afternoon. Sometimes he took tea with a business associate, other times with a well-dressed woman young enough to be his daughter. Mostly he enjoyed this little ceremony alone although his driver-come-bodyguard, Zoran, would always be within calling distance. One afternoon in late spring a poorly dressed young man in a cheap suit and a greasy tie, having got past the liveried doorman by some subterfuge, invited himself to the table and sat down uninvited.

"Mr Vostok, I have a business proposal which I feel you will find irresistible," he said with more confidence than he felt since his talisman pistol had abandoned him on the central line.

"Then you should write to me at my office and not disturb my refreshments," is what Vostok sharply said in reply, but his raised eyebrows gave the signal to Zoran to remove this uninvited guest.

"You would not wish your employees to know anything of my proposal. It would be too dangerous to both of us.

"Even so Mr er ..."

The minder cast his huge shadow over the proceedings but paused momentarily. The visitor made ready to rise but as he did so he leaned over the table and whispered, "ZURICH 18121878."

Vostok's whole body stiffened and his demeanour changed. What an interesting thing to say Mr— sorry I did not catch your name?"

"Brian Phipps. I see that my words are not lost on you. You see I know all about you and your various interests. Might I have a cup of tea and a piece of that cake? I must say it looks most tasty." He took a large piece, which he bit into before moving on in a casual tone which surprised even himself.

"It really is so extraordinarily nice here don't you think?" he said looking around like an out of town country bumpkin totally fascinated by the style and richness of it all.

"Opulent. That would be my word for it. Bourgeois decadence you would have called all this just a few years ago, yet here we are sipping tea and eating some of these excellent cakes. How the world changes."

"You skate on very thin ice, my friend. I do not know how you have managed to become so interested in my affairs, but it is a most unhealthy preoccupation. What is it you hope to gain from such audacity? Money perhaps? Blackmail is it?"

Brian Phipps did not look like the sort of person to bate the Russian bear over a starched white tablecloth, but nevertheless he had somehow managed to acquire the access code to one of his Swiss bank accounts. If he had that he might very well have found a way into his safe deposit boxes also and who knows what else besides.

"Calm yourself, sir. Please, and ask your man here to leave us in peace for a few moments and I will explain."

With a slight twitch of the head the minder was stood down.

"Everything these days is recorded on computers somewhere as you know. Protected by complex codes cyphers and encryptions.

"These systems are about as secure as human ingenuity can make them. But, what one man can devise, another, given the right resources can unscramble and bend to his will. Some systems are easier than others to overcome but with the right equipment and software, money can be moved from one account to another with lightning speed. Nothing new in this but every transaction leaves its footprint behind and the authorities are hot on the trail of this kind of irregularity. Until now that is. I have a system which leaves no trace. No, that is not true, it leaves a million, ten million traces behind. I will explain further if we can become partners."

"That is all very well, Mr Phipps but it sounds rather risky. I am a visitor in this country and wish to remain so, I like it here. I do not know what British prisons are like, but you may be sure I have no wish to find out. Please finish your tea. Good afternoon."

"Yes I thought that you might say that, Mr Vostok, so I have arranged to deposit a certain sum of money in your private account with Lombard Odier whose offices are just a short walk from where we sit now.

"When you have checked with your bank, we shall have tea here again. Shall we say the same time next week? Nice to have met you. Good afternoon."

Andrei Vostok was one of the KGB's newest colonels having received his promotion barely a month before the Soviet Union imploded. Older and wiser heads of department had seen the writing on the wall long since and staked very firm claims to that country's oil, gas, energy, and significant productive resources. He did not leave empty handed however but all the ripe fruit had gone.

He was, notwithstanding the fickle winds of misfortune, still a rich man, even by the standards of the western world yet he yearned to be up there with the mega rich.

The diminutive Galina, former gymnast and would-be pop star, skipped lightly out of the huge circular bed in a froth of transparent pink night attire whilst the waking Andrei wished for the thousandth time that he was still young enough to take fuller and more frequent advantage of this blonde sprite now making coffee with the state of the art Italian machinery that now hissed and gurgled in his expensively equipped kitchen in his expensively furnished West Kensington apartment.

As was usual, and in compensation of his faltering masculine powers, his mind turned to matters of business and still in his silk bath robe he sat down at his laptop computer to see what developments had taken place during the night.

There were, he instantly noticed, an astounding number of transactions recorded on his principle account.

As though drawn by a magnet, sums large and small were being attracted to his business. This was indeed strange. Galina brought in his coffee which she placed by his elbow, but it was ignored, untouched and quickly went cold. He swore several times in Muscovite slang, but not with displeasure, quite the opposite.

He quickly pulled himself together and a fresh coffee, croissant and shower later was on the phone to his accountant, a well-paid and cadaverous Chartered Accountant called Morris Rabin.

10

Within the hour he was sitting across from Morris at his desk in his Baker Street offices.

"Well Andi – it's all valid enough," he said.

"Although these reference numbers, which relate to these transactions, appear to be theirs and not yours. Look at this, all with the same date and time signature. Adjusted for the various time zones, of course, and from all over the world. What do you make of this? Indiana Grain and Feed Corporation have paid to you fifty US Dollars. Wellington Wool Exporters in New Zealand send fifty pounds – Sterling. Atlantic Gulf Oil; fifty thousand dinars. Toys for Pets in Bristol ten pounds 99p and so it goes on. None of it makes any sense. It's all like that, all over the place, and you say that you never did business with any of these people? The only common factor is you."

"Never heard of most of them."

"Well something must be going on that you don't know about. Somebody wants to see that you receive one million pounds. Which is what all these irregular amounts add up to. One million exactly."

"What if they ask for their money back?"

"I suspect that they will not but if they do, we must pay them. But I can't see the New Jersey Paint and Custom Auto Shop sending in the heavy mob for $18.60 cents, can you? Probably not even aware of it until their next audit. These larger amounts look to have real reference numbers. My guess is that it represents a real payment to God alone knows who, been duplicated and somehow has ended up here. Let us suppose that we must return three quarters of the funds here. Yes. Then firstly we have had an interest free loan of £750.000 for however long it takes for them to get their act together and in all probability a gift of £250.000. Free gratis and for nothing, written off in various small amounts as accounting errors."

Greatly relieved, Vostok rose to leave.

"Before you go Andi, my advice to you, which is what you pay me huge sums of money for, is this. That you should run that particular account down to nothing. If the money is no longer there, they will be hard pushed to reclaim it. Move the money in dribs and drabs to other accounts of which you have several and do it quickly.

"If somebody wishes to take matters beyond just asking and starts talking about starting legal proceedings, you must ask for supporting paperwork, an evidence trail in fact. Something which will be difficult for them to substantiate and after a while, which might be years, they will stop bothering you. You mark my words; this is a gift scenario whichever way you look at it."

Greatly relieved in his own mind Vostok turned at the door. They shook hands as it opened, and a petite secretary stepped in holding a print-out of an email in her hand.

"Message for you, Mr Vostok."

He took it, not snatching it from her hand exactly but almost. Nobody knew to find him here at this hour. It read:

"I hope that we can now be friends and cooperate See you on Thursday for tea, usual place Brian"

It is cynically, if reluctantly, recognised that for reasons lost in our evolutionary past, genius and madness are closely related and never more so than in the singular person of Brian Phipps.

It might have been speculated that his remarkable mental powers developed from his childhood because of his family circumstances and social ineptitude.

He was known, whilst at school, as Reg for his resemblance to mass murderer Reginald Christie, which was an apt description, if somewhat unkind. Children can be so cruel, sometimes very cruel, leaving behind mental scars which in some cases take a lifetime to fade away to almost nothing, but still echoes remain.

Small, bespectacled, and prematurely bald, he never discovered the gift of friendship on any level. Men regarded him as prurient and treated him, as far as a workplace environment would allow, with a cool indifference. Women greeted his overtures with a contemptuous disdain little short of rudeness. To children, with the uncanny prescience of innocence he was frightening. To the elderly he came across as vulgar, impertinent, aggressive, and thoroughly unpleasant.

Perhaps, in one respect at least, we all ought to take a share in his nascent socio-pathology. Be that as it may, we now must live with the consequences of whatever part our consciousness did, or did not, directly play in the events which unfolded as his plan came to fruition.

Things were better companions than people he rationalized. You knew where you were with things. There was, or indeed is, a constancy in electronics. Volts and amps will be the same tomorrow as they are today, as they were yesterday, as they will always be and yet in the right hands, guided by the right mind, electrons, upon a ballroom floor of silicone, could be made to dance to almost any tune. Never had a dictator such powerful and willing slaves. Go here, do this, stop that, change this, remember, and now forget.

He would show them. He would have satisfaction. He would have his revenge. If they could live without him, he could most certainly live without them. As a result of his education, his experiences with BT and IBM, and more importantly several subsequent years' service with mobile phone companies, a map of the world and its numerous weaknesses unfolded before him.

It was this map which gave him the battle order of his troops, already armed and poised for an invisible Blitzkrieg the like of which the world had never known. He had his Sturmabteilung primed and ready. All he needed now was a mechanism by which he could procure his Vergeltungswaffe weapons and his Panzer tanks, and for this he needed an ally.

In a new suit and tie, Brian Phipps walked through the tearoom at the Ritz with a renewed confidence. He knew that he had his reluctant ally now.

That Vostok had taken the bait was confirmed when he actually stood up to greet his guest as he approached his table. There was such a change in his appearance that Vostok couldn't but compliment him on his turnout.

"Nice suit, Brian."

"It ought to be, Mr Vostok, you paid for it. You look surprised. You shouldn't. I just gave you a million pounds, did you not think that I would want a little reward for myself?"

Incredulous he replied, "Is that all you wanted, a new suit of clothes? Is that what all this is about?"

"A new suit, and a shirt and tie. Overcoat and shoes too. Several changes of wardrobe in fact. A small price to pay for our friendship do you not think?"

"Very well, Mr Phipps, you have earned them but what I fail to understand my friend is why you need me. You magic up a million pounds out of thin air and instead of keeping it for yourself you give it away, and to me, a man you never knew existed a few weeks ago. Why?"

"Patience, Mr Vostok. Shall we have our tea first?"

"Ah you English and your tea, very well, let us turn our thoughts away from vulgar money and choose some cakes."

They drank their tea and ate their éclairs in silence. After all, what small talk could a madman and an ex-KGB officer have made together? Football, perhaps, but not this pair.

When they had finished the plate of cakes, Vostok continued.

"What puzzles me most is why you need me at all."

"That is easy to answer. Let us say, Mr Vostok, that were a million pounds to suddenly turn up in my current account what do you think would happen?"

Without waiting for a reply to this rhetorical question, he continued:

"Barclays Bank would raise the alarm and before you could sing a verse of the Volga Boatman, the tax authorities would be banging on my door demanding to know where the money came from. The drug squad too I shouldn't wonder, each putting my life and my files under the microscope, and it would not be long before they found a pathway to your door also. And we do not want that do we?"

Vostok shook his head. He had, he began to feel, underestimated this repulsive little man. A thought that frightened him, a man whose previous line of work was the wholesale distribution of fear. An unusual feeling indeed.

"But, Mr Vostok, if various small sums of money, even if cumulatively huge, were to pass in and out of the various companies you control, no one will think it at all odd or unusual."

"And that is your proposal is it? You want me to launder money for you. I really don't think so Mr—"

"Please allow me to finish, Mr Vostok. I do not want you to launder money for me. You keep all the money. But your business acumen is quite correct; I do want something, two things actually.

"Firstly, I wish to obtain some complex and very expensive pieces of computer hardware. You are to buy

15

this from the million pounds I have already given to you. To be delivered to a depot belonging to you from which my agents may collect without attracting attention. I cannot afford for it to be delivered directly to any place connected directly or indirectly to me.

"You said two things."

"To organise the million, you have already, has taken me a week to organise. If we are to make a lot more, I need the tools to do it. Not only will this be quicker, but the degrees of defence it affords will also be many times greater and it is pretty secure already."

"You said two things."

"Ha! Yes, I did, didn't I? I want a job with one of your companies."

"A job? What sort of job?"

"One where I do not have to go to the office. One where my salary can be paid into my everyday bank account. A salary upon which I can pay tax and National Insurance contributions just like any other wage slave. A job which keeps me below the radar horizon of the government spies."

"You have government spies in this country?"

"Yes, but not like in yours with your hit squads and exotic poisons. Don't worry about it. You need not concern yourself. This time next year you might well be one of the richest men in the world."

"And where will you be my friend, in prison?"

"Why should they suspect me? I shall have a steady job in a company owned by one of the richest men in the world, who will no doubt give me an excellent reference should one become necessary. I shall live in some comfort in an elegant mock Tudor house in Surrey some place; Guildford perhaps on the fifty thousand a year salary you shall pay me. I will be fireproof, and if I am, so are you."

"Tell me, there is one question burning in my mind ... why?"

"Why what?"

"Why are you going to so much trouble, dealing with such large sums of money for so little reward? It just makes no sense."

16

"There is, I must admit, an agenda I have not told you of and shall not tell you of, but suffice it to say that there are some companies, some people, who have wounded me grievously in the past and whom I wish to destroy financially, completely and utterly. Their crushing loss will be to you just a small additional gain."

"Do you have a list of the equipment of the items you require?"

Phipps handed over a sheaf of papers from his inside pocket.

"Are we to be partners in this venture, Mr Vostok?"

"Send me an email tomorrow afternoon, and I will give you my answer then. Farewell Mr Phipps."

CYBER BOMB

CHAPTER ONE

The computers at home and at the office had been behaving oddly for some time. Since Easter, at least, but nobody took much notice. Things did happen from time to time. Emails that were apparently never sent, or perhaps erased in a random order, which made no sense at all. On the long train journey from Maidstone to Victoria, one often heard muted curses and screeches as project reports and the drafts of long letters simply disappeared. On one occasion, the passengers witnessed a grown man burst into tears and throw his laptop the length of the carriage. With typical Home Counties insouciance, they did little more than raise an eyebrow before returning to their newspapers. We all felt like that sometimes, but were too cool to react upon the feeling, however much we might sympathize.

The internet milieu, over the last twenty years or so, like a humble but manipulative servant, had become such a part of our lives that we, that is to say the millennium generation, were unable to imagine, much less live, normal lives without it.

I had already postponed my annual holiday twice, but in two weeks' time I was off to Devon to view for the very first time the cottage left to me by my Uncle William who had died in the cold snap just after Christmas. He had lived alone and seemed to prefer the solitude. That is not to say that the old boy was antisocial or hostile to his family in any way, but he lived a fair distance away in a tight little world without computers, telephone, or television. Most nights he would walk or ride his old motorcycle the couple of miles or so to his local pub, *The Coach and Horses*, sit by a blazing fire, or prop up the bar and jaw to the locals. Sometimes he would be asked to clear a stripped thread or perform a spot of welding on a broken piece of machinery. As a boy, I found his stories enthralling. Stories about his time as a merchant seaman, and about his experiences as a fireman in London during the Blitz. He taught me a lot about the use of tools and how to weld with both gas and electricity which is, I suppose, why he entrusted me with the care of his old motorcycle and side-car when he died.

The first I knew of my legacy was one Saturday morning when a lorry drew up outside the house where I owned a flat. The lorry driver, as tall as he was broad, handed me a letter which brought a lump to my throat and an uncomfortable prickling in the eyes as I read its contents.

He had left everything he owned to me knowing that his other relatives wouldn't like it very much. "Serve them right," he had written. "That will teach them that I hadn't forgotten their behaviour."

Though what this long distant family feud was all about he didn't say, and I didn't care to enquire further. Most of my distant relatives were strangers to me now, so why stir up old animosities.

When the delivery driver had gone, I tentatively kicked the engine over and almost jumped out of my skin as it roared into life. It ran until the petrol in the float chamber ran out. The petrol tap was off, but the tank was half full.

There was only one person I could talk to about this, and that was Ginger Hutton, or Chock as we called him at school for no apparent reason. Chock was one of those people who could fix anything from a clock to a tractor. We had shared an interest in all things mechanical since our school days. If it was old, as well as mechanical, so much the

19

better. Only, whereas he took an engineering apprenticeship as indeed I wished to do, my father had other ideas and I was sent to work with his estate agent cousin, which -- as it happened – turned out rather satisfactorily, allowing me to diversify into antiques as well.

Chock and I, whilst not best buddies, kept in touch. He fixed my high mileage cars, and I secured the lease on his business premises.

I found him outside his lock up garage, a railway arch near Peckham Rye station. As I pulled up, I gave a long and unnecessary burst of throttle to attract his attention, for he had seen me coming.

"Well, well, well, what do we have here? Been raiding the bomb sites?"

"Bomb sites, Chock, when did you last see a bomb site? They are all high-rise council tower blocks now and some of them are so old they are being pulled down. Although some of them are so full of mischief they ought to be bombed."

"Model H or a Big 4, I should say. 1948, 49 or 50. I'm more of a Triumph man myself," he said, looking back into the dim interior of his garage towards his much cosseted Triumph T110.

"But these old Nortons have their charm, I suppose. Burning a bit of oil by the looks of it. Valve guides or rings. No horrible sounds, so I suppose the ends are all right. I have a set of cord piston rings about somewhere that ought to fit. A new spark plug and a bit of a de-coke and you ought to get a decent price for her. Well collected these things are nowadays."

"Sell her, Chock? Not a bit of it. I want to take her down to Devon next week to see what sort of dump the old bugger has left me in his will."

20

"Old bugger is it? When we were at school it was Uncle Bill says this and Uncle Bill says that. You worshipped that man. Without Uncle Bill you wouldn't know one end of a spanner from the other. You couldn't have told a valve lifter from a shirt lifter, or a spark plug from a bath plug. As it is you are not a bad mechanic. Not as good as me like, but better than most these days. If they can't plug in a computerized engine analyser, they are stumped big time. They have forgotten, if they ever knew in the first place, that it's their eyes and their ears that are the basis of any engineering repair work. End of next week you say. And I expect that you will want me to look at a few other things while I am at it. Brake shoes, oil and filters and stuff."

He paused and sucked air between his teeth the way that garage mechanics will.

"It's a tall order, I've a lot on at the moment, but OK, just for old time's sake mind you. You come back next Thursday, and we shall have to see. How about twenty-five quid on account? I'll get my boy Raymond stripping it down first thing tomorrow."

I gave him the money and he swung the big double doors to. They shut with a hollow thump and he put the big Chubb padlock in place. As he did so an elderly Daimler Sovereign drew alongside, and a grey-haired man leaned out of the driver's window.

"Ah, Mr Hutton. I hoped that I might catch you. Do you think that you might be able to get a new MoT certificate for me? I have to drive down to the Isle of Wight again next week and would be a whole lot happier if I knew that you had given it the once over first."

It was sleek and looked almost brand new, even though it was over half a century old. The red leather seats were immaculate. People who restore these old cars, sometimes spending thousands of pounds, often neglect to pay attention to the leather seats. To replace them would be prohibitively expensive. He saw me looking.

"Are you a Daimler owner yourself? You seem to have the inquisitive eye of a concours invigilator."

"No," I replied. "Always wanted one though, but you know how it is. First, it's one thing then another; wives, houses and mortgages. I was never in the right place financially at the right time. I have always been an admirer of designer Ed Turner's work."

"Sorry to have to correct you as we only just met, but this car was designed by William Lyons."

I smiled; it was pleasant to meet someone who knew a little about cars of this vintage.

"Quite true, but only the body. The V8 engine was designed by Ed Turner." The reason I remembered this little bit of auto trivia was a glimpse of Chock's Triumph T110 Motorcycle at the back of the workshop.

"The first Triumph twin cylinder engines were designed by Val Page, and Ed Turner took over from him as chief designer at Triumph. His engines eventually evolved into the 750 Bonneville, which was about as far as the layout could be pushed. It is a fascinating story but—"

"Yes, yes, we know all about that," interrupted Chock.

"Give this gentleman a little peace or we will be here all night. No problem, Mr Wyndham, just drop the keys in my letterbox when you are ready, and I will soon have it sorted out."

"Thank you, Mr Hutton. See you then."

With the effortless charm of a turning water wheel, the Daimler pulled away, purring softly.

"Well as long as it doesn't interfere with the work on my Norton that will be OK too, Mr Hutton," I said, with the emphasis on the 'Mister.

As he drove away, I turned to Chock, "Who was that? The Duke of Camberwell?"

"Don't tell me that you don't know who that was?"

I must have looked bewildered.

"That was Dr Jack Wyndham. He is on the telly all the time."

Once again it failed to register with me, and he saw it in my face.

"Dr Jack Wyndham, Professor of Futurology they call him. He has a midweek spot on which he talks about all sorts of interesting stuff from birth control to GM crops. Until a couple of months ago he was all for hi-tec solutions to everything, but just recently he has been going on as to how we should all take up basket weaving, clog making and herbal medicine. Stuff like that. A sort of up-market Ray Mears if you like. He has the reputation of being a bit of a genius, but a bit, oh I don't know, obsessive. Well, actually very obsessed. I am surprised that someone like you has never heard of him."

"Perhaps that's because I don't have a television. Not had one for donkeys' years now. What I have seen of it recently I don't like." And I left it at that.

What I might have said was that I was heartily sick of being spoon-fed puerile pre-masticated pap by left wing androgynous presenters in programmes designed for a shallow multicultural audience with the attention span of a kippered herring. Even the small doses one catches in pubs or people's homes made me nauseous. Instead of upsetting him, for he was a TV addict, I walked to the bus stop thinking of rolling hills, cream teas, pasties and country cottages with roses around the door. I was unable to suspend disbelief for long.

I knew exactly what to expect. Cobwebs, clutter, tools left to rust and a sink full of dirty dishes. Mice too I shouldn't wonder. As an estate agent I had seen dozens of similar places where an elderly relative had been left to rot all alone, and I felt rather ashamed. This was someone who had given me my first taste of scotch whisky, taught me to play darts and how to tell cast iron from cast steel from the sparks on a grindstone. I was in a pretty low state by the time I got off the bus. Perhaps behind all this dour grey sentimentality was the realisation that a similar fate awaited me in a couple of decade's time.

A couple of pints in *The Grapes* with the usual crowd did nothing to lift my spirits; neither did the bottle of whisky I bought on the way home. I was sinking into a mire of despondency in the armchair beside a cold grate, and its grim dirty waters were about to close above my head when I heard something on the radio which made the hairs on the back of my neck stand on end.

Had I forgotten to turn it off this morning? Had it turned itself on or had I switched it on without realising?

"This afternoon the prime minister at number 10 Downing Street met with representatives of the Banking and Telecoms industries, internet service providers and scientists from GCHQ to identify the source of the computer virus known as "MEDUSA". Its ability to infect electronic devices which are in contact, or in no more than close proximity to a mobile phone make this a potentially lethal threat to our security and our economy, but a Government Statement released, whilst we have been on air, advises that there is no need to panic, but as a precaution computers should be switched off for forty-eight hours as should mobile phones. Land lines should be unplugged and only used in an emergency. A Ministry of Defence spokesman, General Peter St-John Wilkes, said that all their systems had multiple layers of protection and that there was no cause for alarm. The UK's nuclear deterrent could not be activated without a human finger on the button. It could not be brought to readiness by a cyber-attack of any description."

Suddenly I was wide awake and as sober as if I had not just drunk almost a whole bottle of scotch on top of three, or was it four, pints of real ale.

I knew precious little about computers and even less about viruses, but I did know that biological ones can change in subtle ways to avoid destruction by the body's natural defences. Perhaps electronic ones might behave in a similar self -protecting way. Reason told me that whoever was behind an attack that was serious enough to concern Downing Street had considerable resources at his command and would not stop once started.

I turned my computer on for one last time to see my bank balance. Last night there was £1275 in my current account.

Tonight, there was £12750. I was not hard up by a long chalk but who keeps more money in a current account than is necessary for groceries, petrol and the like?

If it was still there the following morning when I visited my bank, I would draw out as much as they would allow and go shopping, for an idea was beginning to form in my mind which might turn out to be rubbish, of course, but the seed once planted in my imagination refused to go away.

If what I feared should turn out to be true, then the theft of a couple of thousand from Barclays Bank would be neither here nor there.

I told the bank clerk it was to buy a car and the seller wanted cash. Though I'll be damned if she had any right to know, or the impertinence to even ask, but they can hide a lot of unnecessary nosiness in the guise of money laundering regulations these days.

Amongst the stuff I brought that day was a sleeping bag. A gillie kettle, a Swiss army knife, motorcycle gloves, boots and a Belstaff jacket. About a ton of freeze dried ready to eat meals, and three jerry cans, and lots of other stuff too boring to mention like bandages and plasters, TCP, and aspirins.

There is a whole community of people out there calling themselves "Preppers" who have been stockpiling this sort of stuff for years. Most of them have cabins in the woods of rural America and are waiting with their guns and bear traps for zombies to attack, or until World War Three has blown over.

I, on the other hand, was going on holiday, pandering to a new personal paranoia, and taking along a few precautions just in case things did get worse. I fully expected that some nasty stuff was about to hit the fan, and I wanted to be well out of it, brushing away the cobwebs and cleaning the windows in Uncle Bill's little cottage.

Chock and his boy must have worked overtime on my behalf. Not only had he replaced the old glow-worm of a headlight with a modern quartz halogen one, but added two powerful spotlights, one of which was on a swivel mounted on the roof of the side-car. To power this extra illumination, he had wired in an auxiliary battery in the foot-well of the side-car.

"Well there it is chum," he said with a wide smile, looking at my new Belstaff jacket and boots. "Guy Martin had better look to his laurels."

"Well he might," I replied.

26

I tested the compression with a couple of kicks. It felt much better.

"New rings?" I enquired.

"New cord rings. De-coked. New plug. New plug leads. Blew the dust out of the brake drums. The shoes are fine; almost new by the looks of it. Pressure is holding up in the tyres and the oil in the engine and gearbox has been changed. All in all, it is now pretty roadworthy. If you could let me have it for a bit longer, I could have found you a new set of tyres and inner tubes. Where is it you are off to? Devon. Round trip of about 500 miles or so. It should do that run easy. Just check the oil every hundred miles or when you stop for petrol or a call of nature."

He paused and looked up at the sky where grey clouds were gathering over to the east. He was silent for a few minutes and then said quietly, more to himself than to me, "I wish I was going with you."

"You know where I am going, Chock. Just give me a couple of weeks to get the place sorted out and pay me a visit. About three hours if you leave that old Triumph under its dust sheet and come on the big Honda. Bring Caroline if you like."

"Didn't you know – Caroline is history. She left me for her yoga teacher. Bitch. But you never know what's around the corner. Now there is this neat little maths teacher called Miss Zimmerman. I don't know her first name yet but..."

"Chock, you amaze me and always have. You dog."

"I really don't like the look of that sky. It is going to chuck it down any moment now."

We shook hands and I wondered if I would ever see him again. Chaos in the banking sector and at the tills could ruin a small businessman. Big ones too as I was soon to find out.

CHAPTER TWO

The sun rose a little after 6:00 , but I was up and about a good two hours before that loading up the side-car with all the useful stuff I had so recently purchased, and just as the light flashed over the chimney tops I was on my way. It is hard not to use the words mystical or magical when starting out on a long motorcycle journey early in the morning, sometime in late summer or early autumn. The dawn chorus in full throat only serves to camouflage and highlight the silence and the stillness beneath. It took two or three firm kicks to rouse the Norton from its slumbers, but once awake it settled into a determined stentorian rhythm.

At a twenty-four-hour Tesco supermarket I filled up the tank full to overflowing and then the three large jerry cans. The cashier speaking over a loudspeaker announced, "Cash only – No cards". I raised a friendly arm in acknowledgement and walked over to pay. She gave me a weak smile. She was a pretty girl with a fair skin and bright green eyes. Pretty that is, apart from the tasteless piece of trash jewellery in her nose, and the hideous, ugly tattoo on her slim white neck. Who on earth tells them that this is in any way attractive, elegant or smart?

It being still early, there were few people about and the traffic was exceptionally light on the South Circular. The Wandsworth one-way system was uncharacteristically clear, and I was soon on the Kingston bypass heading west. This was the gateway to freedom.

An illusion of course, but whenever I passed the Robin Hood Roundabout, I always felt that London was behind me and that Devon with its green hills and wild coastline was but a stone's throw away.

The picture stayed with me until Guildford when the chill crisp morning air compelled me to pull over into the *Hogs Back Café* for coffee. I was not intending to stay, but the smell of frying bacon and sausages persuaded me that I had a long haul in front of me and that I ought to eat something.

And eat something I did; a full English breakfast with an extra egg and fried bread, tea and toast but it was not just appetite which made me spin out my stay. The other customers were, for the most part, van and lorry drivers whose conversations I was keen to eavesdrop.

"How you off for Derv, Wayne with just about every petrol station having Cash Only signs up?"

"Me, well I'm all right. Filled up last night at the pump at the depot, but how I will get back is anybody's guess."

"Before the radio in the cab went off, I heard a part of the Today programme on Radio 4. Martha Kearney was giving the Home Secretary, what's her name, a right grilling. Mind you she gave as good as she got. Yes, it was serious. Cobra would be in continuous session until it was all over. Experts in this sort of illegal hacking, from Scotland Yard and GCHQ were expecting to have the situation under control shortly. Or so she said."

"Yeah shortly. What's that mean? Twenty-four hours, a few days, a week?"

"Who knows. But there will be some right bloody fun and games before this is over. If I were you, I would take your deliveries slow and steady. Save the gas or you might never get back home."

"That's the idea, cheer us all up why don't you. Miserable bleeder."

Wiping my mouth on a paper napkin, I paid up and started to leave, but on an impulse, I turned and brought a whole box of Kit-Kats from an astonished waitress. I paid full price too.

Out on the road I swept past Farnham, Bently and Alton, and pushed on through Winchester still keeping to the A roads.

It had been a long hot summer for a change and the countryside of Surrey and Hampshire never looked better. Fields of yellow stubble where the crops had been harvested lay awaiting the plough and high in the branches horse chestnuts hung, not quite ready to drop. My mind drifted back to my school days for miles at a time. From memories of secondary school, it was but a short and invisible step to evening classes and my first meeting with Sonia. Then came our marriage, not all bad and the subsequent bear trap into which I walked all unknowing when introduced to Miranda Palmira. A largely one way love affair which wrecked my marriage and drove my sanity to the edge of despair and settled the grey frost of melancholia upon my grasp of reality which the passing years managed to thaw but little.

Morbid introspection is dangerous in any vehicle in normal times, but the roads were for the most part deserted and at the sort of snail's pace the old Norton had committed me to there was time enough to take in the scenery and indulge in an orgy of nostalgia.

Perhaps a few days in Uncle Bill's cottage amid dust, dirt, and decay against a backdrop of mortality might shock me out of the feeling of pointlessness once and for all.

All men seek spiritual renewal through catharsis in one form or another and some through raising a family. Well I had left it a bit too late for that option. How could I ask another woman to share my life and bear my children with the spectre of Miranda dormant like the larva of the Dutch Elm disease beetle burrowing away just out of sight below the hardened bark of my existence knowing that as with the elm tree the end result was an inevitable hollow death? In truth my life was a shambles beneath the cool, sardonic Pagliacci like exterior.

I had planned to take a break at Dorchester, but there were people fighting in the street outside some of the shops. One man threw a bottle at me as I passed, which missed me by a mile smashing into a thousand shards in the road behind me. Not a riot exactly, but perhaps a rural echo of what was probably happening in the large towns. I pressed on, not stopping for another ten miles in a lay-by, where a red headed woman was talking into a mobile phone and not getting much joy apparently. She tossed it with a contemptuous disdain through the window of her car, a Porsche. New by the look of it. We looked at each other for a few moments.

I dismounted, stretched and fished out my Thermos flask from the overloaded side-car.

"Excuse me."

I looked up. She was a stunner. I am no expert in women's clothes, but I figured that what she was wearing must have set her, or someone, back four figures in Bond Street if not Paris.

"Hello," I said. "Trouble?"

"My car just stopped. All of a sudden, although I have plenty of petrol and now, I can't get a signal on my mobile phone. We must be in a dead spot."

I shook my head.

"That funny looking pylon thing in the field over there is a mobile phone relay station. We ought to be swamped in signal here. Even if one operator goes down the others will always pick up a 999 call. It's an industry wide protocol."

"Perhaps I ought to try to dial 999 then."

"Worth a try I suppose, but I suspect that they are all down. Something or someone is playing havoc with computer systems just about everywhere. Car engine management systems and mobile telecommunications included."

I sipped my coffee and let this sink in. I could feel that she was going through the options in her head. Eventually she spoke.

"Where are my manners? My name is Josephine Pelton-Forbes." The way she said it I gathered that the name was supposed to mean something to me. It did not. Back then, many people were famous for being famous and I took her to be one of these.

"I don't suppose that you could give me a lift on – that?"

I have to admit that I didn't care for the emphasis which she had placed upon "that", as if I were driving a dust cart full of rotting fish heads.

"Where to? A hotel or something? I don't recommend Dorchester in this moment. The natives not being exactly friendly."

"Yes," she said as if piecing things together in her head for the first time. "Basingstoke was in chaos when I drove through as quickly as I dared do. Cars all over the place parked every which way with doors left open and police everywhere." She paused and with a sigh continued, "Has the world gone mad?"

I nodded, not knowing what response might be appropriate.

She pulled the thick sheepskin jacket tight around her thin shoulders. A sudden chilling breeze had sprung up.

"Well I can't possibly stay here all night. On my own," she said as she viewed the sham fortress of safety that is a sports car.

I couldn't help smiling inwardly. Here was a woman at the height of her powers. who probably had an expensive education. Loving, overindulgent parents and a secure home. Perhaps a flat in town somewhere fashionable. The sort of girl who could, and probably did, command the adoration of army officers and academics alike, leaving them scattered and broken by the wayside, finding herself suddenly dependent upon the goodwill of a passing motorcyclist aboard an obsolescent motorcycle to save her from a most unpleasant night of, if not exposure, something far worse on an unlit road miles from anywhere.

Once again, I could hear the cogs turning. This time they were the gearwheels of a child's mind frightened of the dark.

There is a Don Quixote in all of us I suppose.

"Where are you supposed to be going?" I asked.

"Devon," she replied.

Devon. It would be Devon. I almost knew it would be Devon.

"Whereabouts?"

She told me. On the edge of Exmoor.

"My friends have a farm there. They invited me ages ago and it was only last night that I made up my mind to go. A couple of hours would do it I reasoned. The Porsche can really fly if you push it. Over 100 easy. Asking for trouble, I suppose but that's how it goes."

She carried on in this way for several minutes while a degree of relief flowed back into her veins.

"As it happens it is on my route. I have recently inherited some property down that way and was on my way to inspect it. The motorcycle combination was a part of the bequest and I thought that it might be an adventure to ride down on it."

I nearly said my other car is a Mercedes, which was true, but it could so easily sound like a lie cooked up to impress.

"Super," she said. She did not exactly clap her hands, but I imagine that she wanted to. "Aren't I supposed to wear a crash helmet or something?"

"Not on a combination. The police regard it as a sort of inferior car. But you ought to wear something on your head."

"Just a moment. Don't go without me." She rummaged in the boot of her car returning with an equestrian hard hat and a small Louis Vuitton suitcase.

"Will this do? Can you find room for my suitcase?"

How could I refuse? I got the feeling that if I should have much to do with this woman I was going to become putty in her tiny hands and become as soft and malleable as any subaltern of her acquaintance in the Blues and Royals.

I topped up my tank with the remaining petrol from one of my jerry cans which I abandoned, and squeezed her case in. Even riding two up I reckoned that I had enough petrol in reserve to get us where we were going, but not nearly enough to return to London.

Every thirty miles or so I pulled over, ostensibly to check the oil level in the engine but really to give my passenger a respite and a shot from the large stainless-steel Thermos. She looked half frozen. I gave her my scarf to keep some of the wind off of her lower face and told her to put her hands, which were turning blue, in the side pockets of my Belstaff jacket. Even at thirty miles an hour it can get very cold on a motorcycle once the sun starts to set, and I could sense that she was on the point of tears when we eventually neared our destination. It started to rain while we were still a few miles off. The lanes became narrower, and then we turned into the narrowest of them all with grass growing between the wheel tracks. A neat sign picked out by my directional spotlight announced:

WINDRIDGE FARM VETERINARY PRACTICE &
EQUESTRIAN CENTER

Alice Westcliff MBHS & David Thomas Westcliff
RCVS Proprietors

As we passed through a five-bar gate, the dark mud turned into wet cobblestones polished to slate grey silvery brightness in the beams from my modified headlamp and spotlight.

We had, it appeared, reached our goal.

The sound of my single Gold Star silencer brought a woman to the front door of the farm building. Dressed in a Burberry raincoat and Wellington boots she carried a dim

36

torch in one hand and a hurricane lamp in the other. Whatever she expected to see it was not her old school friend soaked through to the skin in the act of nearly falling off the pillion seat of an elderly motorcycle.

I pulled into a lean-to beside the barn out of the rain, which was heavier now, turned off the petrol and as the engine retired for the night, duty done I took a second or two to stretch my cramped legs and breathe in huge lungs-full of farm-yard air. I smiled inwardly, remembering my childhood once again in the smell of horses, hay and wood-smoke.

If I could bottle nostalgia, I could make a fortune.

From out of the stable block, a tall gangly figure emerged, apparently indifferent to the rain, and walked over towards me.

With the cool demeanour that only a public-s c h o o l education can provide, he didn't bat an eyelid at this dripping apparition in his yard and said, "Just sorting out a spot of bother between Bonny and Clyde. Had to put Poppy in quarantine for a spell and they quarrel if she isn't there to keep the peace. My word you look like you need a stiff drink, and if you don't mind, I think I will join you. Can't bear to see a chap drinking alone. Terribly bad form as my father would say." We introduced ourselves.

As we entered through the front door, my eyes fell on the huge open fire with the unmistakable smell of burning fruit wood.

I heard our hostess say to Josephine, now steaming in an armchair, "What we need is a strong cup of tea," as she rose and headed toward the kitchen; a kitchen which smelled strongly of petrol.

"The power has been going on and off for a couple of days now," she continued, "but it went off this morning about eleven, so I dug out this old Primus stove. Cleaned it up a bit with Brasso and filled it up just before you arrived."

I heard her strike one match which went out, thank God, and as she fumbled to get another from the box I grabbed the Primus from the table and threw it out through the open door into the yard, and quickly did the same with the petrol can, which fortunately only contained a pint or so.

The face of our hostess was a picture. "W –W – Why did you just do that?" No doubt she believed that this was most inappropriate behaviour in a guest she had yet to meet.

"Sorry if I shocked you," I said with perhaps an edge to my voice. "But a Primus stove runs on paraffin not petrol. You were about to light a bomb, which would have exploded and killed us all. Even so the fumes from the open petrol can might have spread across the floor and caught from the open fire with much the same result."

"Oh," she said. "No pun intended, but bang goes our supper. It was to have been soup. Only tinned, of course, but now I don't know what else to offer you and Jo."

Beside the fire in the living area were a copper kettle and a brass trivet.

"Well, if you can fill up that kettle with water and set it by the fire to boil, I have some ready meals in the side-car which only require plates and hot water. The sort of stuff soldiers take with them into battle. There are puddings too. So, if you have some instant coffee, we can conjure up quite a little dinner party. Sorry I can't provide any port or Stilton."

"There I can help you," said David. "We have half a case of Taylors 1985 in the larder which ought to be overdue for drinking about now, and I think there might even be some Stilton to go with it. But first things first, that drink I promised you.

"Scotch all right? Only cooking I am afraid but good everyday stuff, and then you can tell us how you came to befriend this lovely lady, and where on earth did you get that monstrous contraption you rode in on."

He poured us all a decent measure of whisky and handed them round.

"Monster. Well perhaps Nortons are a bit unusual these days, but monster is a bit harsh. She has the heart of a pedigree long case clock, the trustworthiness of a bishop and even if she has all the grace of a dancing walrus, she did not let us down once in two hundred and fifty miles. She swept us through Dorchester without a qualm although the natives were being less than friendly, chucking Guinness bottles about for all they were worth."

They sat wide-eyed in disbelief, looking to Josephine for confirmation.

"He loves that old motorcycle. He inherited it from an uncle along with some property hereabouts, but it was only one bottle they shied at him, and even he can't swear it was Guinness."

For a moment, our eyes met and well, I couldn't help thinking what any red-blooded man might think under similar circumstances and rose to get the rations from the side-car.

Supper was not half bad but perhaps my opinion was coloured by the scotch and the port. My eyes became very heavy and I nearly dropped off to sleep in the warm glow of the firelight. From the kitchen, I could hear Josephine and her school friend Alice Westcliffe talking in hushed conspiratorial tones and without hearing a single word I knew that they were discussing the sleeping arrangements.

I was eventually given a duvet and a stone hot water bottle, then left by myself to curl up on the sofa by the fire.

I had every intention of stuffing my wet boots with newspaper and placing my jeans near the fire to dry, but I dropped off to sleep before I did either chore.

I awoke to the sound of a toasting fork being dropped in the hearth and a muttered curse.

"Oops sorry. Didn't mean to wake you," said my host, David Westcliffe, looking as though his project of toasting sausages was not going quite to plan.

"Oh," I said yawning. "What time is it?"

"About eleven. You were dead to the world and it seemed a shame to wake you."

"Thank you. I suppose I must have needed it. Yesterday was quite a long day one way or the other. What exactly are you trying to do?"

Beside the fire was a rack of sorts, upon which hung four large steaks.

"Well the power is off and things in the deep freeze will spoil if we don't eat them soon. So, I thought that whilst the girls are off on the horses, I might get dinner started."

"Where have they gone exactly?"

"Taken a couple of horses out for exercise down to the village to see what's going on in the world and shall probably call in on our neighbours, the Emersons, who farm over to the east, or they might have gone the other way and stopped off at the Brandons. You'll like them, real eccentric artistic types. Loads of money in the background somewhere. Enough to play at being back-to-the-land farmers anyway."

One of the sausages started to smoke.

"I don't think that you are making too much progress, do you?"

"Well no, but I am not used to this sort of thing. My father spent half of WW2 under canvas and would not allow me to join the Boy Scouts so I suppose I missed out on all the backwoodsman skills they are supposed to teach you."

By this time, I was fully awake.

"Is there any tea or coffee? If there is, and if you have any kitchen foil, I will make a start on lunch while you fetch me some coffee."

While I dressed and pulled my still damp boots on, he returned with the coffee, but without milk or aluminium foil.

"No foil I'm afraid, and we had the last of the evaporated milk last night."

"Do you have an earthenware pot of some sort, with a tight-fitting lid by any chance?"

He nodded and went to fetch it. It was a decent size.

"If we put the meat and the bangers in the pot together with a few potatoes and heap hot ashes around it, we should have a hot meal ready by supper time or thereabouts. I can't say for sure. I've never done this sort of thing before. We shall have to wait and see how it turns out. We must remember to keep the fire going though."

41

We walked through to the kitchen as we drank the hot black coffee.

Although I must have seen it the previous evening, I gasped in surprise at the sight of the Victorian stove. It was an original Larbert range, the sort with a central grate, an oven on one side and a cistern for boiling water on the other, with a brightly polished brass tap.

"Here we are buggering about with earthenware pots and toasting forks and you had a range all along. What a couple of muppets."

"Well we tried to get that thing going when we brought this place, but it smoked like the devil and the fire would never stay alight. I wanted to rip it out, but Alice said that it looked decorative and wouldn't hear of it."

"Good for her," I said.

"I expect that it just needs its chimney sweeping."

It was beginning to dawn upon me that if I left these people to their own devices they were going to starve or freeze to death in short order but said nothing just then.

"Let's have a look outside."

Behind the kitchen there was a little cast iron door set in the wall at about waist height. I tentatively opened the door. The opening was packed tightly with soot.

"Er David, do you have a trowel and a bucket?"

Some of the soot must have been there since WW2. I filled a wheelbarrow full.

"I don't suppose that there is a sweep in the village by any chance?"

"No. Do you think that we could get it going before the girls return?"

"I don't know. Do you have any flue brushes or drain rods by any chance?"

From the look on his face I assumed not.

"In which case I will need a brick. A decent length of string and a long ladder."

Cinderella must have looked just as mystified when the fairy godmother called for a pumpkin and six white mice.

The ladder turned out to be one of the old wooden sort, which had probably not been used in decades. A few of the rungs showed signs of woodworm and these I reinforced with some battens. It creaked alarmingly as I tested it with my weight. The rear part of the farmhouse was lower than the central area and by climbing onto the thatch at that end I was able to work my way along the ridge to the kitchen chimney, and drop the brick down on the end of the twine. From below David shouted up.

"That's good, some soot is coming down, quite a lot actually."

He was standing by the inspection hatch when a great block of soot landed and was turned to dust just in front of his face.

He gave a sort of snort and began to cough. I looked over the edge and saw him spitting and spluttering.

I had no wish to see him hurt, but I couldn't help but laugh, under the circumstances. I fought to keep it to a minimum.

"Can you see the brick yet?" I yelled down.

"No, but I can feel it," he answered, with his arm through the inspection hatch.

"Good. I'm coming down."

On the ground once more, I cast around for a suitable brush. The top of a Christmas tree would have been ideal, but I had to make do with a miserable little shrub, which I pulled up roots and all.

David Westcliff looked a right sight. It was with great restraint I stopped myself breaking into Mammy or Way down upon the Swanee River.

With the line now tied to the shrub in place of the brick, I climbed back up onto the roof and began to pull up the line. It worked a treat. Sticks from some historic bird's nest came down with the next consignment of soot. David had stood well back this time, but it still made clouds of black dust.

"We make progress," I said. "Now, while you clean up I will light the fire in the range and with any luck we shall have a kettle on and steaming away by the time the girls return, earning numerous Brownie points for our endeavours, but if I were you I wouldn't go into the house in that state. There must be a tap in the stables. Perhaps you ought to clean up or we will both be in deep trouble. I will bring you out a change of clothing directly."

You can have endless fun looking after a fire. Must be some primeval compulsion I suppose, lighting fires keeping the darkness at bay. By the time I had it drawing nicely two things broke into my reverie, one was the frantic calling of David from the stable block, and the other was the sound of horses' hooves on the cobbles.

For long moments all was stillness. The kindling had caught the split logs alight and the fire in the range was drawing nicely.

44

I had not forgotten grandmother's instructions to never let the cistern beside the main oven dry out, but there was no knowing when the water would be hot enough for shaving or washing up.

There was, I discovered, a laundry room on the opposite side of the kitchen wall, backing on to the larder with a copper cauldron for boiling clothes and a sturdy iron mangle. The rollers were rotten but not a difficult project to renew them, perhaps with elm if I could find one that had not fallen to disease. The chimney which served the copper would need sweeping too, but that could wait for a bit. For a fleeting second I thought that I could teach David to do such running repairs to the farm's equipment when I had moved into Uncle Bill's cottage, but in my heart I somehow knew that I would not be moving on for a spell. At least not yet.

Why I suddenly felt protective about these people, who were at best complete strangers to me a few hours ago I had no idea.

Suddenly the kitchen door flew open with a crash and Alice stormed in.

"And what do you mean by getting my husband to strip naked and stand in the stables looking extremely foolish half-wrapped in a horse blanket?"

I had completely forgotten all about David, preoccupied as I was with the fire in the range. I must have gulped open mouthed like a goldfish.

She tried to look cross, but couldn't keep a straight face, falling about in girlish giggles, which is of course, contagious. Between laughing and fighting for breath, she said,

"He even had soot behind his ears and I had to scrub his neck like a little boy with a piece of rag we keep in the stable, and just like a little boy he began to holler that I was hurting him. What a scream. I will remember that scene until the day I die."

I didn't escape censure completely as though it was all a prank, and I had put him up to it. Even so, I thought that we had done very well, all things considered, and said so, having got the evening meal prepared and cooking by the time they returned and had finished stabling the horses. Apart from Bonny and Clyde, the heavy horses, and Poppy, there were three others that belonged to locals who, having no facilities of their own, fostered them out to Alice and David.

The oven part of the range was not hot enough for cooking just yet and would not be ready for some time. Then once it gets hot, it's a steep learning curve working out how to manage the fire for best effect with the minimum of fuel. A hard-enough job using coal which burns slower and hotter than wood. Each log had to be of a size that would be small enough to fit in the grate, but not so small as to burn away quickly. Still, it soon had the Georgian copper kettle steaming, if not boiling, and the dinner plates were adequately warm to the satisfaction of our hostess.

After about an hour, the water in the cistern was hot enough to wash up the supper things. There would be enough hot water there for me to shave with before turning in.

Whilst we were playing at being Henry Kippin up on the roof, the potatoes in their jackets were slowly baking in the hot ashes of the living room fire. Others, together with carrots, were cooking in a metal bucket placed beside the fire. I didn't make a note of the time, but I suppose that they must have been cooking for several hours at a relatively low temperature. They turned out all right. The steaks looked a bit grim, but the sausages – apart from those ones with bits burnt by our previous efforts – were just about edible. All in all, it didn't turn out to be too bad. We had apples for dessert and by the time we had opened the second bottle of Malbec we had forgotten for an hour or so that the world we had unquestionably taken for granted was falling to pieces around our ears. We were not to know it, but fly-by-wire aircraft were crashing into the sea out of control. Super-tankers were drifting lost and helpless, eventually being washed up on an unforgiving shoreline. Had we known how universal, and how devastating, the situation had become and how it would become even worse, I think we might have agreed to end it all there and then, but we did not know anything of the sort.

We took our drinks over to the sofa and the armchairs by the fire, which David stirred into life and put a large log and two smaller ones into the ashes. The evening had turned suddenly chill and a fresh wind could be heard in the sycamore trees outside; a gentle warning that we were on the cusp between a long summer and autumn. Winter would not be late in coming. We exchanged our wine glasses for balloon glasses. I'll say one thing, David Westcliff was not mean in dishing out the brandy.

I am not an expert by any means, but it was not run of the mill stuff but soft with an unusual and delightful finish. I could have sat there before the fire drinking all night and drifted off into a world of imaginings, but now was really the time for a council of war. What had the girls found in the village?

Alice who had lived in the area on and off most of her adult life and knew many of the villagers by sight if not by name, spoke first.

"The village was as quiet as a grave. The few people that were about walked with their heads down lost in their own thoughts.

47

"I said good morning to Richard the postman and later to Mary who arranges the flowers in the church, and little Jimmy Lee who steals our apples. He ran off, but the others just ignored us. There was no motor traffic at all that we saw and none within hearing distance."

The fire crackled and the wind sighed in the chimney, and the long-case clock struck the half hour.

"It was creepy," continued Alice, with a shudder and took a sip of brandy.

"Yes," said Josephine. "I am not easily frightened but—"

Her eyes flickered towards me for a split second. It was almost a glance of conspiracy. I knew it was a lie. I had seen the fear in her eyes when she thought that I might leave her to her own devices to face the night all alone in an unlit lay-by.

"But what I felt was not so much fear as tension. The little shop had its shutter down and the pub was closed and in darkness.

"A little further along the street someone was venting their frustration by shouting and kicking on the door of the newsagent, and when that failed to attract attention threw a bottle at the window. We gave him and his broken glass a wide berth. We rode up the hill and along Coppice Lane to call in on our nearest neighbours. Andrew and Polly Brandon. Are people still referred to as hippies? I don't know, but they certainly look and act the part.

"To a very large extent they opted out of the rat race ten or twelve years ago. They have a radio but no TV, phones, mobile or otherwise. No computers of any kind. Their tractor and battered old Land-Rover are both diesels, not that they get about much. They seem to be very happy just to be with each other. Quite romantic in a pastoral, rustic, bucolic sort of way. They will be OK for a while, at least until the food runs out. They grow their own vegetables as you might expect but, what do they have? Two or three acres at most. You can't feed two adults on that and whatever he can shoot. Have you ever eaten rook pie? It is an acquired taste. Andrew said that he would call over in a couple of days and if he was lucky he would bring us a couple of rabbits, and as we were about to ride off Polly gave us a dozen fresh hens' eggs as a parting gift. It was about then that I realised that there are going to be lots of things in short supply, or even unobtainable to us, in the short term or—"

She took a sip of brandy, which was followed by an even bigger sip, and drained her glass, "or even in the long term." She sighed slowly and with a sad resignation continued,

"Or, perhaps, forever. Afterwards we rode around by Nibbs Cross and took the bridle path up through the woods to Home Farm."

Mr Emerson was pleased to see us, hungry for any news of the outside world of which we had none to give the poor man. He was on the point of pulling his hair out, and small wonder. A herd of eighty cows in lactation, no parlour staff to milk them and no electricity to power the milking machines and chillers. He was working on the stand-by generator when we arrived, but that thing, brand new and computer controlled refused to start."

"What a bloody awful mess, Alice," said her husband.

"Even if he managed to produce some milk it's a pound to a penny that the tanker isn't going to turn up, leaving him with a holding tank full of milk going bad. I shall call over tomorrow to see what I can do, which will be not a lot. If a cow isn't milked her udders swell up and they become vulnerable to mastitic infection.

"The teats can rapidly develop secondary complications from any number of pathogens but fortunately about a handful of really lethal ones. All of which I could treat quite simply with antibiotics, if I had any. They are not the sort of things a vet would keep on hand in any quantity. I keep a few doses of wide spectrum antibiotics in stock, but with the pharm' companies giving a next day service nobody holds much of anything any-more. The kindest thing would be to cull the herd of the sick ones. A few will escape the worst of the infections and get through it unharmed, but not many. It will be like foot and mouth all over again, but worse."

"How come worse, darling?"

"With staff being unable to get to work, drive tractors, JCB's etc., what is going to happen to all those rotting carcases? With a few small differences it will be the same all over the country, Europe and the world. A few herdsmen in the third world will get off Scott free of course but even they will get their share of problems resulting from this. Only the carrion creatures, rats, crows and the like will survive and flourish. The rest of us will just have to make the best of it while the central government get its their act together. If they ever do."

On that happy note we all went quiet for a while. The fire spat and the larger log settled down on its bed of grey ashes.

David refilled our glasses, and returning to his seat, said,

"The little bit of land we have here is not going to be able to feed four people, not with the resources we have."

"Three people darling. You forget that tomorrow, or the next day, Mr Marsh will be off to collect on his inheritance."

"Well, three people then, none of whom have any hands-on skill or experience of arable farming. Such

50

foodstuffs as there happens to be hereabouts are going to be fought over tooth and nail by people with less tender sentiments than we have. People will kill to protect their own and to stay alive as they always have done, and we must be prepared to do the same even if it goes against the grain. For a start we must take stock of what resources we have and formulate some sort of plan.

"It is a reasonable assumption that the government, law and order are going to be minimal for a while, if – that is – they do not disappear forever."

I rose to take a look at the fire in the range. It had settled down nicely, and I added a small log which I hoped would burn all night.

That they were talking in hushed voices, which fell silent as I returned to my chair, told me that I had been the topic of their conversation.

I broke the silence with some remark about getting in some more wood before we turned in for the night. A range like the Larbert needs a lot of fuel before it heats up, but once up to temperature will hold its heat for quite a considerable time, and just needs to be kept going. I continued, "It's none of my business, of course, but if I were you, I should throw in my lot with your hippy neighbours, I forget what you said their name was. If I read their position correctly from what you have told me they grow their own crops, catch the odd rabbit, a pheasant too I shouldn't wonder. They keep chickens and it would be no surprise to me if you told me that she makes her own butter and cheese. With your little orchard out back, home-made cider would also be a possibility if you had the time left over from simply staying alive that is."

I had their undivided attention.

Who was this city boy who knew all about ranges and cider and who knows what else besides?

Having started my lecture, for lecture is what it was, I continued.

"What's the alternative? Beef from the culled herds? Well that's not going to last. Everyone will want some before the rats get what's left. Next thing is that you start consuming your capital. The horses. Lot of meat on a horse."

"250 to 1000Kg," contributed David who, as a vet, ought to know such things.

"Clyde is the biggest and ought to weigh approximately—"

"Shut up darling let him finish."

"Thank you. As I was about to say, it hardly matters if you butcher the largest or the smallest first for without some means of preserving the meat it is going to spoil and you will have to throw most of it away in any case. I dare say you could live for a bit on the oats they don't eat because they are dead.

"I would suggest that if you were to let hippies, Andrew and Polly, manage your land, with your help of course, you would have an equitable basis for sharing in those eggs and cheese."

David stood up and went round with the bottle once again, but only he and I took a refill.

"Look," he said. "We have been talking it over while you were out of the room and would like it very much if you would choose to stay with us, so how about it?"

Alice gave me the prettiest smile.

"Look here, Mr Marsh. David is a fine vet but he can't knock a nail in straight to save his life and us," she said glancing at Josephine. "Well, the sort of expensive education we received hasn't equipped us at all well to face life in the rough. David is not going to need an office as such for a while and if we take one of the beds out of the guest room and move it down, you could have your own room on the ground floor. So, is it a deal?"

"It's very kind of you to offer to take me in like this, but you hardly know me. I might be a mad axe-man for all you know and walk in my sleep with murder and lust on my mind".

"Kindness, utter bosh. It's self-preservation really. Can't you see we need you, Peter? We need you so much that we can put up with whatever strange proclivities you may have. Apart from the axe murdering habit that is."

"Do I have to give you an answer right away? I should really like to see my inheritance, which is why I came here in the first place. It's only thirty miles or so to Uncle Bill's cottage. If I pop over in the morning, I could be back by teatime if all goes well. I will give you my answer then if that's OK."

With that thought in the air we all went to bed. Them to their rooms, and me to the sofa. I was tired but couldn't drop off to sleep, at least not right away. One thing played on my mind more than anything. Josephine was a very attractive woman and imagining myself living in close proximity, working together, it would only be a matter of time before I made a move towards her. But if she rejected me, life here would become intolerable. Even worse, what if she conceded to my advances, for no better reason than they needed my contribution to group survival? When sleep did come it brought with it dreams of the office and being taken to court as a result of a compact for some property sale, I was unable to complete.

I was awoken by the sound of thunder as lightning lit up the room as bright as day. The wind and the rain hammered on the windowpanes, telling me, although I did not need telling, that it was not going to be a day for motorcycling.

Pulling on some clothes, I padded barefoot to the kitchen where the fire in the grate still glowed but with no great enthusiasm. I woke it to life with a handful of twigs which I followed up with a couple of split logs. The water in the side cistern was still warm and I had a quick wash and shaved with a disposable razor. I wondered where I might get an old-fashioned strop razor. Perhaps Uncle Bill had one stashed away. I made a mental note to look one out.

Afterwards, I started to get breakfast ready as a thank you for my hosts. The remaining raw sausages went in the pan first although they would not begin to sizzle for a while yet, not until the heat from the grate had worked its way up and into the heavy cast iron Creuset frying pan. When it had done so, I sliced some of the cooked leftover potatoes and set them beside the bangers to brown. The eggs could wait till last when there were signs of life coming from upstairs. The coffee grinder, being electric, was useless, so I crushed the beans with a flat iron on the top of the stove.

Not perfect prep but it would serve. The DeLonghi coffee machine was just as useless as the electric grinder. With no percolator in sight, I put the crushed beans in a saucepan and hoped for the best.

Whatever it might eventually taste like, it certainly smelt wonderful as it perfumed first the kitchen and then the whole house. They had, apart from the beans in the jar, about two kilos in stiff paper bags from Café Meo, the coffee specialist a few minutes' walk from the Gare du Nord railway station in Paris. Coffee was one of the things we were going to have to learn to live without for a long time. Tea too I suppose, although you can make a refreshing hot drink from mint and pine needles; other things too if you know what you are doing.

Standing there breathing in the grand aroma, listening to the ticking clock on the mantle-shelf and the shuffle of feet overhead heading for the bathroom, I easily and unintentionally found myself imagining that I was at home in the days before my divorce on any one of a thousand Sunday mornings cooking breakfast for Sonia before strolling down to the village for the Sunday papers.

What I did not need now was entanglements of any kind, commitments, or obligations. All things being equal, it would be better all-round if I moved on as soon as the rain let up. They were good people, but what chance did a handful of over-indulged city dwellers hope to have playing at being The Archers? At best it was a brave attempt at producing a facsimile of normality, and at worst an agonising long term way of committing suicide, which I did not want to be around to witness, much less participate in.

CYBER BOMB

CHAPTER THREE

It rained on and off for the next three days. During the breaks in the weather I explored the smallholding, its barn, stables, and outbuildings. There was a disused forge with bellows, a grindstone, and some blacksmith's tools. A pile of coke, about half a ton would be my guess, and other useful things like a pitchfork, several axe heads, a hay rake and a scythe with a worm-eaten haft.

There was a hand operated pump in the stable block which they said had never worked. I unbolted the cap and lifted out the plunger. The leather seal had rotted, as had the clack, and these I renewed. I reassembled and primed the pump with a bucket or two of water and it worked as well as it had on the day it was installed, which was sometime after 1889, the date cast into the body of the pump. The tap in the yard, and those in the house, still worked but who could say for how long or how clean the water would eventually become?

On the fourth morning, the sky cleared and such clouds as there were, were high and thin. I wheeled the Norton out from under the lean-to, and having already said good-bye and checked the oil, I turned on the petrol, retarded the ignition, set the choke and swung down hard on the kick starter. It humped itself into life and once again with that mixture of pride and admiration, I felt that small childish thrill which I have always experienced at the start of any journey by motorcycle.

Slipping the clutch, I turned the combination around and was about to thunder off along the lane when Josephine appeared wearing Alice's Burberry trench coat, jeans and Wellington boots.

"I thought that you might need a hand cleaning out the old boy's stable," and before I could object, she had swung her leg over and settled lightly on to the pillion seat. It was, I suppose, one way of ensuring that I was sure to return to Windridge Farm.

I had been an estate agent most of my adult life and dealt, on many occasions, with property related matters of probate so I had a pretty fair idea of how people let things slide towards the end of their lives when housework and hygiene becoming secondary considerations. Uncle Bill, for all my fond early memories of him, would probably have been little different, living all alone in a tumbledown ruin of a cottage. If it was really bad, I should lock it up, turn around and retrace my steps back to the farm and the friends who awaited our return, and take them up on their offer.

At the end of the lane, I took the right hand turning and drove down to the village, as even if it did add several miles to our journey I needed to see what, if anything, was happening.

The village was a ghost town, the steady pomp-pomp-pomp of my engine echoing off the still neat white walls of the shops and cottages.

I had half intended to visit the church, where I knew from experience of churches elsewhere that it was where people often left messages on the noticeboard in the porch. I had almost rolled to a halt when I saw a man slumped against a wall asleep, or so I thought until I saw his bloody shirt and the blood splatter above and behind him on the wall. Someone had given him the full blast of a shotgun in the chest. Who or why I had no wish to find out. Josephine, leaning forward said in the calmest voice imaginable, "I think it might be better if we were to move on now."

I could not but agree, and in spite of the horror we had just seen in a quiet village street, I almost smiled at the imperturbability of the woman.

The journey to Uncle Bill's cottage proved uneventful, which was something to be grateful for at least. Nearing our destination, I picked out various shabby cottages set back from the road believing each and every one to be his and now mine of course.

What I found came as quite a shock. A huge shock, so certain was I that Bill had ended his life in a hovel. His cottage, I had not imagined it to be anything else, was situated at the end of a long cul-de sac where a rustic gate let into a field and beside the gate, a short driveway curved up to a modern bungalow with a double garage sporting solar panels on the roof. I let myself in with the key his solicitor had sent to me, and apart from a pile of unanswered and unanswerable post, a little dust and a musty smell, the house was in apple pie order. The things which struck me most were the coke fired Baxi back boiler set in a tiled fire surround in the living room, beside which sat a scuttle full of coke. A Calor gas fired Aga cooker in the kitchen, which was supplied from a tank in the overgrown garden. By foresight, habit, prudence or chance there was enough tinned goods in the kitchen cupboards to last for months, and a good supply of coke in a bunker by the back door. Like nosy children, we opened cupboards and peered into drawers.

"Why is that stove in the fireplace called a Baxi back boiler?" Josephine asked.

"Because at the back there is a boiler which heats water for the radiators and the hot water."

"So, we can be warm and have hot baths tonight," she said half-expecting me to say that's impossible.

"Yes, if we light the fire and if the flue isn't blocked, and if there is water in the system and it has not been isolated and drained down. Yes, we might. Go upstairs and look for towels and soap and such while I fetch some kindling in."

Opening up the garage looking for kindling I couldn't believe my eyes. It was a fully equipped mechanics workshop and if that wasn't enough there were six completely restored motorcycles from a giant Royal Enfield Constellation to a little B S A Bantam. I could just imagine that as he lay there in his final hours, he would have pictured the look upon my face as I discovered this treasure trove in his lair. This was not something I could abandon just like that.

I had to think things through carefully. But not in this moment. I wanted a hot bath, a cup of tea and a decent meal in any order I could get them. I broke up an empty crate for kindling and screwed up a great handful of post that looked to be mostly bills of one sort or another. With the doors shut on the Baxi and the vents wide open it began to draw with a vengeance. I only hoped that there was water in the system. Thankfully, there was.

Josephine returned with towels and a blue bathrobe. "Look what I found in the airing cupboard," she said, and with a flourish produced a pistol.

A service revolver, which I took charge of straight away. It was fully loaded. God! Where on earth did he get this? He was never in the army. Speculation was pointless. There were other guns too in a steel cabinet in the garage. A shotgun and a Lee Enfield rifle with enough ammunition to fight a war. Later, while Josephine took her bath, I unloaded the pistol and made like Clint Eastwood for five minutes before the mirror in the hall, "Do you feel lucky? Well do you? Make my day punk."

Then, remembering the corpse propped up against the wall opposite the church, I suddenly felt ashamed at playing such a childish game. Guns kill people, tearing great holes through flesh and bone, turning vital organs to mush. I hoped to God, whose existence I strongly doubted, that I was never to become enmeshed in a fight for survival with guns.

Tinned lobster bisque for starters, followed by tinned ham, tinned peas, tinned carrots and tinned potatoes with tinned fruit cocktail for desert. Uncle Bill had, it appeared from the quantity of stuff in his kitchen cupboards, no intention of starving to death.

As we ate, we talked, and got to know each other a little better.

She was surprised that I had once made a million pounds speculating in property, and almost as quickly as it came, I lost it doing exactly the same thing. I was only slightly less surprised that she had trained as a ballet dancer and had reached a very high standard before breaking a leg beneath a horse at a gymkhana. Turning to television she became known as Judo-Jo teaching women to look after themselves. From talking of my property dealings, I soon drifted onto my true love – antiques.

"How strange you should be occupied in both," she remarked as if I had said that I was a brain surgeon with his very own window-cleaning round.

"Quite a practical, if somewhat cynical, choice really," I replied.

"When the economy is on the slide and people are strapped for cash, one of the first things to go are the family heirlooms. When things start looking up once again, they buy houses and fill them with antiques. Well some of them do."

"How clever of you," she said with a yawn. What was I to make of this woman's turn of phrase Was that a put-down or just the sort of off-hand condescension she was accustomed to dish out to everyone not blessed since birth with her privileges. That is one spoilt miss in need of a long hard dose of reality and a smacked bottom to put her in her place. Haughty. That was the word I settled on. Yes haughty.

Had I known how to do it we might have gone to bed by electric light fed from the solar panels on the roof, but I never found the control box. I did find a bottle of Bells Whisky though and was asleep the moment my head hit the pillow. I may have been asleep an hour or a minute, when I was awoken by a creaking board, or it might have been a hinge.

"Yes – what's the matter?" I asked, my eyes half open.

"There's a spider in my room, a big one."

"You woke me up for that? Whack it with a towel or something."

Well I had just been fast asleep, so I can be excused for being a bit slow on the up take. In a split second she pulled back my sheet and slipped in beside me.

"Oh!" I said, "You're naked."

"So, I am. So are you," she said. "Would you like me to find a pair of Uncle Billy's pyjamas?

"Er- no, that won't be necessary."

"Are you cold?" she said almost flowing around me smelling sweetly of soap, one hand rippling down my spine the other stroking the nape of my neck.

"No, not cold – boiling," I replied.

Then, as if to restore my faith in a vagrant and absconded God, the moon, a little less than full, appeared through a rent in the clouds and a gap in the curtains to give its argent blessing to the work in hand.

It was a honeymoon of a sort, and for the next three days we were lost to the world. We made love a lot. Laughed a lot. Argued sometimes about nothing. Made imaginative meals together and with a shotgun for company walked in the local countryside. If there were any game birds about, I never saw them. I did not even carry any cartridges.

There was never any question that Bill's cottage would provide a more comfortable retreat than the farm, at least in the short term, but we now felt that David and Alice were family, dependent relatives if you like, to whom we owed a responsibility of sorts to look out for them. It was a strange, and not particularly welcome feeling, but one I had to acknowledge.

With the side-car packed out with boxes of provisions and lots of other useful stuff, we locked up and set off back to the farm. With Josephine's arms tightly around me I wanted the trip to last forever. It lasted less than a mile. On the pavement outside a group of run-down terraced houses a large man was laying into a child with his belt. He was bigger than me, a lot bigger but I could not let this pass. I had a pistol in the waistband of my jeans but could not get to it quickly. In any event it was not loaded. Before I had even braked to a halt Josephine was off the pillion and running towards them. Not waiting for her to say a word, he turned his attention to her and gave her a heavy swipe across the face with the back of his hand, knocking her down. I quickened my pace, but I need not have bothered. In a split second she was up. With the highest high kick, I had ever seen, she caught him beneath the chin with a green Wellington boot.

It got his attention, but his temper flared, and the next blow would not be a slap as a reward for her interference, but a punch. He drew back his hand, his fingers clenched into a huge fist, but it never connected. As he moved his weight forward, she struck again with a lightning fast kick to the side of his knee and over he went with a bellow. Unsatisfied with this, her next kick caught him squarely in the crutch. At this, and my arrival on the scene revolver in hand, he lost all interest in chastising the child and the martial arts and staggered to get up. Not to be out done by a mere girl I gave him another kick in almost the same neighbourhood to send him on his way. It felt really good. Josephine made a sign that we should turn around.

With this thin child perched between us we returned to the bungalow and I got my first real look at the little girl. About seven, eight or nine years old I should guess. I know next to nothing about children. It might have been more or a bit less, it was hard to say, she was so skinny, half-starved I should rather say. Barefoot and wearing a thin nightgown through which her ribs showed, her face filthy. Strange, but one detail I did notice was that there were no lines in the dirt made by tears. Perhaps she was all cried out.

Josephine put her down on the kitchen floor and turning to me said, "Don' t just stand there you clot, heat up a tin of soup."

Running her hand under the hot tap over the sink she nodded and added, "While I give this one a bath and find something for her to wear. A T-shirt or something."

"A long-sleeved sports shirt would be better, warmer, there's one in the chest of drawers."

The hot plate on the Aga was still warm, and I hoped that it would get warmer in a hurry.

63

I stood around waiting for the chicken soup to boil, but you know what they say about a watched pot. After long minutes Josephine called out from the bathroom, an edge to her voice, "Peter will you come here a moment."

With half my mind still on the soup I stepped into the bathroom.

"My God. The bastard." There was hardly an inch of flesh on her entire little body not covered in welts and bruises. Her face was unmarked, as they are, I suppose when such people wish to practise their cruelty in secret.

"The bastard, the bloody bastard," I said again.

"That's quite enough of that thank you," said Josephine with her usual lofty composure. Feeling uncharacteristically paternal I said as softly as I could, "That is never going to happen again. No one will ever hurt you ever again, sweetheart. Josie and I will not let them. Not over my dead body and er..."

Josephine silenced further conversation with a look. Funny how some women can do that.

The soup was just about warm enough when they entered the kitchen. Without the dirt, and with her hair washed and brushed, she looked a picture and for the very first time in my life I regretted that Sonia and I had never had children. There was a world of gratitude and perhaps disbelief in those sad eyes as she looked from Josie to me and back again as if we might take the soup away as yet another punishment. Had it all not been so strange she might have smiled.

After the soup she ate a whole tin of pineapple chunks in evaporated milk before falling asleep in an armchair.

"Can we keep her?" I said entreatingly earning another of Josephine's strange looks.

"Of course, she is going to stay with us darling." It was the first time she had called me that. "What do you want to do, return her to that brute or turf her out on the street like they do in Calcutta? She would be dead of exposure within the week. Doesn't it break your heart?"

"It beats me why people have children and treat them like that."

"Alice will be delighted; they have been trying for a baby for ever so long. Our little visitor has certainly landed on her feet. She might have lost one parent, such as he was, but has gained a whole new family in the process. A place to stay, sleep safe and warm at nights with regular meals. Well, as regular as those we can contrive for ourselves."

"I think that I ought to unload the side-car. She is not dressed to ride pillion. I think that you might like to ride in with her, out of the wind for a change."

I paused and finally said, "You called me darling."

That look again.

"Yes—darling, and one other thing."

I waited for the bad news which I knew would almost certainly follow.

"She can't speak."

Coddled in a duvet, they settled down in the side-car and I closed the hood. I had no reason now to keep the speed down and sped off homeward, off to the farm which was to be our home for the next five years.

Over supper we told our story, well most of it, but our happiness at being together was manifest as was their relief that I was to stay permanently, and Alice just oozed maternal affection. "What's her name?" she asked as if we had some way of knowing.

"We must call her something."

It became a bit of a game thinking of a suitable name "Margot, Amanda, Camille, Rebecca, Clementine.

Do you remember we had a Miss Clementine at school who took us for deportment? Some of the older girls said she was quite a bit, you know."

"We were all a bit – you know at fourteen."

"As interesting as all that is, it is of no help to us now. I have always liked the name of Elvira myself," I added pointlessly.

David spoke for the first time in this part of the conversation.

"I think that Rose is a very nice name, or Susan. I think it should be a short name, English and uncomplicated."

We all exchanged glances, and Susan it became. We raised a glass of Hock in salute to the child who was fast asleep in her chair. Welcome to Windridge Farm and your new home, Susan." She was still asleep at the table when we put her to bed on the sofa. I now had a comfortable place upstairs to lay my weary head. But not for long. About three o'clock or thereabouts we were woken by a scream from the living room. Josephine hurried down. Susan had had a nightmare. Returning with her wrapped in a duvet she said, "Do you mind if she sleeps with us?"

I didn't think that was a good idea by half and dragged the still warm duvet downstairs, raked over the ashes in the fire, added a log or two and curled up once again on the sofa.

David and Alice had promised to turn the practice office into a bedroom for me, but now I suggested that it ought to be Susan's room, which was fine but Susan wouldn't be parted from Josephine, so it became my room after all. We had to be content at snatching a few moments of intimacy when Susan was out in the stable helping with the horses. She had made a particular friend of the pony, Poppy, which was understandable, and I could swear that she spoke to her in whispers with her lips close to the animal's ears.

When I mentioned this to Alice, she said that she will speak again, when she is ready, and we left it at that.

The nights were drawing in, the weeks were slipping by and the need to get ourselves properly organised was pressing. I calculated that we should need ten cords of wood to see us through the winter and about a ton of coke or coal for the range in the kitchen, but that was just a guess and easier said than done. Gathering in wood became my prime preoccupation. A cord is quite a lot and ten cords a tremendous amount for two men to cut, carry and stack. About the end of October, the Brandons, arrived bringing with them a mobile home, their Land-Rover full to bursting with recently lifted potatoes and root vegetables. With these transferred to the barn, he and David disappeared and returned with a horse drawn plough which had been left outside a pub as decoration ages ago. It needed some attention and a replacement coulter, but I could make one of these with little difficulty. My thoughts soon turned to the welding equipment and steel bar stock in Uncle Bill's workshop. There were other things there too, not the least of which was the stack of coke in the bunker outside, and the tinned goods we had off loaded the day we brought Susan home.

We set off early one morning, the dew still on the grass, and in the hedges, spiders' webs were picked out in diamond like beads.

The autumn was well advanced now, but we saw almost no smoke from the chimney pots of the houses as we passed by. Where had everyone gone? Some must have died from hunger and despair but not everyone. Lying low, fearful of intruders, carefully rationing their mere stock of food there must be thousands of people out there just getting by. If there were to be no initiative by the authorities these self- same people were going to perish in their own homes. The isolated, the infirm and the disabled had most certainly already done so. At least we had each other for company, fodder for the horses and Polly's goats now, of course, but our greatest asset was our intelligence, imagination, and unquestioning belief that we should see this thing through. Sooner or later little groups like ours would link up, and we might have a more realistic chance of survival based on something more substantial than a bloody-minded faith and raw hard work.

It almost broke my heart when we drew up at Uncle Bill's bungalow and found it a blackened ruin. Had we left something alight when we departed with Susan? I didn't think so, and when I saw the broken bottles all around the house, some still with bits of charred rag wired to the neck I knew that the bungalow had been fire bombed. But who would do such a thing, Uncle Bill had no enemies? Then like a punch in the chest it dawned upon me that the only person with a grudge was the man we had disturbed in the act of beating Susan with his belt. How had he discovered my connection to this place I had no idea, but it could be no one else. The ashes were cold long since and the property ransacked before it was set ablaze. The vintage motorcycles so lovingly rebuilt by my uncle over long winter evenings just so much worthless blackened metalwork. The coke in the bunker amazingly remained undisturbed, and this we laboriously loaded into the rear of the Land-Rover. It took us several hours. We worked as quickly as possible for I had no wish to be stuck here in the dark, unarmed, and it was possible that the perpetrator was still lurking in the vicinity wielding a grudge like a cudgel.

CYBER BOMB

CHAPTER FOUR

The winter when it came, came early, and came hard. It began to snow on November 5th. Not much at first, but it was bitterly cold with a cruel wind from the east. Polly made tallow candles, while I shut myself away with the aim of making a beehive. Two, if the first one turned out all right. Polly asked me if it would be difficult to make a smoker. I did from an old oil drum. It was simpler to make than I had imagined and simple to operate so we had smoked meat and fish as an addition to our larder. Andrew swept the chimney which served the copper and wash days became slightly less of a chore.

Unable to turn pieces of wood large enough to replace the rollers of the old cast iron mangle, I improvised with two pieces of steel pipe which worked very well. Most evenings after supper we sat beside the fireplace or in the kitchen reading or attending to repairs of one sort or another. There was always something worn or broken. We ought to have made more of an effort to find some clothing for Susan. Josephine and Alice did their best, but the result was nearly always comical. One night, for no particular reason, Susan stopped on her way up to bed and turning gave me a great hug; something she had never done before. To have earned the unsolicited affection of a child is a wonderful thing and it kept me in good spirits for days afterwards, whenever I thought about it.

Although he showed willing to lend a hand, it was clear that David believed that he was not pulling his weight and wished to make a contribution which was all his own. Whenever he went out walking on his own, he always returned with a couple of rabbits or pigeons and on one occasion a thin reluctant sheep on the end of a piece of twine. The range was just the thing to cook things slowly.

Every night after supper at eight on the dot, he would sit down in the kitchen with a wind-u p radio and scan the airwaves. He had a regular routine. Long wave from one side of the dial to the other, then medium wave, and then VHF. Then he would return to long wave and start again. He kept a log of everything he heard. Morse code faint and distant sometimes. One blustery evening just before Christmas he shouted, "I say come here listen to this." We rushed into the kitchen. There was a steady flow of Morse code. Some passages louder and longer than others. "Great," I said. "What are they saying?"

"No idea," he replied. "It's all in Morse."

"Well where does that get us?" I asked, my interest waning.

"What makes this so important, Peter, is that although I can pick up bits and pieces from time to time it is always just the one operator sending out messages, hoping that someone will pick them up. This is different don't you see. This is a conversation.

"Operator "A" is faint and either distant or operating on very low power, whereas operator. "B" is louder, meaning that he is either local or has a very powerful set. Now here is the thing. Although we can't talk to either, because we do not have the equipment and would not know how to operate it if we did. There is the additional problem that we do not know the Morse code.

"Now, thinking ahead. If we had two radios like this one, set about a mile apart. we might be able to fix their position on an ordinance survey map. As you will see by looking out of the window this is not the weather to be hanging about on hill tops with a paper map likely to be blown away any moment, but what I can do is to learn Morse code. I am sure that I have seen it in a book hereabouts somewhere, a dictionary or an encyclopaedia. It may be that these are people we would not wish to meet under any circumstances, but if we could read their correspondence it would at least give us a heads up. What do you think?"

"Well David, do you think that you can learn to read Morse code?"

"Certain. Doubly certain if you can all help me. We might even make a parlour game of it for these long winter evenings. Are you up for it?"

We were and a game it became. At times I thought that we had all gone mad. Dar dar dit dit. Dit dit dar. The easy one was:

Dit dit dit - Dar dar dar - dit dit dit which was S O S of course.

It got a bit silly sometimes with some of the messages we sent to each other. "I want an ice cream" "Anyone for tennis" "Who's round is it" "Merry Christmas"

No sooner had David mastered the art, and we had become reasonably proficient, than the two-way traffic came to an abrupt halt.

David continued his vigil, but the after-dinner game had died away.

We had other things on our minds just then, as the blizzard started. Light powdery snow that drifted into huge piles against the sides of buildings and hedgerows. One windfall, quite literally, was the tree which was brought down across the entrance to our lane. Some of the branches had snapped like glass with the bitter cold and these we were able to saw into manageable lengths and cart home for the fire.

Another gift of the gods was a little flock of sheep who wandered into our yard and into our barn without force or invitation. If we ate two a month, we would have mutton stews and curry at least until May, by which time there would be other options. When in April the last of the snow melted, we decided to have a party, setting perhaps a new tradition for future generations. By June we honestly believed that we had got the hang of this survival business, and Andrew and I ventured further and further afield on salvage expeditions. We would note the routes we had taken, recording everything that might be of interest to us in the future. There was nothing to stop us now breaking into shops and houses in search of tools, clothing, fuel, and preserved food. Lorries that had stalled and were abandoned when their electronics packed up, frequently had nearly full tanks of diesel which we pumped out with a hand operated pump. Here and there were dead bodies to be seen, but not many. Most people, I suppose, died at home trying to keep warm, eating whatever came to hand. There were stray dogs; lots of them, but no feral cats that we were aware of. In some places there were thousands of rats seemingly unaware of what the Land-Rover could do, and we ran over them in droves. No doubt in due course nature would find a balance.

The furthest we ventured that summer was Instow, a village beside the River Torridge estuary where there was a Royal Marine base. Royal Marines are famous for their ability to survive under any circumstances. If there was to be anyone alive in this part of the world it would be here.

A ripple of machine gun fire rent the air as I tried the gate. I stood stock still until a corporal walked cautiously forward, assault rifle at the ready. In that moment I would have bet a pound to a penny that there were other guns covering me from behind cover. I was not wrong. After a brief exchange of words, the corporal swung back the gate. There were six marines in residence, and they did pretty well for themselves. Enough sealed meals-ready-to-eat to last for years. They had guns, fuel, trucks which wouldn't run and an RIB boat which would. They had scouted the coast from Bude to Ilfracombe and the Island of Lundy. They dined on fresh fish from time to time and even had a rescued cow shortly to be butchered. They did not know, and why should they, that a cow must be in calf to give milk.

"So, we need a bull then."

I nodded.

"Hear that George? We need a bull."

"Does it have to be any particular sort of bull?"

"Not as far as I know. Any bull will do."

"Well I'll be buggered, here we sit with no milk for our tea all these months and just over the road are hundreds of wild cattle in the grounds of Tapeley Manor; ugly great brutes with horns as long as your arm. We were going to shoot one if we got really hungry."

"So what do you guys want to do? Stay here or move on some-place else?"

"What for? We can survive here for years, or until somebody sorts things out."

"I think that it is the same everywhere. No government. No law and order. The only chance we, any of us, have in the long run is to meet up with a larger group, but so far apart from a bit of radio traffic in Morse, I don't think that there are any large groups."

"That Morse you picked up might have been us talking to a Royal Navy training ship somewhere in the

Med. It's lost power and has been trying to rig up sails. Been aground twice. Silly buggers."

"There is one largish group, mind you, centred on Barnstaple. About a hundred I should say. Kids on scooters. Kill you soon as look at you. They tried to break in here once, shotguns blazing. Only kids, but a kid with a gun can kill you as quickly as anyone else.

"The guy leading them though wasn't a kid. A big gopping son of a bitch, he hung back and sent them in to do his dirty work. If I could have got a clear shot, I would have blown his bloody head off, no sweat.

"Sergeant White, before he buggered off with some scrubber from Appledore, wasn't going to give these mugs an inch and opened up on them with an LASM. I guess you would call it a single shot bazooka. It hit a scooter and blew it to hell. That took the heart out of them and they never came back, although we see them ride past now and then. The remains of the scooter are still there over on the grass, but of the rider no sign.

"I reckon the seagulls ate whatever bits were left. Greedy creatures, gulls. Good luck to them. Fancy joining us for scran?"

"Scran?"

"Scran – nosh, grub, food."

"Oh yes, thanks."

Of all things the "meal-ready-eat" was lamb curry. We had been eating lamb curry for weeks and would have loved a bit of fish and chips.

After lunch, George, Harry, Sid and the others topped up our tank and asked us if there were any bits of kit we might need. I asked for an LASM and a couple of SA

80s rifles and if they could spare one, a trailer would be handy. All of which they gave us without question, wished us well and waved as we drove out of the gate. Driving cross-country we avoided any possible roadblocks on the main roads. Stopping where we thought we might pick up some useful item, we arrived back home with a full load, including another radio for David, some books and an old treadle operated sewing machine for Alice, new Barbour overcoats for Andrew and Polly, a BSA 22 single shot bolt action rifle, together with a scope sight and a silencer, which Andrew insisted was a suppressor. Also 1400 rounds of Remington hollow point ammunition sealed in an unopened plastic bucket, several cases of wine (various), some Gucci shoes, perfume, and a silk headscarf for Josephine. And, as a special present, a full-face crash helmet. I was unsure how she would take this eclectic mix, but as I explained later, scavenging in rural Devon was not the same as shopping in Knightsbridge.

The thing which gave me the most pleasure, however, was the ensemble I had put together for Susan. Ignorant about children's sizes I took lots of everything. Jeans, shoes, socks, Wellington boots, party frocks, woolly jumpers, and a bright red raincoat. All of which earned me a kiss at supper time when she appeared in a mismatched rainbow costume which touched my heart in its artless innocence. I was beginning to feel more for this child and her future than I did for any of us.

Josephine, in whose life clothes, style and the latest fashions played such a large part looked amazed at the concoction, but said nothing; no doubt she would teach her about colour balance and proportion in due course, but for now it was enough just to see her happy.

The following winters were not nearly so harsh, and we settled into a routine of ploughing, harrowing, sowing and harvesting. The bees were hard at work in the hives I had made for them and the hens were doing good business. Once a week Andrew and I would stroll out just before dusk and try to bring in a couple of rabbits, and occasionally a pheasant. Although for a very long time I let him do all the shooting, I did warm to it eventually and became, as he said, "A rotten shot bordering on better." We had sheep, and lambs too in their season, and a choice of three kinds of milk: ewe, goat and cow, and for the present at least a stock of tea bags which we kept in airtight Kilner jars. What we would do when the rubber sealing rings eventually perished, I had no idea. It was just one of those small things which we were leaving behind and would distress me disproportionally when already worried and unable to sleep.

Returning from one shoot the back way through the woods, some sixth sense told me that something was not quite right. I slowed our pace to a crawl. I signalled to Andrew and he chambered a round. We had been expecting a raid from one of the packs of dogs which ravaged the area, but so far they had left us alone.

Mims, the Brandon's terrier who was usually skulking about looking for rats was nowhere to be seen. Andrew gave a long, low whistle which normally brought him running. He tried again.

"Come on, Mims, you must have heard that," he said, when we were suddenly both surprised much more than I can express.

"Daddy stop! He is here. Please, Daddy, you must stop."

Susan who had never spoken a word was now entreating us to stop and with some urgency. Panic would be a better word. She beckoned to us from the side door to the stables.

We slipped in as quietly as we could.

Who was here? Who was he? "And darling you can speak again," I said excitedly. I so wanted to hug her there and then and ask what had happened. She silenced my questions with a finger to my lips as she whispered in my ear.

He was. Barney Mason her stepfather, yes, the one who regularly took his belt and his fist to her. He was here with five of his gang. Four were in the kitchen eating everything in sight. The youngest had slapped Polly about and dragged her upstairs. Andrew stiffened and drew breath. His grip upon his rifle left his knuckles white with frustration and fury.

"Where is David?"

"They hit him. He is dead, I think. They left him lying out by the back door."

We eased over to the window facing the house where the orange light of several candles flickered.

"Susan can you be really brave, and do exactly as I tell you?" said Andrew with a surprising and uncharacteristic air of command.

She nodded.

"What I want you to do is climb up the ivy by the bedroom windows and with a stick bang on the glass. Lightly at first, then louder until somebody comes to the window. Let him see you then climb down as quickly as you can and then run and hide in the woods until I call for you. Can you do that for me?"

She nodded again.

"You won't let him take me, away will you?"

I kissed her lightly on the forehead. "Not in a million, million years my darling. Now off you go."

As light as a feather she climbed the ivy and tapped with increasing urgency on the bedroom window with a stick. First on the one to her left, then to the window on her right.

A face appeared; a youth no more than seventeen perhaps. He opened the casement and as he did so Andrew calmly shot him cleanly between the eyes, his old-fashioned rifle making little sound. The boy, whoever he was, slumped forward without a murmur.

"Andrew, that was some shot," I whispered. "Where did you learn to shoot like that?"

"At school; Marlborough actually. Never good enough to compete at Bisley, but I can usually hit what I aim at."

There were four more and Barney Mason to deal with now.

Swiftly we moved in the failing light to Andrew's mobile home where he swapped his rook gun for one of the Enfield SA 80s that the Royal Marines at Instow had given to us. Our plan was simple. Andrew was to slip in by the back door. I would stand outside by the front. After a count of twenty I was to make a noise with a bucket. With their attention on the door Andrew was to appear behind them in the kitchen and distract them further by cocking the bolt on his assault rifle. In that self-same second, I would come in through the front with a shotgun in each hand.

One of the gang was too quick and reached for his sawn off shotgun. Too quick to live and too quick to die, as Andrew pumped five rounds of automatic fire into his chest. The others froze. Josephine sat petrified at the noise and recent events, her T-shirt torn exposing a bare breast, her mouth blood-stained from a split lip.

"Stay still, stay very still." Josie made to move. "You too Josie, just for a moment. Where is Alice?"

"Upstairs. She took a tranquilizer and has missed all this fuss."

"Andrew. One at a time remove their guns. Josie move slowly towards me staying out of my line of fire. That's it good girl."

"David is lying outside. See what you can do for him. Easy now."

"You lot stand up one at a time and go over there and sit on the floor facing the wall."

Barney Mason opened his mouth to say something, but I was in no mood for conversation and hit him over the shoulder with the barrel of one of the guns.

"Andrew give me that rifle, now go and see if Polly is all right."

I set aside the shotguns and retrieved Uncle Bill's pistol from the drawer of the Welsh dresser. A pistol is much handier in a confined space like a kitchen, so much more so than even a short-barrelled rifle like the Enfield SA80.

Andrew returned, "She's OK, just shaken up. He didn't do anything. He couldn't. First time nerves, he was just a kid, I shouldn't have killed him."

"You did what you had to do. She might have been dead by now. You had no way of knowing."

"But I feel so guilty."

"If anyone should feel guilty it's this one," I said giving Mason a poke. OK you lot, outside."

"What shall we do with them, Pete?"

"Lock them in one of the outbuildings for now while we sort ourselves out. Perhaps we can feed them to the pigs one at a time tomorrow."

We didn't have any pigs, but they didn't know that.

David needed both of us to get him on his feet and had a nasty gash on his head which needed stitches. He had the kit in his bag, but we had never done such needlework before. Still we did our best. At least it stopped the bleeding.

Josephine put on a clean T-shirt and went up to see Polly.

With the bumper of Andrew's Land-Rover against the door of the outbuilding we were pretty sure that Mason and his gang were not going anywhere soon. We buried the boy whose name was Patrick Webster, and Mims in the same shallow grave.

CYBER BOMB

CHAPTER FIVE

The following morning was dry and bright and we were all up and about by seven o'clock, but it was ten before we cautiously moved the Land-Rover, released our prisoners and had our first good look at them. Just big kids, in their twenties maybe. You could have seen their like any day in any run-down area in the country, out-competing each other in doing bunny-hops on little child-sized bicycles or skate boards. No self-respect, no ambition, and no prospects; just the kind of dumb cattle that tattoo parlours and shops selling legal highs were there to serve. We opened the door. One nearly fell out.

"Come along sunshine, move. You're going home, that way, quick march."

"What about our scooters?"

"You are lucky. I have been thinking about taking your boots and belts, but mustn't be cruel, must I?

"Your scooters are now our scooters. You are walking home. Put some zip in it and you will be home this time tomorrow. Down the lane, turn right and keep going."

Sluggishly they moved through the gate. Andrew with his assault rifle and me with a shot gun in my arms, and a pistol in my waistband, a few paces behind. We reached the veterinary signpost that was just before the entrance to our lane. That should have been the end of the matter, but no. Barney Mason turned to face us, his features full of hateful spite.

"Just you wait, you fucking bastard, I'll be back. And when I do, I shall have a hundred others with me and then we shall see who will be kicking who around."

"Leave it out, Barney, it's not worth it. Phil and Eddy are dead, and we lost the scooters. Let's get a move on. We don't want to spend another night out here." This from one of his reduced gang. He turned on them with some venom.

"You shut your fucking mouth. I say what we do."

"The boy's right you know. There is no point in looking for more grief. Now get a move on. We don't want to stand here all day talking to the likes of you," I said.

"Likes of me, eh? We will see about that when I come back mob-handed."

"Now don't be silly, Mason. You most definitely do not mean to come back here and cause further trouble. Listen to these boys, quit while you still can."

"I will come back, not for a bit, but when I do I am going to burn your little farmhouse to the ground. A petrol bomb through each window will fix your bloody hash once and for all just like I did to the bungalow you visited recently."

"You did that?" I asked.

Something unfamiliar was stirring within me, which I did not like, and which gripped my throat making speech and breathing difficult.

"Yeah."

"And you are really going to come back here to hurt my family?"

"Yeah."

"When?"

"Don't know, but soon. Very soon."

"All of us?"

"Yeah, and that little bitch my stepdaughter, I will find her wherever she is hiding."

"You know that I can't let you do that don't you."

"Fuck off."

With that I drew my pistol and pointed it at his face.

"You don't have the fucking bottle."

But I did have the fucking bottle and shot him in the chest at point blank range.

I do not know who was more surprised, he or I, or Andrew, or the gang members who feared that they might soon be next.

He didn't fly backwards as they do in the films. He just collapsed drowning on his own blood. He slumped down onto his knees, his lifeless head bowed as though in prayer or supplication. It was then that I shot him again, this time with the muzzle in contact with his skull which burst spraying blood, bone and slime in all directions. He fell over into a heap.

This opened some strange emotions. For me very strange, which I did not have the words to frame into thoughts at that time. With the first shot I had felt nothing but relief that this evil son of a bitch was gone from our lives and that my sleep would never be disturbed by visions of him lurking in the hedgerows waiting to fling petrol bombs at us.

But when I shot him a second time, clean through his head and the back of his skull blew out, I felt a pleasure I am unable to describe.

My hands were trembling, and I had to put them in my pocket so that Andrew wouldn't see. God alone knows what he thought of me now. He whistled and signalled to our remaining prisoners to go.

Turning the pistol upon them I said, "Before you go, drag – that --- into the woods as deep as you can. If I should ever see you or anyone riding motor-scooters up this lane again I will shoot on sight. You have seen what I can do when I am cross. Wake up! You are still young, don't go the way he did, dead in the dirt of the road and all for nothing. Now get going."

They only dragged the corpse a bare ten yards into the woods before running off.

I knew, without knowing that I knew, that things had changed. That I had reached a punctuation point in my life and that from here on my life would be very different. Perhaps everyone who kills for the first time feels the same; I had no way of knowing.

I wanted this kept secret, to shield Susan from the fact that I had murdered her stepfather. No other word for it. But Andrew told Polly. Polly had told Alice, and Susan had overheard.

That night in the hay loft of the barn Josephine and I made love with a passion and fury which shocked us both. I apologized afterwards if she thought that I had been a bit too rough, but not a bit, it made a nice change I

85

was told. It transpired that I could be too gentle, too sensual sometimes. I could not help but think that killing Mason had in some way affected my behaviour towards her. That and other things were still very much on my mind the following morning as I took out my self-doubts on the stack of firewood with an axe. I didn't hear Susan approach, which is dangerous when someone is swinging an axe.

"Daddy, he is dead, isn't he?"

"Yes, darling he is dead."

"And never coming back?"

"He is never going to come back to hurt you or anyone ever again, my dear."

"I want to see the body to make sure."

"No you can't do that. It would be wrong."

"But why?"

"It just is, that's why. Now please I have to get on with my work if you want to be warm this winter. Watch if you want but stand over there. Please. I have such a lot to do."

She moved as requested.

"Daddy, where do bad people go when they die?"

"Oh, I don't know. Hell probably."

"Daddy, if there is a Hell is there a Heaven also?"

"I suppose so," I said throwing the split pieces to one side and setting a new log up on the stump.

"If there is a Hell and a Heaven will God be there to keep an eye on things. See that no one escapes Hell and sneaks into Heaven on the quiet when everyone is singing or playing their harps?"

"Sounds reasonable to me. Have you collected the eggs all up yet?"

"Yes, but you said that you didn't believe in God only last week."

"Did I? Oh. I don't know darling. What do you want to know for?"

"Oh, no reason. Can we talk about this some more when you are not so busy?"

"Yes of course any time, now run along there's a good girl."

She went a few paces, stopped and turned on her heel.

What now? I remember thinking.

"Daddy?"

"Yes?"

"I think that it is time that I had a room of my own. If you are sure that he is not coming back, and then of course you and Mummy can cuddle up together all toasty like proper married people do even if you did not actually get married in a real church.

And that was that. Theology, ethics, and morality all in one package.

It did get me out of my gloomy introspection though, and also reminded me that there was a remote chance that Susan might stumble over Mason's rotting body one day. I lay aside the axe and exchanged it for a Devon spade, the sort with a pointed leading edge and a long handle. The sort gold miners have in the westerns.

The ground in the woods was hard and full of roots. I made several attempts before giving up and looking for some place else. I had no wish to carry or drag a large dead body any great distance.

I found a spot beneath a drystone wall and dug an egg-shaped hole large enough to take his body folded in two. I stamped the earth around him as I backfilled the grave and scattered the surplus earth far and wide. I wanted there to be nothing to mark it as a grave in any way. Finally, I gathered up armfuls of last year's leaves to cover the wounded earth. It would not fool a determined investigator, but it might fool a child who just happened to stumble upon it. The exercise had taken the better part of the day.

"Where have you been to all day, Peter?" asked Jose at dinner.

"Erm." For a moment I was lost for words.

"Servitium pro defunctis," I replied hesitatingly dragging that up from God knows where.

"My, my," she said taking an elegant sip of elderberry wine.

"The things you must have learned at that Secondary Modern School of yours."

She could be an awful snob sometimes. Actually, it was a Comprehensive.

"What did he say, Mummy?"

"Nothing darling, now sit up straight if you please."

"But what was it, I want to know?"

"It was Latin."

"What's Latin?"
"Nothing for you to worry about, poppet," added Polly who knew Latin when she heard it but didn't comprehend a word. "It's a dead language." Susan's eyes opened wide.

Suddenly the table went quiet and Josie blushed for the first and only time in my experience.

"You mean a language to talk to dead people?" said Susan excitedly as if thinking that this might be a useful thing to learn.

I was about to explain when there was a loud yell from David, up in bed with a stitched- u p skull. "Come quick, everyone."

We ran for the stairs and burst into his room.

"Come in all of you, quick, listen to this."

He wound up the little radio as far as its spring would allow and switched on once again. There could be no doubt about it

We were listening to a recording of *The Last Night of The Proms.*

Someone, perhaps only one man alone in an attic room somewhere, had assembled the bits and pieces to broadcast sound and with quite a broad bandwidth according to David.

There followed a short period of dead air until a quiet, educated voice announced:

"Good evening ladies and gentlemen. Thank you for joining us.

"This is Radio Albion. Broadcasting from Eastleigh on 96.1 FM, for two hours every evening from eight to ten, and this is your host Albert Murry-Piper welcoming back all of our regular listeners and all newcomers hearing us for the very first time. Here is the news. Four new families joined us at the reception centre this morning.

"They have reported that between Guildford and Gosport they never met a living soul. Many of the main roads and most of the minor ones are closed to traffic due to localized flooding, abandoned vehicles, and fallen trees but some routes are usable with extreme care. Dr Aubrey Morgan, who runs the quarantine facility tells me that one of the new adults is a chiropodist. No doubt we would have preferred a dentist or a vet, but we must be grateful, for this brings the number of people with some professional knowledge of the human condition up to eleven."

There followed various bits and pieces about food stocks. Births and deaths and a weather forecast. He ended the evening's broadcast by saying. "Although we no longer have a Royal Family, some of us, myself included, find it reassuring and optimistic to end the day with the National Anthem followed by a quiet moment of reflection. Good night and God bless you all."

David switched off the radio with a firm click. "I say did you all hear that too. I thought that I was going bonkers. You know that whack on the head. Music, Edward Elgar of all people, well I never, and did you hear that bit about needing a vet and what do you know here we have a vet and no clients. Where is Eastleigh anyway?"

He began to perspire, and Alice had to make him lay still or those crude stitches might split.

We left the room as quickly as possible.

Downstairs once again, I poured myself a large whisky, slumped into an easy chair and tried to pull my various thoughts together.

In spite of what was unquestionably good news, there was an air of gloom in the room. Rather than force a discussion, much less a decision, I suggested that we had had enough excitement in the last couple of days and that we ought to give some thought about what this sudden piece of intelligence could mean to us all.

Andrew started to say something, but I stopped him with a raised hand.

I picked up an unlit taper from the dresser and lighted it from a candle on the supper table and went to bed.

Josie, sensing my mood, quite wisely said nothing but snuggled up close until we fell asleep. Even before it was clear in my own mind, I had begun to work on the logistics of moving the entire establishment south.

The sheep we could turn out to rough it on the moor. The horses were a must, as were the stocks of food, seed and fodder. David's veterinary kit was essential, as were our guns and personal items. If possible, I wanted to include the Instow Royal Marines in our party, big healthy lads undaunted by any problems. I would ride over next week and make them a proposition, one which I hoped they would be unable to refuse.

The next morning, I was up before first light divorcing the Norton from its side-car. I had to be very circumspect before taking it out on the road. One steers a side-car outfit, but one has to ride a motorcycle and I had got out of the habit. My plan was to make my way south on two wheels, on my own at first, find a suitable route, see what set-up awaited us and report back. We still had the confiscated scooters and I rode around a bit on one of those. I was impressed. Not only were they quicker than I had imagined but burned very little petrol and were almost silent. In the end I decided on one of the scooters; one with very low mileage and pannier boxes. At supper I outlined my plan. Everyone was in favour except Josie.

"We came into this together and we will face whatever comes our way together until we decide otherwise. I am coming with you," which I found most reassuring and not a little flattering to have earned so much trust and confidence.

That was just about that. Over the next couple of days, we listened in to Radio Albion and put together things for our journey. You would think it was an expedition to Timbuktu instead of a round trip of about 150 miles.

If we broke down and were in need of overnight accommodation, I had house breaking tools, and if something more serious arose I had Uncle Bill's revolver and a sawn off shotgun taken from our attackers. With these things, and the big sheath knife in my boot, I felt like Davy Crockett.

On a dry day before the crisis we could have done the trip in three or four hours. As it turned out it took all day.

Radio Albion gave out a special announcement that evening to the residents of Windridge Farm in Devon that Peter and Josephine had arrived safe and sound and would be returning in a day or so.

It all looked very well organised. There was a Bobby on the gate by a red phone box although the line only served the central office. There was a cafe serving fried meals. I ate Spam for the first time in years, and Josie ate it for the first time ever. She didn't like it.

How someone who will happily eat snails and oysters can turn her nose up at Spam is beyond me. Had it been called, 'Jambon hache epice' on a smart menu at a seriously high price she would have loved it, but that is neither here nor there. A pretty little junior nurse with a name badge which read "Alison Barnes" came out to see us and answer any questions we may have. If we wished to go beyond the gatehouse, we would have to undergo a medical and stay for a while in the isolation camp as a precaution. By all accounts Covid-22 so called Gambian 'flu had killed off millions who were already weakened by a restricted diet and the exceptionally long cold winter. We knew nothing of this.

"It's not so bad here," she said in a charming little Welsh girl lilt.

"It was a holiday camp once. It has all the usual amusements. A juke box, a swimming pool, crazy golf and a library."

"How many people are here at the moment?" I asked.

"Here at the Hayling Island Reception Centre, about a hundred. Over on the main island, a little over ten thousand with more arriving every day, in ones and twos mostly. We have no shortages of food or supplies at present which is nice isn't it? We will fit you out with new clothes when you arrive officially and burn your old ones. It's less labour intensive than fumigation. We have hundreds of empty houses so you can take your pick of whatever suits you best. More or less that is. Some buildings have been reserved for special projects by the Council though. It's funny but what you might call working people like to live fairly close to the central parts of town and the others, professional people like, prefer to be a bit more secluded if you know what I mean. I expect that you would be the same. She looked at Josie with a look that had something of the guarded, even worshipful admiration of a menial about it. Even in motorcycle waterproofs and boots with her hair a greasy mess beneath her helmet, she was every inch a woman of substance.

"If you want to stay overnight, there are any number of small hotels outside of the compound. They have all been cleaned and the cadavers removed long since. You might like to try the Regency. It has a bar and a radio so you can catch our nightly broadcast if you like and have a few drinks. All the drinks are free, but if you want tea or coffee you have to shift for yourself and if you want breakfast before setting out on your return trip the cafe at the gatehouse opens about seven. That too is free.

"Well, I must go there's quite a panic on at the moment. A ship of some sort is heading in this direction with several hundred people on board, some are sick already. We can quarantine them aboard, but you never know what to expect these days."

We rode away from the security gate and parked outside the *Regency Hotel*, an unprepossessing Victorian four-storey building in need of fresh paint. We made for the bar. A man at the bar got up to introduce himself. "Miles Waterhouse, international affairs journalist on the *Telegraph*, or was before all this happened. Didn't even draw a pay cheque. Came over from *The Economist*, asked to write a piece about the proposed Baltic Tunnel and then Barclays, God bless 'em, lost all my money down some infernal electronic black hole. Cyber-attack some called it and blamed the North Koreans; others said Sunspots. So, they didn't know how to react. My guess is that it's Martians or some spotty dyslexic kid holed up in Harlem with a grudge against the world and an Oedipus complex. But we will never know now, will we? Can I get you a drink, on the paper of course?"

"We were told it was all free."

"So it is, so it is, force of habit."

Under other circumstances he might have been a bore, but apprehension about his present circumstances combined with too much free gin had made him more than usually garrulous. That is to say more than was normal in a senior member of his profession whose stock in trade is to drink, question and listen. It was not until we were making for whatever vacant bedroom, we could find did we discover, quite by accident, that he was being eaten up by not knowing what had happened to his wife of thirty years.

Afterwards Josie said that his story was one of millions and millions and that we were very lucky to have found each other and a ready-made family on a well-founded farm as far as may be from any civil disturbance and rioting gangs with guns. This made me think of Barney Mason, and the strange way that recalling his execution always left me aroused. But it was not to be. I wanted to know what's wrong.

"Nothing, darling. It's been a long day and I am so very tired. Let's stay like this with your arms around me. Good night."

And that, with a chaste kiss on the cheek, was that. But there was something wrong. I could sense it. Something that was to come between us and our lovemaking for a long time. It was to be a very long time indeed.

We topped up the tank, although we didn't really need to and after a late breakfast and a stroll around the perimeter of the outer camp, set off home. After an hour or so it began to rain. We sheltered beneath the canopy of a garage forecourt to catch our breath. We could have found a place to lay up but decided to push on and spend the evening beside our own fireside.

Susan had dry towels ready warming before the kitchen range and Alice served us hot Bovril in a Pyrex glass, laced with sweet sherry. A curious but agreeable mix I can truly recommend.

We made our report over supper and continued it afterwards by the fireplace.

The decision to move over was not one which needed much debate. The benefits of living in a settled community were obvious, but even so we were sorry to be leaving this place, which had been, with one exceptional episode, a happy home.

CHAPTER SIX

The Royal Marines decided, having given the matter due consideration, to throw their lot in with us. The society which they had trained so hard for no longer existed as such. The command structure had vanished as had so much else, and regular pay-days were but a thing of fond memory. Like Hernan Cortes before them they quite literally burned their boats as they left, and set time delay charges in the armoury and fuel dump, having first topped everyone up with petrol and diesel and hitched a full bowser to Andrew's old Land-Rover. The Barnstaple gang would get a rude awakening if they tried to force the door to the armoury to get at the weapons stored there. There was a smoke grenade triggered as a warning. The demolition charges would follow within minutes.

Not that the remaining fuel would do them much good either diluted with estuary water.

It was a strange collection of old vehicles which we had assembled at Windridge and packed to capacity with everything we could imagine might be useful, and which we might not be able to replace later.

The journey along the route I had picked out previously was uneventful and as we eventually rolled up to the entrance we were welcomed at the gate by the police officer on duty, who introduced himself by telling us that he was not a real policeman but he said it gave the new arrivals a nice warm feeling to see a Bobby loitering outside a red telephone box. "See that lady over there with the pram?" I looked and nodded. "That's Maggie. She is the one really in charge of the gate. It's not a baby in that pram but a Sterling sub machine gun. I have an automatic pistol in my lunch box. We have to be ready for anything here."

"Yes," I said. "We have had some problems with a gang of armed youths ourselves."

"No, it's not just gangs we have to worry about. There are packs of dogs, some quite large, that make their appearance from time to time. Quite a fuss they created last year about lambing time. Our job is to hold them at the gate until the sound of gunfire brings out everyone within hearing distance with a shotgun. Then we have to clear up the bloody mess. What a life eh?"

We did not need to stand about very long for soon we were welcomed by the staff at the Hayling Island Reception Centre with hot food and mugs of tea. The stock was led away and we were shown to our quarters in quarantine.

The medical officer that day was a young, fresh faced staff nurse that Susan took to instantly and who showed us to our quarters.

There were three degrees of quarantine here. The first compound was for people like us who had escaped the ravages of the 'flu epidemic by virtue of our isolation. Even so our clothes were confiscated and burnt first thing, and we were given new when we moved into our huts. The second was for people who had lived in close proximity with infected people but never contracted the illness. These people remained longest under observation. The third group were people showing signs of the 'flu or something else potentially lethal. Their compound had more in common with a Prisoner of War camp than a Holiday Camp. People that could be treated with the limited facilities available and subsequently cured were, after six months or so, allowed to join the general population.

Those that would never recover were treated with respect and kindness, for that was all that they were able to offer. As we were to learn, it was policy here not to waste what few medicines we might have that could be used on those with a longer life expectancy.

The dead were driven to a field a mile or two away, buried with little or no ceremony, and covered in quick lime. There had been so much death in the last few years that it was impossible to be overly sentimental about strangers.

Being considered a family unit, we were billeted in close proximity except, that is, for David Westcliff. His head wound was examined and pronounced to be healing nicely. Fresh air would hasten the production of scar tissue. Being the much-needed vet he was kept outside of the wire and put up in a cottage to be near to the sheep, goats and cows. Not only was he happy to be back at the job he had trained for, but I got the impression that he welcomed a break from Alice for a while. Part of the problem for her was to have been wrenched away from *Peter Jones, Harvey Nichols* and *Fortnum and Mason*. At first it had been an adventure, but it had worn membrane thin and it was showing on her nerves in various ways. She needed a holiday, French cooking, fine wine, but most of all she yearned for a baby.

Having power showered under hot running water for the first time for ages, we changed into the clothes provided and burst out laughing

Our jeans, T-shirts, sweaters, and trainers were, apart from the size, completely identical. Couples that lived and died in such close proximity to one another were the object of derision and contempt from us with our cosmopolitan values. If I were to be absolutely honest there was just a hint of envy in my regard for such people who looked and behaved as if they were trying to be just the one person. So utterly close in their simplicity and lack of individual identity. "Shall we have a little fun with the others and finish each other's sentences for them?" said Josie mischievously.

"Perhaps not, that takes years of practice and I don't suppose that we will have the time to play party games."

After we had eaten, we were given our schedules. The first item on mine was to give bio samples. I noticed that they did not say just blood, and I speculated just how many types of sample they wanted.

I was not wrong. Nurse Barnes, in the nicest possible way, took a blood sample then left me to my own devices to produce the others. No great chore, but embarrassing. When she returned it was wearing latex gloves, and a pretty smile. "That wasn't so bad was it? As you will learn when you join the others for the introduction lecture from Jack Wyndham we have a social structure here which is very much predicated to reproduction, and if we are to progress as a society and a civilisation we mean to start with a clean slate.

"STDs, sexually transmitted diseases, are to have no place in the scheme of things here. For some people it will be hard to adapt to the freedoms at first. Particularly if happily married and set in their ways, but for others it is a licence to have fun." She paused to let the implications of this sink in. "I can tell from your expression, Mr Marsh, that you have your doubts. Well we shall see. Now if you just step over here, I will measure your height, and then to these scales. Just a bit overweight I should guess."

CYBER BOMB

CHAPTER SEVEN

This was it, the final leg of our journey and the first day of our new life. We had been pronounced hale and healthy and were cleared for the short ferry voyage to the island. First, however, we were to spend a day at the induction centre which would be the last chance for those who didn't like what they saw, or shunned commitment and society, preferring to try and make out all alone on the mainland. More of a symbolic last chance than a real one. The island was not a prison, but they wanted people to be sure that this was where they wanted to live and work, perhaps for the rest of their lives.

Josephine and I were directed towards a utilitarian looking building. The others, including Susan, would follow shortly.

Two girls dressed exactly like air hostesses stood by the double doors with clipboards and we were handed maps, leaflets of one sort or another and a notebook and pencil. I was about to say that it reminded me of a package holiday to Benidorm when Josie said much the same thing, although I doubted that she had ever been on a package holiday or a coach outing in her life.

Our names were checked off a list and when the hostess got to Josie, she said: "Josephine Pelton –Forbes."

Josie nodded. "I have this for you. It just arrived." With a wide toothy smile handed to her a small pink envelope.

She opened it and she too smiled.

"What is it? What was it? Something medical?" I said rather alarmed expecting the result of some toxins test.

"Oh nothing important," she said with another great smile and a peck on my cheek. Taking my hand and squeezing it firmly added, "It's just that we are going to have a baby, that's all. I hope that you don't mind."

"Mind, why should I mind? I think it's bloody marvellous. That's all, just bloody marvellous. I hope that I can be as good and half as kind as my father was."

My first thought, which ought to have been about giving birth under these strained conditions, was how nice it would be for Susan to have a baby sister. For what must have seemed like ages I just stood there and goggled, mouthing like a koi carp. Then the penny dropped. "Is that why you have been a bit distant recently, you know, when we were you know upstairs together and I—"

"You are an old square, aren't you?" she said, which was true.

Sonia and I were married young. Too young and the swinging party scene just passed us by and then Miranda Almira happened, which blew my stuffy, overconfident little world to pieces and took my home and my marriage with it.

The whole thing was too much for Miranda, who took herself off and I never heard from her again, leaving my heart ringing like a cracked bell.

For three, or was it five, years I threw myself into my work during the day and threw myself into a whisky bottle during the night. That was all water under the bridge I told myself now, though it never really is. The pain of things remains, even if it is only the memory of memory. This, however, was something completely different, something fantastic. What did I know about babies?

The girl with the maps and papers directed us to seats in the front row. We settled down. Turning to Josie I said, "When do you think we—"

"Oh, I don't know. You can be very silly sometimes. Walking in the woods perhaps. Sheltering from the rain when out on the Norton or—"

"Er yes," My mind retracing our intimate history. "Perhaps it was when we—"

"Yes, perhaps."

With Josie needing to share her room with Susan, we had to be imaginative in some strange places which sometimes added to the excitement and sometimes distracted from it totally. Wasps have little or no consideration. No sooner do we have a bedroom to ourselves again than I will be on short rations again. It's an ill wind.

There were about forty of us assembled when they closed the doors, a man sporting a ginger imperial beard, which fairly matched his tweed jacket, walked confidently forward, and mounted the podium.

"Good morning Ladies and Gentlemen. My name is Phillip Berry. Tea will be served shortly, just waiting for the urn to boil. We will stop for a comfort break about eleven. Lunch will be ready for us about one o/clock. The fire exits and the usual offices are at the rear of the hall.

"My everyday job here is to run the various schools, from primary to degree level. That surprised you didn't it? Degree level education is still possible after all that's happened. Not every subject is catered for, of course, so if media studies is your thing you are out of luck, but it's a start towards putting things back together. As you may have guessed I am, or was, a schoolmaster. Head of English at Pepys Academy up the road apiece. As you will find out, books are sacrosanct around here. One of our major projects at present is the consolidation of as many books as we can find in private collections with the library of Southampton University. In fact, every technical book we can lay our hands on, even those not in English. We are urgently in need of people with a consuming interest in books to help us, but Mac will tell you all about the Pergamum project in due course.

"When I am not sorting books, finding pencils and paper and whatnot for our schools I am learning to shoe horses and in the wet season I help to unblock drainage ditches as we all must do from time to time if we want to get about with dry feet. I must stand down now as I see that the boss has arrived. Ladies and Gentlemen, may I introduce to you Professor Jack Wyndham, the leader of our Council" I recognised him immediately. He was the Daimler driver who was at Chock's garage the day I took the Norton in for servicing. He recognised me also and acknowledged my presence with a hand lifted in greeting.

"Good morning everyone, my name is Jack Wyndham as some of you will already know and I am the head of administration here.

"The catastrophe when it happened caught most people off guard although there were a few of us who had anticipated something very much like it happening for several years. Some people went to great lengths to protect themselves and their families, but in academic circles it is ill-advised to get the reputation of being a crank, so we kept our thoughts and anxieties to ourselves. Perhaps with hindsight we ought not to have done so. To me it was obvious that the more stratified and complex a society, or for that matter any structure becomes, the greater the chance of component failure. Those of you who were raised on bible stories will recall the tale told in Genesis Eleven of the descendants of Noah who speaking with one tongue wished to build a town or a tower to the heavens which displeased their God, so he destroyed it and scattered them to the four corners of the world speaking diverse languages.

"What the architects and contractors of the period could not have known was that the compressive strength of sun-dried mud brick was severely limited and that above a certain height it would collapse under its own weight. The bricks that made up the lower levels would simply crumble. The bible does not say that they allowed for earthquakes, but I doubt it. The science of materials as we know it was unknown to them, even though they might have got some idea using weights and levers to arrive at some empiric knowledge of what was possible and what was not. Story though it surely is, it has an anecdotal ring of truth about it.

"Our Tower of Babel was globalisation which has grown and grown without cease since World War Two and a whole lot of people, speaking with the one tongue, that of commerce, derived a great deal of benefit from it. Today I stand before you wearing socks from China, underwear from India, shoes from the Poland and a silk tie from Italy. This level of international trade might have gone on a lot longer yet. There are always new products, new processes and new markets. That raw materials were becoming scarce was always acknowledged, but never acted upon. That the biosphere was under pressure everywhere hardly mattered. Whole countries and cultures were having more children than they could feed, so why not climb aboard the industrialisation bandwagon. Make hay whilst the sun shines, is that not what we said? Well whilst globalisation was having its day in the sun, we, all of us, you and your children were beavering away at every level of society putting all of our eggs in the one basket.

"The basket of which I speak is computer technology. Another single language displeasing in the sight of God no doubt. If you believe in God that is. Had the world's computers been standalone machines we might have had a chance to revert to a paper based economy in the event of singular failure but no, due to the mobile phone and the internet, every computer, every electronic device was linked in theory and in practice to every other piece of equipment in the whole wide world. Just about here I am out of my depth, and after lunch John Kelleher of GCHQ will try to explain what the government was up to and how we came to this inevitable sad pass when we did.

"We, the whole world, were in a most vulnerable position. What I feared most was something called a Carrington event, or mass solar ejection sending a storm of electrons heading for us at the speed of light, which would have had a most serious effect on all of the computers on that side of the world then facing the sun. These events happen all the time, but fortunately not all are very large or pointing at us, and at a distance of 93 million miles the earth is a very small target. The last time we stood directly in the path of a solar mass ejection was in 1859 where there was not much electrical equipment around and no electronic stuff at all, and all the Morse telegraphs went haywire. When the writing appeared on the wall to us a few years ago, some friends, Oxford Dons and philanthropic industrialists started to play a parlour game after dinner, usually at my home in London, in which we tried to project what might happen were such a thing come to being. The one rule was that we had to stick as close to known facts as possible.

"We never imagined for a moment that anybody would have the power, the resources and intelligence to replicate the same effects on a worldwide basis. Why should we have factored in a madman into our calculations? But there again, why not? History has had its share of those, from Caligula to Pol Pot. Why should the 21st century be any different? When the signs became clearer, I invited my colleagues to join me for a holiday here on the Isle of Wight. It soon became self-evident that things were starting to go

106

wrong in the world of computers. Slowly at first, but with an increasing pace the situation could only get worse, and it did.

"Why did I choose the Isle of Wight? It was not too far from Oxford or London and it was surrounded by water and was defendable if things became really hot. The water was both a barrier to aggression by armed marauders, and also to disease. Disease always follows serious social upheaval. Rats, broken sewers, infected water supplies or what have you. I must confess that I overestimated the threat from the first, and under estimated the second.

"My second reason for choosing this place was that this island is very much like a country in miniature. It has almost the entire infrastructure one could need, roads, electricity generation capacity, solar wind and fossil fuel, water and sewerage plants. It has a full complement of public buildings, schools, libraries, an infirmary, swimming pool and so forth. It even has a steam railway with a most interesting collection of locomotives. Not the least of which are the four 0-6-0 Hunslet Austerity Class. Whoever thought up that name must have been clairvoyant, for they are all a hundred years old or thereabouts. Some of the highly skilled volunteers from the Havenstreet workshop also survived, so if we can secure the necessary coal, they ought to be good for another hundred years. The locomotives, not the volunteers that is.

"When troubles come, they come not as single spies but by battalions. Hot on the heels of the computer meltdown came Covid-22, and with no on-line ordering facility, and the phones out of commission, we had nothing with which to treat the sickness, which quickly turned to pneumonia with fatal consequences. Just one of the benefits of an open-door policy to the world's refugees and indiscriminate multiculturalism. That is an error we shall never make again – not ever. With all links to the mainland severed. There remained about eight hundred

107

persons still alive here. Half of us scavenged for food, the other half buried the dead. In a solemn and proper manner at first, but there were just too many, and speed was of the essence for the air was turning foul. The solution was to drive around the island with a container lorry, which when packed to capacity was taken offshore and sunk. Some said a prayer, but we had had too much grief already to show more than lip service to the sad passing of unknown strangers. Even with this novel method of internment it took us six months of nauseating, depressing work to clear the island, and a further six months to deal with the rat problem."

He paused to open a bottle of real ale, with the memory of all those months of hard, dirty work drying his mouth. He raised his glass in salute. "Soon we shall be brewing our own ale, but we will come back to that. We have done our bit to lay down a framework of a society upon which you can rebuild your lives. What we ask of you is that you give us your commitment to make it work. Not just for us, yourselves and your children but for generations yet unborn who will, with great hindsight and wisdom, be able to see where we went wrong and how we tried in our own small way to put things right and make it better for ourselves and them. Can I ask you for that commitment now please?"

He clearly deserved his reputation as a great speaker for the room cheered as one in confirmation of the things he had demanded, and I suppose that I cheered as loudly as anyone.

He held up his hands and said thank you several times before moving on.

"Behind me on the blackboard are four numbers:

11,000

100,000

1900

100

I expect that you are wondering what they signify, I will explain as we go along."

In a conversational, even avuncular tone he continued, "As a first principle, article of faith if you like, I would ask you to agree that our civilisation, our culture and our race are worth preserving. If you do not then you have no place here and I must ask you to leave this place and shift for yourself on the mainland out in the great wide world, where with a hearty spirit, good luck and enterprise you can find enough food and other necessaries to keep body and soul together to last you the rest of your life. Perhaps you will encounter someone of good will who will give you support and keep you company during the long nights ahead. We will provide you with a packed lunch to see you on your way. At least you shall have had a few nights in a real bed, a bath or two, a check-up and a couple of hot meals and clean clothes. So, if you feel that you must go, one of our hostesses will walk with you to the gate and wish you farewell."

Not a soul moved as he knew full well that they would not.

"Secondly I hope that you would wish to pass on to your children and grandchildren a society where everyone has the aspiration to make their lot and that of the community as happy and as content as possible through the passing on of skills and knowledge. Central to our future is the passing on of the things we know and the things we shall take the trouble to learn. Things we simply must learn. From the boot-maker and baker to the chemist and surgeon.

"Much of our time and energy in the past was consumed in commuting to and from work. Paying our taxes and struggling to keep a roof over our heads and not missing a mortgage payment. Well that way of life, if you can call it living, has gone and gone for good. Well and truly. Here there are no taxes, no rush hour, no muggers and for the present at least no shortage of housing. The administration has a little control over who lives where, but not a lot and what there is is guided by common sense. By and large you can live where you wish, but most people like to be near their friends, their work, the shops and the pub. Oh yes, we still have those.

"We have an increasing number of health professionals, and now a vet who can't be with us just yet, his services being in such demand. These people, along with other professionals and specialists, have placed in our hands a precious embryo of a civilisation. If you need boots who can say that a cobbler is less important to survival than an academic researcher or a lab technician?

"We need everyone. We all have the right as citizens to draw rations of food and clothing. If you wish to trade one thing for another if it makes your life more agreeable, then why not. We do not need currency at the moment, but the time will come I expect when we shall. My advice is this, if you do find any gold items, wedding rings, that sort of thing, then hang on to them. Useless at present, but gold takes up very little room and history has shown that as a store of value, it is second to none.

"The third principle of our survival here, which you must accept if you wish to join us is this: Men must work, and women must have babies."

There was a murmur of unrest in the room at this and many unasked questions hung in the air.

He took another sip of beer before adding, "I hope that you are ready for this. Everyone is expected to have three jobs."

This sounded like slavery to some people and one man rose to his feet ready for a heated response.

"Please allow me to continue for this is not as oppressive as it sounds. Do you remember that I spoke of rolling my sleeves up and pitching in with everyone else to clear the island of the dead? Corpses that were in various states of decay. A most unpleasant duty. But we had to do it if anybody was to have a half decent chance. Well it is most unlikely that you will be called upon to perform that service. But there are jobs that need a lot of labour from time to time and must be attended to, usually for quite a short period. For example, cutting back the overgrown hedgerows to keep the roads open, helping to bring in the harvest; rat hunting can be time consuming but with luck that problem is now under control. There are also courses you will be expected to attend, some optional like cooking with limited ingredients, and some compulsory like first aid and the care and use of firearms, pregnancy being the only valid excuse for not attending that one. These are our homes and the longer we are here the more we will have to defend. We shall never court trouble but must be ready if it comes looking for us. Why should we raise livestock and bring in a harvest and then stand by while somebody steals it?

"It makes no sense to gamble with our livelihood and that of our children when we can fight to prevent it. If it is known that we are trained, armed and ready it should be enough to put off any aggressors, but if they come, they come.

"Your second job will be, more or less, whatever sort of work you were trained to do. If you are a trained specialist, then a part of your commitment to the community is to train up an apprentice every five years. I am sure that we can find you some useful task that you can apply your experience to. The man now running our power generation systems once owned and ran his own garage in London. Everyone finds a place to fit in somewhere on the island.

111

"Now I come to the third job. Perhaps it was wrong of me to call it work but I like to spice these talks up with something contentious from time to time, just to see who is paying attention. You have heard that Phil Berry, our head of education services, is learning to shoe horses. The Bobby you would have met on the gate, is – in his nine to five job – a dental technician repairing dentures, who in his spare time likes to walk the beat. Derek Appleby, former long-distance lorry driver, who directs our teams of scavengers is teaching himself to repair clocks and watches. I am the leader of the council, and I lecture on scientific subjects. I will give you three guesses what my third job is."

At this he raised his glass of beer to his lips, although there wasn't much left.

"Yes, you guessed it. I brew beer in my garage. Soon, if someone who would like to learn the craft as his main occupation and is willing to join me, we can scale up production and become self-sufficient in real ale. Now wouldn't that be something.

"Now allow me to draw your attention to the numbers on the board behind me.

"11,000 - this is our population here at the moment; about the size of a small town and perhaps there is an equal number living hand to mouth all around the British Isles, but even taken all together it is not enough to ensure survival.

"Let me say, to all the umarried mothers here. No single parent families. We do not give any particular status to marriage. The institution was in decline anyway with, surprisingly, even a Conservative Prime Minister banging nails into its coffin. Get this. All children are our children. Anyone who harms or neglects a child harms us all. We all have a hand in their upbringing. Together we teach them right from wrong, feed their sense of self-respect and respect for others and the environment. Build in them a

112

thirst for knowledge. We have a duty to look out for each other, it cannot be otherwise if we are to survive and, hopefully, prosper.

"Your special job, ladies, is to have children and our part of the pact is to see that you and they are looked after. The problem, as you will soon discover for yourselves, is that there are not enough men to go around, meaning to be quite blunt about it that some of you, perhaps most of you, will have to share a spouse. How you organise this is entirely up to you, but it makes sound common sense to become part of a warm loving family.

"Whoever you choose to have children with it is of no interest to the administration but you may be sure that he will be free of venereal disease, syphilis HIV-AIDS and, as far as we can tell, no congenital inheritable disability.

"We appreciate that this is a heavy burden to place upon your shoulders, perhaps the heaviest of all. Based upon nascent civilisations from history the minimum population we must have requires a baseline of 100,000 souls. We are not demanding that you parent that many. That would be a bit too much to ask of anyone, but your grandchildren and their children should see it achieved. I will be long gone by then of course. Done in by drinking my home brewed beer you might speculate.

"This is your choice, on the one hand babies, a midwife in attendance and an infirmary with nursing staff to be with you in your hour of trial. A home, a partner – even if you have to share him, – the companionship of another woman. Other children to be surrogate brothers and sisters. Schools and further education.

"It begins to sound not half bad when you consider the alternatives available on the mainland. As I have stressed before, if you want to go and try your luck elsewhere you may do so, if not with our blessing then with our best wishes and a bundle of stuff to see you on your way.

There will be no hard feelings on our part, just overwhelming sadness for the loss of what you might have given and received by being a member of our society.

"I think that this might be a good moment to break for coffee. Shall we say twenty minutes?"

As we lined up for coffee Josie squeezed my hand and said,

"If you give me a wish-list I will start looking for wife number two for you. After all you are going to need someone to look after you whilst I am off work having all those thousands of babies."

"Another one like you? I don't have the energy."

"Come off it, isn't it every man's dream to have a jolly no holds barred threesome?"

"So that's what you got up to at all of those wild parties in Eaton Square and Cheyne Walk. I often wondered."

She knew I was joking, but the look in those wild green eyes said that she was not sure if I believed it or not.

"Seriously though darling..." She never completed the sentence for the professor had remounted the podium and was about to restart his lecture.

"The civil administration here centres on the Council of which I am the head, chairman, president call it what you will. Every member of the council has executive authority and responsibility for a sector of our existence here. The waterworks, the generation of electricity, health services, scavenging, defence and so forth. You already met Phil Berry who runs the education system and is shaping up as a blacksmith farrier in his spare time if he has any, which I doubt.

"We meet officially once a month with written agendas, minutes and so forth, but we are in more or less continuous session on a daily basis. The waterworks people might need a new valve or have an unusual demand for power at short notice. The health people might need more splints or bandages. The greater the requirement, the more departments that need to be involved. We all have a requirement to turn out when needed by the council and we all have, as previously mentioned, three jobs."

A man with a bellicose appearance and a boozer's nose stood up, his hand raised.

"I usually call for questions at the end but as you appear a little agitated and have the floor please continue."

"Who exactly elected this council of yours and when do you hold the next election?"

"That's easy, we do not hold elections."

There was a gasp from some of the audience and a ripple of conversation spread around the room.

"So this is a dictatorship then," continued the questioner, already seeing himself as the leader of an insurrection.

"Not hardly. You or anyone can join the council at any time and in any department if you think that you have something to contribute. However, if you are unable to demonstrate to the other members of your department that you are a constructive member after three months in office you will be asked to leave. If you refuse to do so then a vote will be taken at the next quarterly plenary session and if it goes against you, you will be compelled to leave. You may, however, resume your seat at the table after three years and start afresh should you wish to do so. Does that answer your question?"

The man sat down. It was not the answer he was expecting.

"The same is true with regard to the chairman by the way, except that I cannot resume my seat at will after three years I have to be invited back as a result of a vote taken at full council. There you have it in a nutshell. It's a lot of work on top of whatever other responsibilities may come your way, and all without pay and no more rations than the rest. If that appeals to you, join us at the next session and see how you get on. I am not trying to put anyone on the spot. You have all the time in the world to think about it.

"Settle into your new home. Talk to your family and, if you can find one, talk to other council members. We meet at Osborne House on the last Friday of every month. The general public are welcome to sit in, but questions must be put in writing to the secretary at least an hour before the start of the meeting and will be raised before the full council. However, if the answer is considered unsatisfactory the chairman may call for a sub-committee response; a committee, which must include the person raising the question, who will have an equal vote. What we have here may not be perfect or the finest expression of democracy, but it avoids the two party first past the post system of elections which we once had, and what's more it seems to work. There is only one party here and that's the survival party and we are all members. It is not Utopia and we do not plan to build one. Utopias, however called, need rigid rules and immutable social structures. No wonder none have survived even though there have been numerous attempts, from hippy communes to state socialism. If we can have structures that are workable but flexible, we shall and must abide.

"I am frequently asked at these introductory sessions about law and order. There is only one legal principle here which may not be transgressed. It is based upon our sense of fair play and our desire that our people, our culture and our race survives.

116

"Any interruption of the harmony of our community is an offence. Theft, murder, assault - even noise -- all come under this heading, as does antisocial drunkenness, cruelty to animals and the like. The sanctions vary with the seriousness of the offence. Withholding supplies of sweets, tobacco or alcohol is sufficient for most minor offences, but exile is reserved for the most serious.

"Not punishment enough you might say? Imagine, if you will, being taken out of the Hayling Island compound on a winter's day with only the clothes you stand up in, and let loose twenty or thirty miles away with a north-east wind slapping at your legs. This, we on the council feel, is a very dire and condign punishment indeed, but not one we have been given reason to employ yet and I hope that we never need to.

"Now if I might be allowed to get back on course."

He turned, and with a piece of chalk ticked the top two numbers on the board.

"From about 1950 onwards our factories, which were producing everything from radios to cars, from toys to household appliances, began to design, as a matter of policy, items that were increasingly impossible to repair. First whole component parts needed to be replaced then the whole item itself had to be scrapped and renewed. It was, of course, more profitable to sell a replacement than a repair. In other words, more expensive to repair than to replace. Secondly, we were told; and this is only partly true, that the new radio, car or whatever was better looking and performed more efficiently. Each one better than its predecessor. The result was twofold. Firstly, thousands of tons of scrapped items were sent to landfill on an annual basis, and secondly we, as householders, lost the skills of fixing things. Add to the list of broken, or thrown away items another list of disposable things that need never have been made in the first place, and best described as ephemeral tat.

"Plastic gnomes and windmills. Pathetic nonsense like rooftop Santas. Using up resources like there was no tomorrow. Well there is no tomorrow for that sort of thing now. We cannot afford to waste materials, time and resources on rubbish any longer. Will a child be happier with a toy train or dolls house that Daddy had made especially for them, or a plastic spaceman soon broken, forgotten and discarded? I think the answer is tacit. Sounds Victorian? You are correct. We must put the clock back by conscious choice for if we do not take the initiative in this, circumstances will do it for us and the best and the worst of our culture will be flushed away for ever.

"Just for now it is essential that we salvage whatever we can from the wreckage, particularly things which will spoil if we do not use them. I am thinking here of tinned food but other things also.

"We must learn to repair, make and mend once again. To produce and preserve our own food. To design and forge, not right away perhaps, the tools which we will need for our own comfort, spiritual enrichment and survival. This process I call retrograde transference.

"This brings me to the figure 1900, which is our aim. Some years ago when computers still worked as they should and things might be looked up rapidly, some of my students and I ran an imaginative program supported by some complex arithmetic to see at what level of economic activity might a civilised lifestyle be maintained in the long term. With a little fudging of the figures the year 1900 was agreed upon. The late Victorians, in spite of their many social injustices and environmental nightmares, all of which we can avoid, did actually build a world which was stable yet evolving. It was a period of unbridled prosperity. More people lived longer, in greater comfort, ate better and were cared for better in sickness and old age than at any previous time anywhere on earth. It was not all grime and oppression though it would be foolish to claim that these did not exist. These are ills we are well placed to avoid completely. Many people, in what was until recently contemporary society dismissed the Victorians out of hand, never stopping to consider the many things we took for granted. Railways, roads, public libraries and recorded music had opened up worlds previously closed to most people. It has been said that iron bedsteads, cheap cotton sheets and mass-produced soap did more to promote public health than almost any advance in legislation with the same aim.

"I could go on all afternoon about all the other things we must thank our Victorian ancestors for, the telephone, the bicycle, anaesthetics, Bovril and the safety razor. Not to mention the sewing machine and the cinema. The list is almost endless. With 1900 as our aim we can aspire to herds and flocks large enough to fill our need for meat, milk, cheese, leather, glue and wool.

"In 1900 nearly all the heavy work on the farm was done by huge horses bred for the purpose.

"Thanks to Mr Marsh's party, here this afternoon, we now have two of the best, sturdy Shires at the peak of their strength. Horses to plough the meadows with the Norfolk plough he also brought along with him. Sooner or later we shall be able to grind our own corn, find or build a steam oven to bake bread on a viable scale. We are working on rebuilding an old cyder press and have an ambitious eye on a distillery, and did I mention that I brew my own beer, and jolly good stuff it is too.

"Somewhere here today, I notice from my list, there is a fitter -welder from a firm who once made aircraft furniture. There he is over there with his girlfriend all the way from Germany. Well, sir, how would you like to build some ploughs for us? The first horse drawn plough to be made in England for generations. We need more than one. We will also need all the associated harnesses and fittings, so

119

there must be someone among us with a feel for leather work. It is surely within our imagination and resources to make these too. Are you up to the challenge, sir?"

A voice from the rear of the room shouted out in an amused tone, "We'll give it a go."

"Certainly, give it a go. Is that not what we are all here to do? Give it a go.

"Above the doors you will have noticed two clocks, one of which has stopped because its battery is exhausted. The other old one has to be wound up once a week. It may be a little inconvenient, but it works and is more or less correct, most of the time. A useful reminder, or metaphor, for our life here on the island.

"Now, if there are no questions, I think that we might stop for lunch."

Hands shot up everywhere. A serious looking woman in clothes that did not suit her in shape, style or colour, asked, "What religion do you propose to establish here?"

"That's easy, madam – none."

She looked shocked.

"Let me put it to you this way. We do not recognise the authority of any church, religion, faith or sect. Nor do we regard ordination as having any particular value in and of itself. Nor is it an excuse to avoid the necessity to hold down a job or to help out along with the rest of us when called upon to do so. If people wish to dress up in antique garb, follow meaningless rituals, profess to believe in miracles that happened thousands of years ago or imagine that we have been spared because we are a chosen few or that I am some sort of Noah, then good luck to them. We do not promote such self-inflicted delusions and refuse most definitely to allow them to be taught in our schools. The churches and chapels hereabouts are public property, an established part of our history and shall be preserved as and when we can spare the resources and cannot be commandeered by any one organisation.

"If you or your friends wish to hold prayer meetings in these buildings, you can of course do so. While you are deep in prayer you might seek out a sign which might indicate to us all why countless millions had to die to fulfil the Lord's plan for humanity. Millions of good – pious, and bad – mad people to perish without any discrimination whatsoever."

Another woman with the same demeanour in the same row stood up, "Are you saying that this is no longer a Christian country?"

"My dear, young lady. This is whatever kind of country you want it to be, but I fear that you will be unable to convince a voting majority on the council, most of whom have lost loved ones, that they should bend the knee to a beneficent God, much less make it in any way compulsory in our schools."

She was not done yet, and continued, "If what I hear is correct, a boatload of refugees was recently refused permission to dock and land its passengers. If so, and even if you dislike being called a Christian, it was a vile and inhuman thing to do."

"Madam, by your lights would you consider it a Christian gesture to increase our population by nearly a tenth with people from an alien culture so very different from our own? People whose most earnest desire was to flee a dysfunctional society that has thwarted even their slightest aspiration to change their way of life, yet would – if allowed to do so --- bring their old ways with them here to us. Tribalism, honour killings, arranged marriages and female genital mutilation are among the things you would be asked

121

first to tolerate, then accept as normal. Add to this, demeaning codes and conduct or laws you could not live by and would not accept for a moment.

"Many of the hundreds of people crammed aboard that miserable vessel were ill and half-starved. How long do you imagine that it would take our hard pressed medical staff to examine, take and analyse blood samples and whatnot, even if there was an interpreter on hand it would take longer than many of them had left to remain on this earth. There was dried blood and sputum everywhere on the steel decks. Were our roles reversed, and had a boatload of diseased consumptive Christians turned up in their territorial waters, how long do you think it would be before their gunboats sent it to the bottom believing in their hearts that it was God's work ridding the world of just so many unclean, imperialist unbelievers?"

He was beginning to get a little heated.

"Would you consider it Christian to use up what little medicines we possess on such a cargo and then if we did so what words of consolation would you have said to a mother who had just lost a child because you had given away the medicine, which might have saved her, to a thankless alien who might well have died anyway. Do we not have sufficient problems already? I am not as ignorant of Christian teachings as you might imagine. Is it in Matthew Chapter five of six where Jesus says, "Sufficient unto the day is the evil thereof"? We have had all the evil we can contend with for now thank you very much and need no more."

He paused to collect his thoughts and, taking another sip of his home brewed beer, continued: "Now before you give voice to the thoughts which are forming in your mind, together with the names you will soon begin to call me, let me add that one of the hallmarks of a true civilisation is tolerance. Tolerance is essential until it is perverted by those

122

who ought to know better into indiscriminate approval, encouragement, and support.

"I am sure, Madam, that with your trenchant interpretation of Christianity, you tolerate things, thoughts, and actions of which you do not approve. The confluence of a benign tolerance with abject approval was a foolish characteristic of the world we have been forced to leave behind. It is not something I plan to replicate here. The line is drawn. We can ill afford that which will cause us harm in the short, or the long, term.

"We will only approve of that which will enhance our chances of survival or add to our collective happiness and well-being. Have I made my position clear, Madam?

"As far as the ship you have referred to is concerned, we gave them some flour, salt and rice, fifty tons of marine diesel, and sent them on their way. We will do no more or no less for any similar vessel which attempts to land here. But if I have not spelt it out to your satisfaction and understanding as to what we are about here, let me reiterate. We have certain rules which are predicated on survival. The survival of everyone here. Every one of us is of value, as is our culture and our peaceful disposition. Anybody finding our ways abhorrent and intolerable is perfectly free to go and find somewhere else to live. They go with our good wishes and no doubt with the blessing of whatever version of God they prefer. Now as time is rapidly moving on and we all need our lunch, I will briefly say a few words about the final figure on the blackboard. One hundred.

"One hundred years. Many of us in this room now have lived through half that number already. It sounds a lot, but it isn't. Not really. How many new generations will that length of time witness? Four or five. Unless we all pull together and agree upon the common aims of which I spoke earlier, the next generations will be scavengers, behaving much as we are doing now but without our plan for the future. Conserving our culture, teaching our children, encouraging crafts and practices which will keep us alive for decades to come. Generation one. Young poorly educated scavengers raking over the bits and pieces we left behind. Within the next one or two generations the notion of even a simple education will have taken second place to the need to hunt for food. Winters will take a heavy toll, and those alive in the spring will have to fight tooth and nail for subsistence. Add one or two more generations and our descendants will be savages, pure and simple. Only the fittest and the strongest will survive. Nothing decent, kindly and just shall remain. And this, ladies and gentlemen, frightens me more than anything else on this planet today. More than rampaging gangs, more than food shortages and more than sickness and disease.

'These things may come and go, but a relapse into stone age barbarism will condemn future generations to a million years of want and suffering without even the glimmer of light at the end of the tunnel. We, traumatized as we may be, at least have that light; the light of hope shining firmly before us in the darkness. Remember this. One hundred years is all the time it will take to get us back to the stone age unless we all work together.

''Now shall we go off, break bread together and each in his, or her, own way give thanks that we are together and of one mind.''

We met up with Andrew, Polly and Susan in the canteen where we told them our good news. Susan's reaction was that she wanted a baby too. I was on the point of saying in about seven or eight years' time darling, when Josie said, "Let's get settled into our new house first" which was not the answer I would have expected from her in my role of self-appointed guardian of Susan's innocence. No doubt I had read too much into it. Reflecting on what the professor had said I wondered how Alice was going to take it. She and David had been trying for a child for years now without success. She was a very attractive woman, but I

124

could not imagine that she was the sort to take a string of lovers in the hope that one might hit the jackpot.

But one never knows with women; faithful unto death one moment fast and loose the next. Their fidelity can turn on the point of a pin when the mood takes them. I tried hard not to think of my sad marriage to Sonia and the fatalistic way it ended.

CYBER BOMB

CHAPTER EIGHT

If the luncheon was nothing much, the desert was excellent, and even the highly selective palate of Josie thought so. I went back for seconds, which I had not finished when the bell sounded for the afternoon session.

Philip Berry took the stand once again to introduce us to John Kelleher of the National Cyber Security Centre –– a division of GCHQ. He was small, scruffy and in need of a new suit and a haircut.

"Good afternoon, everyone. Lunch was a bit civil service wasn't it, but the bread pudding and custard certainly brought back memories. Jack Wyndham has asked me to have a word with you all to try to throw a little light on all that has happened. What it was that went wrong that made our world fall to pieces, but first a little about me and my qualifications for being here.

"For ten years I worked as a senior analyst with one or another of the large telecom companies. We tend to move about a bit in our profession. Hi Tec or E Gipsies someone once called us, which is true enough for it's the only way of expanding one's knowledge and one's prospects. Then seven years ago I was head-hunted and ended up working for GCHQ at Cheltenham. It was a hush-hush high security institution set-up to glean intelligence from the airwaves, something it was particularly good at. Some say the best in the world. I can't disagree. The government quickly realised that in the internet age the potential for cyberc rime and international terrorism was enormous, and

126

my section was formed by pinching some of the best brains in the computer and telecoms industries, most of whom knew each other either personally, or by repute. We were given a pretty wide brief and were not starved of funds, which in itself was rather unusual.

"When you are looking for the bad guys, black hats we call them, it is important to have some idea of where they are operating from and what it is, they want. With criminals that is the easy part. What they want is money and lots of it, and we had developed a range of weapons to deal with this. With government sponsored mischief they go to great lengths to distance themselves from the actual hands-on perpetrator, so if confronted they can hold up their hands and say with some degree of honesty, "Not me, comrade. I ain't done nuffink." A large part of our effort was focused towards Russia, Iran and North Korea. So, as you can imagine we were shocked when strange patterns of disruption appeared, which seemed to come out of nowhere, all of a sudden and everywhere at once. None of it was very complex to start with, but for one thing, it had the ability to self-destruct if you looked at it for too long. One feature of these disturbances was the singular fact that they might start in one place and hop around the globe, making it very difficult to learn the point of origin. The closer we came to the source, the more complex became its behaviour. We called it, amongst other things, the virus with a death wish. We were not alone in our curiosity. The Chinese called it the many-headed demon, or the devil with a thousand heads. Every country in the industrialised world had teams looking into this phenomenon. It was moving faster than we could follow. It was only our policy of having our computers at GCHQ effectively isolated from the outside world that we were able to monitor what was going on at all.

"What we found out was this. I can tell you this now, but back then to have done so would have been in breach of the variously amended Official Secrets Acts and got me chucked into the Tower of London for my trouble.

127

What we eventually deduced was that this was the work of one man, or at most a handful of men, resident in England and having a tremendous amount of computing power at their command, which means having the money to purchase the necessary equipment. He or they could, and did, move with lightning speed, which led us to believe that this threat had been a very long time in the oven, and that means an expert and probably someone we know, or knew of. Ours is a small world.

"For want of a better name we referred to him as Jonah, just in case we let something slip in public or over the telephone. Jonah was always one step ahead of us. We had to collect information and see what the patterns were before we could even speculate upon the why and wherefore. Jonah could, and did, move with supersonic speed, leaving poor plodding investigators like us scratching our heads. However, we were able to discern that there were three phases in this: some by inference and all too much after the event.

"The nuisance stage came first, followed by the money stage and finally the coup de gras.

"The nuisance stage. The purpose: to infect every computer with a benign piece of programming which did nothing but prepare the way for subsequent small elements, which could lay dormant until activated. Larger pieces required the computer or mobile phone to be dormant for a while. It could do this in the middle of an email or phone call and nothing you could do would bring it back to life until it was ready. Its mission was to be enabled to pass on another different stronger virus when the time was right.

"So, for several weeks, phones and most computers went crazy. GB£ changed to US$, emails were redirected at random, numbers on a spreadsheet erased or modified. Some lists erased; some phone numbers substituted for others. Within that time-frame every mobile phone or computer, not isolated from the world-wide-web was infected, but with what we had no way of discovering. Were we to run any sort of diagnostic programme the virus would disappear. Place an infected phone next to an uninfected one or a computer, and you were back to square one for it was air mobile and very infectious. And then things really started to happen. Sums of money would start to appear and disappear all over the place. Sometimes between a company's own internal accounts and sometimes to a customer anywhere in the world. We could tell from some of our monitoring programmes which companies were most affected by eaves-dropping their telephone conversations. Money might be moved between branches in ways that were not strictly legal, and then become split into a thousand smaller bogus transactions which were impossible to follow. It was easier to try to see who was not being targeted, bearing in mind that we were trying to untangle millions of money movements. One person whose activities in the UK we were following most closely for a variety of reasons, was ex-KGB colonel Andrei Vostok. We kept an ongoing watch on all ex-Soviet game players because we could never be sure what they were up to or what agenda they were following. We were lucky. Money was pouring into his bank accounts far too quickly to be legitimate; small sums for the most part, but thousands of them.

"Our National Cyber Security Centre was coming under increasing pressure from the banking industry, who were threatening to take their businesses off-line after having spent so much effort proclaiming how safe their services were. We had meetings, of course, and sub-committees were formed, and we were literally running from one meeting to another. Special branch, MI5, MI6, COBRA, and all the rest had us standing in each other's way and buzzing around Whitehall like blue-arsed flies. What I strongly suspected at the time was that all this activity, all this fuss, was just a diversion. I began to think that we were being given the run around just to take our minds off what really might be about to occur. Then something strange happened. We, that is all of us at NCSC, the Cabinet Office and New Scotland Yard, all received the same message over the intranet which is supposed to be hyper secure and very restricted, telling us where the money had all gone. Who had it. Where it might be found, and where Andrei Vostok was exactly. This piece of information was being updated in real time. Vostok had no way of knowing that his mobile phone was in fact now contaminated with tracking software. He was in the Holiday Inn Hotel at Heathrow with the lovely Galina resting while awaiting a flight to Singapore.

"More plain clothed policemen than he had ever seen in his life since leaving Lubyanka for the last time burst into his room and, not distracted one little bit by a squealing naked Galina, had him in handcuffs, downstairs and through the lobby into a dark grey Volvo estate with blacked out windows in no time flat.

"Worse was to come. By the time the police convoy arrived at Paddington Green Police station, every penny and every trace of every penny had vanished from all his bank accounts, both legitimate and clandestine. He was now as broke as the rest of us. When we informed him of this, he went ballistic and told us everything he knew about Jonah, now called Brian Phipps, which was not a great deal having only met him in person a few times. We could not even tell if Brian Phipps was his real name. Holding Mr Vostok on the basis of no tangible evidence at all was not my problem, and I returned to Cheltenham happy that the panic was at last over. How wrong can a person be? Before I had even taken my jacket off, one of the team said that there had been a breakthrough and that the computer at the heart of this web of confusion was located near the Dartford River Crossing, most likely on the south side somewhere in close proximity to the huge complexity of telephone lines, fibre and copper, running beneath the tunnels which link the Midlands and the North with the South of England and the Continent. I called for large scale maps of the telecommunications network, but before they arrived the meltdown had started. Computers, telephones, engine management systems, radar satellite navigation equipment were, one by one, erasing their own memory, including all trace of any virus that there may have been, and setting everything at zero. All the affected equipment was as undamaged as the day it left the factory but would require total reprogramming if it were to have any further use. All perfectly possible of course given time, but we did not have the time and people began to die in hundreds of different ways as the lynch pin of our existence, the silicon chip took a holiday. Fly-by-wire aircraft fell from the sky, people died of thirst stuck in lifts, or crushed in the panic on the underground as power systems were shut down by their safety trip switches.

"Modern hi-Tec cars would never run again. Petrol could not be sold, pumped or metered without the controlling hand of a computer somewhere in the supply chain. A few of us stayed at our posts at GCHQ for longer than was necessary while the food in the canteens lasted and the back-up systems still put out power, but it was pointless and in small groups we drifted off, and the rest you know. We never discovered the whereabouts of the perpetrator we had previously called "Jonah", but at this point in time who cares. Punishing him in whatever way you might think of would not put the world back where it was. Almost certainly as mad as a hatter, what had he to live for now having achieved his fantastic goal? It is unlikely that he had any end game in mind, support group or even many friends to help him survive the chaos that followed and even he, genius he might be, could never have imagined the Covid-22 epidemic, or the harsh winter which followed. He certainly had a good working insight into the RSA algorithm invented, they claim by Ron Rivest, Adi Shamir and Len Adleman of MIT, although like the cavity magnetron and so much more was developed in England first. By one of my predecessors actually. Cliff Cocks of GCHQ. Not that it matters one whit now but given another six months or a year to complete our work on LEMON FACTORING PROBLEM IV we would have had something fireproof as far as outside tampering was concerned Not to mention the risk to life and limb posed by the plague of rats and the dog packs which roamed London in their thousands ready to fall upon anyone or anything which looked like food. Rest assured that his power to cause havoc is now a thing of the past."

CYBER BOMB

CHAPTER NINE

We were all gathered together, excluding David, waiting for the motor launch to take us the five or six miles across to the big island. We must have looked like poor pilgrims as we stood there in the matching anoraks that had been doled out to us. Me with one arm around Josie and one around Susan, I felt every inch the paterfamilias. Andrew and Polly were deep in conversation a little way off and Alice was wistfully quiet and thoughtful, looking out at the grey, wind-ruffled Solent.

The crossing was a little choppy, but I don't think that anybody gave it much mind. In due course we stepped ashore at Cowes. To our amazement street lights were coming on in the high street which runs more or less north to south. People were strolling about and a nearby pub was open with laughter and music spilling out into the street. The pavements were swept and there were a few cars about. There were one or two motorcycles which caught my interest, being pristine museum pieces, and the cherry on the cake, so to speak, was the wonderful aroma of fish and chips. Josie was the first to express our unspoken wish,

"Fish and chips anybody?"

It was all so normal. So utterly normal until you chanced upon the date on the newspaper in which the portions were wrapped.

Not being in the least able to pay I said, "How much do I owe you?" to the stout lady behind the counter.

"You must be newcomers. They all say that. It's like this my dear. I get the fish and the oil and potatoes for free, fresh every day, and the electricity to cook them, so we don't charge either. Back in the day I ran a wallpaper and paint shop. My day job here is to help run the archives, but in the evening, I do this. I enjoy meeting people; we usually have a good old chat while the fish is cooking and last year, I met my partner here. Complaining he was, that there wasn't any saveloys, cheeky beggar, I soon put a stop to his moaning. Love him. I would not change him now for all the tea in China. You probably met my Darren on the way over. He steers the launch. The space shuttle he calls it."

With fingers blue in the cold evening breeze we ate our supper as we walked along, looking in the shop windows all run just for the fun of it as third jobs. Wiping my hands on the newspaper I began to read the headlines, until Josie took it from me, screwed it up and threw it with hers in a litter bin.

"That was yesterday's news, Peter. We have to start thinking about tomorrow. All our tomorrows," she said, softly patting her stomach, although there was no sign yet that she was pregnant.

From the directions given to us on the map supplied, we made our way to a rather splendid, if a little run down, hotel.

Mrs Martin, or Dotty, as she liked to be called, handed us keys and said that we better have a full night's sleep. We would need it as we would be very busy tomorrow, restocking our wardrobes and house hunting, and would we prefer eggs, kippers or oatmeal for breakfast?

The room was warm and the bed very soft, an ideal place to spend a honeymoon, except that we fell straight asleep and only awoke when the sun hit our eyes and the seagulls started crying about drowned sailors, as they always do.

Seaside towns always look different when the sun shines. More alive. More like a holiday destination than a working harbour, which many of them were of course. We decided to split up our day as follows. Josie, Susan, Polly and Alice would go off in search of clothes, foodstuffs, household items and the like, while Andrew Brandon and I went to look for a house and some transport. The girls shot off right away, while we lingered over our coffee, the freshest we had had for ages. A boy in a baseball cap entered and walked up to the reception desk. Mrs Martin pointed to me, and he handed over a brown envelope. I thanked him and he left sorting out other envelopes from his backpack.

"How about that Andrew? Not here five minutes and the bailiffs have found me out already." I gently opened the envelope; we might need to reuse such a thing later.

"Listen to this Andrew. It's from Jack Wyndham,

"*Dear Peter.*

Far be it from me to tell you where to live, but I have a place in mind which you might feel is suitable to your needs and interests.

On the quay you will meet Kevin Jenks who once drove tourists around in a horse drawn coach, more correctly a Brougham. Nowadays he runs a taxi service for the Council. Introduce yourself to him, he knows where to go.

In a few days' time please join me for lunch I have a lot to discuss with you, and I should like to point you in the direction of a job which I think you might like. A letter handed to Dotty will find me, and whatever date suits you will suit me.

135

Best wishes

Jack Wyndham."

"Sounds intriguing," said Andrew.

"Do you fancy a jaunt in a horse and cart?"

Andrew nodded and drained the last of his coffee. "I could have sat here all morning drinking that. Funny how one forgets how normal a cup of coffee was. You know, beans from the other side of the globe, picked, roasted ground and percolated. A wonder of transport and commerce, yet we took it for granted. Not just coffee, but everything."

Kevin Jenks was on station as advertised and in a vehicle with only one gear clip-clopped off. Being my first trip on the island, I paid more attention to the houses and gardens which we drove past than the route we took. There were some amazing contrasts. Out of the town itself nearly all of the houses we passed were substantially built and sat in large plots. Some looked neat and cared for, most of the others run down, with brambles and weeds starting to overwhelm the lawns and tennis courts. Almost any one of these large bungalows could be made to serve. What we needed was a place with four bedrooms. Doubles preferred, but one might be a single. I had no bigger ambition than that. After we had been on the road for about half an hour our coachman turned off into a narrow lane in the direction of the sea. Past tall pines and fields of sheep only to stop at a pair of iron gates at which Kevin our driver climbed down to open wide. A couple of hundred yards beyond stood the most amazing ivy-c o v e r e d house, before which the driveway turned back on itself.

"Here we are, gentlemen. This is as far as I go. I must be off. I have other people waiting."

"But how shall we get back?" I asked.

"Oh, I'm sure you will find a way." And with that, and a flick of his whip, he cantered away.

It was certainly a lovely house. One I can best describe as a mansion in miniature with its stone mullions and leaded glass windows. The grounds seemed to be well kept, with a moss-covered fountain and a sundial on the lawn.

"Well we can't stand here all day like a couple of Jehovah's Witnesses," said Andrew pulling the bell and knocking on the door, which went unanswered. I tried the handle. It turned and we stepped inside. The hall was panelled in oak and a small fire burned in a fireplace set between two eighteenth century chairs upholstered in well-worn brocade. Several doors led off the hall and we opened them one by one, shouting 'hello, is anybody home?'

The more I saw of this house the more I feared that we should never make our home here. The living room was dominated by a huge cast iron American Franklin stove pumping out heat for all it was worth, the dining room set out with china and silverware for eight. Doors off this led onto the drawing room, and a library with floor to ceiling books, a gun room with a glass-fronted case full of guns. We progressed further, breakfast room, kitchen, the pantry full of foodstuffs, and a conservatory. As a former estate agent, I was mentally taking measurements and writing copy in my mind as we went. Already I had settled on a price of over two million pounds before I realised that nobody had that sort of money any more. Money was just so much paper in this economy. Upstairs were six large double rooms, three with en suite bath or shower rooms. Above these, under the eaves, were the servants' quarters, smaller unheated rooms which must have been murder during the winter back in the day when the house was first built.

We moved about in silence, half-expecting to be evicted at any moment when the owners returned. On the kitchen table next to a bottle of scotch and three glasses on a silver tray there was a large iron key with a paper label marked, "GARAGE" in felt tipped pen and underneath in smaller lettering, "Worth a look." We slid back the bolts on the back door to the kitchen. Away to the right and invisible from the front of the house, a walled garden, and to the left a stable block, and next to that the double doors of a large garage. It all began to feel unreal. Some sort of set-up; a leg pull or a test to see if the newcomers would pilfer the silverware. They were heavy wooden doors and it took both of us to get them fully open, but with the daylight streaming in I knew that this was more than a test of our honesty. At the back stood a short wheelbase Land-Rover not too different, but younger, than the one Andrew had on his smallholding and before that – my Norton. Not just the same model, but the very same. The Norton left to me in Uncle Bill's will, cleaned and polished with what appeared to be a set of brand-new Avon Road Runner tyres. This was a set-up, but it was clear that somebody was looking after me. The thing was, what did they want from me in return?

We closed the doors and slipped back into the kitchen. The silver tray and the scotch had vanished, and I could hear music coming from the front of the house. I entered the lounge with some trepidation. A man was sitting in a high-backed leather wing chair.

A voice rang out, "Put the wood in the hole, Boggy, there's a terrible draft round the back of my neck. I had not been called Boggy for donkey's years, since school in fact where I was always called Boggy Marsh. It must have taken quite a time for all this to sink in, and when it did, I exclaimed, "Chock is that you?"

"Of course, it is you, silly beggar. It took you long enough to cotton on. How are you? You have a family now I understand, and one on the way too."

138

How he knew that I have no idea.

"How, er, what, er, um..." I was a bit lost for words, which is unusual in an estate agent, but after I had introduced Andrew, we exchanged our tales of escape and survival. His was hair-raising. It seemed that as soon as society began to break down, gangs of youths from east and south-east London had taken to the streets smashing, burning, and stealing anything which took their fancy. God help any woman who came their way. Two boys entered his garage demanding money. He hadn't any. They did not believe him and held a knife to his throat. His hand fell on to his propane blow-lamp, he lit it and thrust it into the crutch of his attacker who jumped back in surprised anger bumping into his partner. This was all the chance Chock needed. He pulled a Dexion storage rack down upon them and ran like hell. Leaning against the railings outside a police station he found a bicycle which he stole and, peddling like mad, never stopped until he had reached Wimbledon. He had had no real plan, just to head west into open country. Some intuition told him that things were not going to return to normal any time soon. By some strange coincidence, he took much the same route as I, pushing his bicycle, riding it where his sore legs would allow, or cadging lifts on lorries but there were fewer and fewer of those. At Alton he had stopped to relieve himself when an Austin Cambridge pulled into the lay-by, its elderly driver seemingly having a heart attack." Take me home, son. I have money. I can't drive like this. Portsmouth. You know where that is? Please. Olive will worry herself sick if I am not home by seven."

Chock poured us all another scotch before continuing with his narrative.

"I tried to ask him for his address in Portsmouth, but he passed out. I went through his pockets but there was nothing but credit cards and about fifty pounds. I turned on his ignition and saw that he had nearly a full tank of petrol. Unless you try it you can't imagine how hard it is to move an unconscious man of some fifteen stone from the driver's seat to the passenger's seat of a car. I did it, but I was worn out. I put his seat belt on and suggested to him that I find a pub or a garage and call an ambulance. I found a pub almost right away with people still drinking outside, but their phone was out of order. The publican's wife had been a nurse and came out with me to have a look. "I'm sorry," she had said, and I believed she meant it. "He's dead. Was he your father?"

"I shook my head and said I needed a drink. In fact, I had several. Too many to drive, but I was past caring by then. All the customers in the bar could talk about was the poor signal on their mobile phones and the non-existent Wi-Fi coverage. That, and those awful race riots in London. They didn't know the half of it. With Mr M Eldridge, a customer of Barclays Bank and an organ donor, folded over beside me, held safely in with a seat belt, I drove to Gosport, locked the car and in due course my path crossed that of Jack Wyndham still behind the wheel of the car I had so recently serviced."

The Thomas Tompian long case clock in the hall struck the hour and I jumped up with a start. "How time flies. I clean forgot about the girls. I must get back."

"What's your hurry, you don't have to go home. You are home. Provided you like this place of course. Shame if you didn't like it after all the trouble Jack and I have gone to. Not to mention the small army of helpers who turned out to clean this place, cut the grass, stock the pantry, make the beds and get that bloody great motorcycle over without you seeing it arrive."

He walked out to behind the garage, where a 60's vintage Mini was parked.

"So long, Boggy, Andrew, see you both in Jack's office in a couple of days' time. I will call in on the girls and sort out some transport for them and all their shopping. I hope that there are enough coat hangers in the house that's all."

With that and a wicked laugh he headed back to town.

"The girls are certainly in for a pleasant surprise," said Andrew.

"Why do you call him, Chock?"

"I haven't the foggiest idea. We just did at school."

"I understand why they called you Boggy. Boggy Marsh. That seems to make sense, but Chock makes no kind of sense."

"I wouldn't worry about it if I were you. Let's see what we might have to do before the girls get here."

Josie walked into the hall as if she had been born here and looked as if she was about to admonish the servants for the dust on the inlaid walnut hall table. There was none. She tried to pretend that she was not delighted. She failed. Susan in a new frock ran up and down the broad staircase laying claim to the bedroom with the pictures of horses. She did well to be so impressed.

Two paintings were by George Stubbs and one by Horace Vernet, together with several others of excellent quality by artists unknown to me.

Although every light in the house was switched on, we ate by the light from two grand silver candelabras. Cheese omelettes, with a very acceptable white Burgundy followed by tinned mangos and fresh cream.

What made the meal unforgettable for me was the contagious feeling from Josie that here we should be safe; a place to settle down with optimistic prospects for our children. Alice put on a good show of happiness for our sake, but her feeling of loneliness at being separated from David was almost palpable behind the laughter and smiles. Andrew and Polly were also keeping something back, but I was in no mood to pursue it just then, reasoning that there were things between couples which, from time to time, take on an inflated importance only to disappear as quickly as they arrived. Whatever it was, was no business of mine and pushed it to the back of my mind where it would have stayed had not Josie raised the matter as we were climbing into our immense four poster bed.

"Honestly darling. Can you see them, but mostly her, being happy in these surroundings? Afraid to make a mess, walk in with Wellington boots on to chase out her goats or chickens. She misses the homely clutter of her caravan. It was different at the farm where we had our house and they had their caravan home next door. We met up at mealtimes and that was about it socially. They are wonderful friends, but I can see us getting under each other's feet in no time. Polly just couldn't stand there being any sort of atmosphere between us. She would submit meekly every time there was a difference of opinion and that would drive her crazy. This is something we must attend to sooner rather than later."

It had been a long, exciting, and exhausting day. My eyelids with a faltering will of their own began to droop as I slid my arm around Josie's naked waist and pulled her close to me in the bed's cool, crisp, starched vastness. Then, after the fashion of every married man in the world at one time or another, said, "Yes dear," and promptly fell asleep.

I was alone when I awoke. The curtains were drawn, and the sun filled the room with optimistic rose gold light. I stretched and yawned. There was food in the house and a roof over our heads, and what a roof. I had nothing planned. This was to be a day off. A day for myself if I could manage it. A gentle run around the island on the Norton would, if nothing arose to spoil it, fill the bill quite nicely. Lunch in a pub if I could find one open. Watch the sunset. Then home for supper and feet up in front of the fire. Perhaps find a little gentle Chopin in among the records by the Radiogram. A glass of something civilised and a book from the library room.

Standing at the window overlooking the drive, a pretty girl in a white coat was delivering milk from a pony and trap. Looking up she waved I waved back and smiled too.

As visualised in Jack Wyndham's vision, we were on the road to 1900 already and I realised that I had not been happier in years.

Whatever they might say to the contrary, women make the best housekeepers. Within no time flat Josie had procured horses for the stables, complete with tack, a pony and a governess cart, a school for Susan, a delivery of logs, regular deliveries of milk, eggs and bread, a part-time cleaner and a helper for the kitchen, a gardener and a window-cleaner. Alice had found a Morris Minor Traveller, not is the best condition perhaps, but a runner with decent tyres and brakes, ideal for small trips to the shops and the distribution centre.

Andrew and I kept our appointment with Jack Wyndham, curious to know what he had in mind for us. It was hard for us to imagine what he might possibly have to offer to an estate agent in a place with hundreds of unoccupied houses, and a middle-class hippy drop out.

"Come in Peter, Andrew," he said in a friendly and informal manner. "Please sit down." From a slim leather portfolio case he took two files.

"Right, Andrew let's sort you out first. My time with Peter is likely to be a bit protracted and I wouldn't want to keep you hanging around more than necessary. It says here that you went to a good school, left with a whole bunch of A-levels, good grades too and went on to become a fully qualified Chartered Accountant, then just when you were starting to rise in the profession chucked it all in. Is that true?"

Andrew started to explain, but Jack silenced him with a raised hand.

"No Andrew. We do not need to know who or what upset you so much that you threw your hand in and frankly I don't care. I know all too well how oppressive it can be working within a monoculture, don't I just. Living the good life, which wasn't very good at all. The rat race for promotion. The daily trudge into London. Shallow office gatherings you felt obliged to attend so as not to give the appearance that you were not a committed team player. I am not surprised that you dropped out. Here you will find it different. We need people like you. It's all a bit seat of the pants at the moment but as we get bigger, administration will become more and more important. How would you like to join the council and take on all day to day administrative matters? What I am saying is taking on a good portion of my job. You will have every support from all of us. Sound good to you? Is it an offer you can't refuse?"

Andrew seemed to tense in his chair. For a moment he did not answer, as if there were difficult things he wished to frame into words.

"Mr Wyndham, Er -Jack. I appreciate your confidence and the great honour you do me, but I must respectfully decline. Firstly, I have had it up to here with being a link in the chain of command. A cog in the machine is just a cog, even if it is an important one and years ago, I said this far and no further. After I had washed my hands of the whole business I bought a caravan and a few acres, found a partner who felt the same as I and before the catastrophe we had found our level and a place in the world. There is no way I can go back now to a different, and for me totally unacceptable, mindset. Now, and at this point in time, the best way I can further your aims and help the community is to find another little farm. Well perhaps not so little and not too large either."

"I see Andrew, and I would guess that there is nothing I can say that would change your mind."

"No, Jack there is not a lot."

"Hum. I guess that this part of our interview is about over," he said looking up from beneath stern and beetling eyebrows.

Andrew looked about fifteen, and as if he had just been told off by the headmaster.

"On your way out, ask Brenda to direct you to Mrs Warboy's office.

"She holds all of our maps and will help you find another farm, and give you letters of introduction to Don Slack and Jeremy Blight, they control the distribution of seeds, feedstuffs and livestock. What can I say? Sorry that you don't want to join us at the hub, but I would rather that you were happy".

Andrew left to find Brenda, Jack Wyndam's secretary.

"Now Peter, it's your turn to be put to work. Humm...

"It says here that you have a love of old buildings. Is that correct?"

I nodded.

"We have a couple of old buildings here on the island I am particularly keen to put back into commission. One built in 1863, and the other more recently. Perhaps you have heard of them. One is called Parkhurst and the other Albany. Do you know I thought of calling our settlement here Albany at one time, but we talked it over in council and opted for Albion, the old poetic name for Britain, white cliffs and what have you, also a Celtic baby name which I thought quite appropriate for our little settlement here, which can but grow to maturity under our guidance. Let us hope that it grows straight, clean and strong. Wise too."

"Yes Professor," It was the first time I had ever called him that.

I did not like by half all this talk of prisons.

"Ah yes, sorry Peter. I get carried away sometimes. I so often feel the heavy hand of history at my back pushing me forward. It may not feel like it now, but we are making a new chapter in the history of these islands." He paused and pressed the switch on his intercom with the outer office.

"Can we have some coffee now please, Brenda?"

"To return to the subject. Prisons. We want you to take charge of them for us."

"Me, a prison warder? I don't think so. Not on your life. Not my sort of thing at all. Besides I understood that there was no crime here. You had other ways of keeping people in line."

"We do."

"But I don't understand."

"Forgive my little jest, I really must stop pulling people's legs like that just to get a reaction. A hangover from my student days you know."

I smiled but is was not much of a smile.

"Isle of Wight prisons, erstwhile population at the last count 1500 souls, most of whom died locked in their cells.

Don't ask me what went wrong. There could have been a dozen reasons why they were never fed and watered. Who knows? Some rather nasty pieces of work among them; murderers, rapists, perverts and the like. What chance would we have had to build anything if that lot had broken loose?"

I still wasn't catching his drift.

"Criminals stole valuable things and if caught were locked up. What I should like you to do is steal things, with the blessing of the council of course, bring the swag here and then lock it up. Rather ironic don't you think"

At last I was beginning to understand what he was getting at. He wanted to turn the two prisons into a secure depository of as many of the country's works of art and cultural objects as I could find. Working with the regular scavenging team, I was to travel with them in ever greater circles around the perimeter of the previously searched areas, recording and collecting as we went. It sounded like a job made in heaven.

"Your old school chum, John Hutton – Chock I believe you call him – will look after the fabric of the building with his team of builders and electricians. They have made a start and all the bunk beds have been moved over to the Hayling Island Reception Centre, the mattresses fumigated or burnt. Chock has nearly as fine a grasp of history as you have. He tells me that you would play truant together, usually on a Friday afternoon, and hang around garages and antique shops."

"They were mostly junk shops back then, but we learned a thing or two."

"I say you did. You have Chock to thank for the choice of furniture, paintings and silverware in your new house. I helped pick that out. Any questions? No. You will have to make up your plan of operations as you go along. When you get yourself sorted out come and see me again,

147

and I will see who we can spare to help you. Look at that, you let your coffee get cold. Can I get you another?"

CYBER BOMB

CHAPTER TEN

So started my career as Arch Scrounger, and during the following few months I began a collection to rival that of Hans Sloane and Richard Wallace. Some of the galleries and museums had been broken into and vandalised, but much that such places collect is locked securely away in vaults and out of the reach of the casual intruder. If it were generally known I would have to feel some responsibility for leaving behind a great deal of gilded French Rococo furniture, which I find gaudy and over-elaborate but if I had to make excuses we were constrained by the limited amount of space in the lorries; food and drink taking priority of course.

As our search area widened, we would be away for days at a time. I would always try to bring something for Josie and the baby of course. She was not alone, for Alice was there with her and the midwife made regular calls. Mrs Beaumont, the midwife, was there one evening as I returned with a Land-Rover full of plunder much of which was destined for Billy. At least that was my choice of name; Josie wanted something else of course but we never argued about it. Well not much.

"Mr Marsh, may I have a word?" said the midwife looking very serious.

"It will be soon now, tomorrow or next week at the latest and although we don't expect any problems, primagravida, first child that is, is always a worry but she is young and strong. You will wish to be there, with her at the delivery?"

That was something that had not even presented itself on my mental horizon.

"On hand, of course, but you want me to be there when er— "

I had to sit down; my legs felt that they wouldn't support my weight. I knew exactly what to expect to see when a woman gave birth.

It took me an awful long time to learn to kill a rabbit, even longer to catch and behead a chicken. I remembered in vivid colour the sight when I shot Barney Mason. That was then. The bastard deserved to die. Who knew what carnage he might have vested upon the heads of my family had I let him go pumped full of angry spite and yearning for a bitter-sweet revenge? This was different. This was someone I had made love to with great passion and tenderness over the last few years. I could not bring myself to see her in pain, her features contorted by strain surrounded by instruments, blood, slime and—

"Mr Marsh, Mr Marsh, can you sit up for me please. That's it. Good boy. Now just put your head between your knees for a moment. Hold that pose. Now I do believe I saw a decanter of spirits somewhere."

She returned directly with an over-generous shot of my best Delord Hors D' Armagnac in the wrong glass. When this bottle was gone, I wondered if I would ever find another. Logic told me, yes, somewhere perhaps, but emotion said never.

"Here, drink this. Not current medical practice, mind you, but I find it works wonders with expectant fathers."

I sipped it and as always marvelled at its gentle strength and complex flavours. Father, expectant father. That was something I was going to have to get used to. Daddy. Susan had always called me that ever since she got her voice back. Right on cue she entered through the back door having forgotten to remover her muddy Wellington boots.

"Has she come yet?"

"Not yet darling now just go back. Hose those boots off before you come in again. There's a good girl. I'll let you know if anything happens."

Feeling better, but not perfect, I put the glass to one side meaning to finish it later, but the midwife picked it up and drained the glass in one.

"My word that is warming, Mr Marsh. I dare say that it's as good for midwives as it is for fathers. Perhaps when you get the chance you might pick up a bottle or two for me."

I may have grunted and stood up and went up to see Josie. She looked blooming propped up in bed reading *Middlemarch*.

We sat talking about not very much and I mentioned one or two of the things I had collected on my trip; a very fine, period, ebony bracket clock and a seascape by Winslow Homer for us and a Gainsborough for the prison. I would have to think up another name for our public collection but hadn't just yet. I will raise the matter with the council. Moving downstairs, I made us all hot chocolate, glanced through Susan's homework project, kissed her good night and packed her off to bed. I did my usual round of checking doors and windows. No point here really, but old habits die hard. Changed into my pyjamas, and with a little soft hug and a gentle caress of Billy's hidden head, dropped off to sleep.

I was awoken by Josie moving about in the bathroom.

"Peter, it's time. Can you get on the telephone to the midwife please?"

151

The telephone came with my job. An old fashioned 1940's pyramid phone. It worked, but only to the council offices at the moment. If there were someone up late, I could get a message through to the infirmary fairly quickly, but if not I would have to go myself. No one answered. I ran, half-fell, down the stairs and out into the night to my Norton. Like the civilised lady she was she started first time and riding faster than was prudent, I headed for the infirmary. It started to rain. I was not dressed either for rain or for warmth and was soon wet and shivering. The porter on duty who opened the door was not in the best of moods, and when I explained that I needed to see the midwife he said, "Would you be Mr Marsh by any chance?"

I nodded.

"They said you might turn up. Mrs Beaumont had a phone call and left for your house just ten minutes ago. Are you all right? Soaking wet, dripping on the carpet like that you had better come in and dry off."

The porter, Ken Danniels, immediately went up a few notches in my estimation. He rose a further couple of notches when he appeared with a hospital-sized bath towel and a mug of tea with rum in it.

Squeamish coward that I am, I welcomed the excuse to be out of the house in that moment although Josie was permanently on my mind. It was almost sunrise, when in overalls and a borrowed raincoat, I returned home. The midwife gave me a broad smile as our paths crossed at the front door. "It's a fine strong baby you have there, Mr Marsh, and a fine brave girl. I hope that you have the sense to look after her."

"Yes, I shall. Thank you, Mrs – is it a boy or a girl?"

"Not for me to say. Now up you go, your wife is waiting to see you."

152

I flew up the stairs two or more at a time.

Josie was sitting up in bed with this strange little visitor in her arms, Susan sat on one side of the bed and Alice on the other.

I stood stock still for a moment taking the scene, which would last forever in my mind.

"Darling," said Josie. "Would you mind if the name we choose were to be Will instead of Bill?"

My mind raced ahead. Did she have a relative or a past lover she wished to remember?

"No, my dear, Will is fine."

"Are you sure?"

"Yes, I suppose so."

"Good. Then please allow me to introduce you to Wilhelmina, our daughter. Are you terribly disappointed? I know that you so wanted a boy."

"Oh, I dare say I shall get used to having her around."

On that happy note, and with the care and assistance of her two guardian angels, both mother and daughter dropped off to sleep and I was not far behind in doing exactly the same.

CHAPTER ELEVEN

As in any social situation anywhere before the catastrophe, life settled down into the routines of work and home.

As from the beginning, we were plagued by rats on the mainland which were a constant nuisance taking up valuable manpower to deal with them when they became intolerable. We would have bred up some terriers, but all the small dogs had disappeared in great packs of mostly large dogs which ranged the countryside on the mainland. Everyone in the scavenging parties was now obliged to go armed. I had exchanged Uncle Bill's revolver for a Browning 9mm automatic, but still also carried in the cab of the lorry the sawn-off shotgun which I had recovered from Mason's raid upon the farm. We ran into one pack outside Aldershot whilst trying to load a consignment of vegetable oil aboard the lorry which already contained; packaged in about a thousand blankets, a rich and ornate harpsichord by Jacob Kirkman from a private house, which I fell in love with at first sight. It was, to my eyes at least, as if its marquetry were in ardent competition with the music it was designed to produce, so rich and vibrant and baroque. Where had this concerto, this confection in timber been hidden all these years? There was no way on earth could I allow it to be eaten away by insects and fungus in an elegant house, reluctantly but gracefully, surrendering to the elements.

It took over four hours of hot work to get it securely aboard to my satisfaction when the dogs struck, falling upon Chris Leather relieving himself in the shrubbery. His scream froze my blood.

Ken Watson the driver dropped four of the dogs with his automatic rifle. I shot and killed another two and wounded two or three more with my pistol. By the time the others had woken up and unslung their weapons the raid was over and the pack running off followed by much noise but few certain hits. We administered as much first aid to Chris as we could, but he had lost an awful lot of blood. Even if he had lived, he might well have considered that his life was not now worth living. One moment screaming, another cursing, finally whimpering like a child, he died on the way home, but not before I had retched over the tailboard of the lorry several times. Retched until my stomach hurt. He was no special friend of mine, but for days afterwards all I wanted to do was shoot dogs.

I reported to Jack Wyndham over tea in the canteen and agreed that the time must come when we must take decisive action against the dog menace. He asked me to sketch out some ideas of containing the peril, but with no great urgency from his perspective here in his ivory tower. There were no dogs on the island. Our conversation then turned to music.

"Peter. There is one thing which has occupied my thoughts on and off since this business started. It is this, I should like to see us lay on a complete orchestral concert."

He must have noticed from the look of amazement on my face that I thought that given the resources at our disposal that this was a very tall order indeed.

"Bit of a tall order, eh?" he said, reading my thoughts.

I nodded, "And then some."

"Not only would a concert signal to our population that we were getting our act together in a controlled fashion,

155

but that we had constructed the foundation course of a real civilisation, one with depth."

I could not but agree. "Where on earth are we going to get enough musicians? The instruments do not pose a problem. I have been bringing them in piece by piece for some time now, and we do have several first-class orchestral class performers. Anne Girling, for example. I gave her a Giuseppe Guarneri violin to take care of; one of the very top Classic Cremona violins and almost priceless. That little girl can make it sing."

"Exactly what I wanted to hear, Peter. Do you think that she would give an on-air solo recital for us?"

"Yes, I think so – but ..."

"No buts. After the performance we shall request other classically trained artists to come forward. We will also say that if distance presented a problem, we will be happy to arrange transport. With me so far?"

I wasn't but he continued.

"Our little radio station can be picked up for at least 250 miles. That takes in the Home Counties and as far south as Normandy. With a bit of luck, Paris also. There are plenty of venues on Hayling Island so quarantine will not be a problem, and if our visitors wish to stay with us permanently it will contribute greatly to our under-population problem, which brings me on to the next subject I would like to discuss with you.

"The number of live births is increasing all the time but, as you will realise, we started with an ageing population. Consequently, with an increasing number of deaths every month. If we do not take steps, we may find ourselves with a shrinking population. The youngsters are all at it, copulating like rabbits and good luck to them. They have sex and hygiene classes at school and starting at a very young age are encouraged to explore each other's bodies.

"I know exactly what you are going to say, Peter, because it's what I said when the subject was first raised in Council, and a modified Montessori system with elements of the Summerhill education system was proposed by Phil Berry.

"Oh, brave new world that has such people in it." Huxley sketched it out as a means of social control. For us it is a mechanism of social survival. If in a few generations time society reacts against this free and easy life style then it will hardly matter because the population will be large enough to accommodate almost any perceived changes in morality and we shall have fulfilled our obligation to the future. The problem before us now is that there are far too many women still fertile who remain childless. Too frightened, too frigid, or too unattractive to find a partner, even a temporary one."

What did he expect me to do about it? I wondered.

I was not to be in ignorance too long.

"Have you met Claire Blackwater, she is the chairperson of The Albion Sorority, a sort of mutual support group for women, young mothers especially?"

"Yes, I believe that Josephine has mentioned her name in some context or other, but I can't for the life of me remember what."

"Excellent, Peter. We may need to sit down with this woman over dinner one evening because we shall need to have her very much on-side."

"On-side about what?"

"The artificial insemination programme I have in mind to instigate. Tell me, what do you know about the process of Ai?"

"Only what everyone knows. As far as livestock goes you select a preferred progenitor or sire, depending on your needs. You may want to breed for milk or meat if its cattle, or speed or strength if horses. A specialist company will send you sperm of the right specification, deep frozen in little straws. These you thaw out as required, then you, or the vet, place one of these in the cow's uterus and nature does the rest."

"And with people?"

"On the one hand it is an incredibly simple procedure; something a woman can do on her own at home. She will still need a male of course to donate the sperm. I understand that she could order a kit to do the job from almost any high street chemist, sperm excluded. The only draw-back is that hygiene can be a bit hit or miss. Blood cells and God knows what getting into the wrong place.

"On the other hand, the best method is to enlist the aid of a trained nurse in a dedicated ward of a clinic where the sperm can be processed and cleaned up a bit where necessary. Not too expensive. I am sure that even with the people and hospital space we have we could organise something along those lines."

"Yes, Peter, I am sure we could. Is there any way we could weed out the unfit ones? You know, those with inherited genetic conditions, deformities, missing chromosomes – things like that?"

"Not without a bigger laboratory facility than we have.

"'That's bordering on in-vitro fertilisation which allows you to play God, and for many people eugenics

158

sounds a lot like Nazi policy and I can't see them buying into that lightly."

"Oh! Curse that man Hitler. Not content with killing two of my father's brothers on the beaches of Normandy and blowing up my family home on Blackheath with one of the last V1s to land in London, but he had the diabolic gift of taking many a good idea and turning it into an evil one. May he rot in hell. Never mind all that guff about a master race. We are struggling for our lives and our civilisation and we cannot spare the resources, human and material, looking after anyone who cannot make a net contribution to the commonweal."

"Does that include the decrepit elderly too?" I said manifestly tongue in cheek.

"Yes! You impudent young devil, it includes the likes of me as well. Of course, it does. When the time comes, and if I am unable to take matters into my own hands to slip away silently, then you will find a written authority in my desk at home to allow you to put an end to my suffering. You would do no less to a sick beast would you?

"All joking aside, Peter, if we are to embrace eugenics, we must also accept euthanasia and weave both concepts into our philosophy.

"But enough talk of death for today. I have found two assistants to help you with your conservation work. One is a fabric restorer from Boston, the other a graduate student writing a book on Messrs Bolton and Watt of steam engine fame. Couldn't be better. There were four of them who managed to survive the worst of the flu and the long winter. One stole a boat from somewhere and set sail for her parents' home in Norway. Two you will meet as soon as they clear quarantine, and the other is a microbiologist who will be working with the infirmary team until we can find a better job for her."

159

"Might not be a bad idea for her to look into why so many of our children are girls; four to one in some areas. The time might come when men are bred like bulls, fed on the best of everything and kept caged as sperm donors to be milked on a routine basis."

"Is that the sort of job you fancy, Peter?"

"I think that I will recommend that my old friend Chock applies for that one. Mind you with five wives, all under twenty, he is unlikely to notice any difference."

The next day being Saturday I loitered around the depot where the scavengers' vans and lorries were serviced. Being, on average well over 20 years old, they had to be handled with kid gloves and serviced regularly. Finding nothing to do, I took the Norton home with every intention of changing the oil, checking the chain tension and the air pressure in the tyres, but it was not to be for as I stepped through the door Susan grabbed me by the arm wishing to talk about Geoffrey Chaucer and Silas Marner. A weaver who finds a little girl and calls her Eppie and loves her to distraction, so the story runs, bringing out other issues like honesty and witchcraft as the narrative progresses.

"Do you love me as much as Silas loved his Eppie? You gave me my name, didn't you?" I gave her a hug. She was still pretty much a bag of bones.

"So, I did, because you couldn't speak. Susan, do you remember what your name was before Susan?" I asked.

She looked sheepish, shaking her head; a sure sign that she did remember.

"Tell me, just whisper. I won't tell anybody, honestly."

She brought her face close to mine and whispered.

"But that is a nice name," I said. "A pretty name. It means— "

She silenced further comment with a hand over my mouth.

"It's a horrible name. It reminds me of him and the time before you fetched me and became my daddy and we are all happy together."

"What was that name?" I said. "Oh, I forgot already, let's have some tea."

She reached up and kissed me very hard on the lips.

You may not know this but it's very hard to hold a conversation about Chaucer and George Elliott when there is a lump in your throat the size of a golf ball.

Behind the house was a large garden, or rather several interconnected ones. The top garden was the formal one.

Bulbs in their season, roses and rhododendrons, clipped lawns, and a sundial. Behind the house, a walled kitchen garden which now earned its keep as it had not done for perhaps a century, its soil well worked and manured, its stone walls always warm to the touch. It was a tranquil place to be alone with one's thoughts and to work off a headache. The deep green lawn led onto a semi-civilised spinney which gave way to a wilderness of dead, wind-felled trees and brambles. We were content to leave it to the birds and butterflies, before Susan had discovered that beneath the carpet of leaf mould was a stone footpath which it fell to me to clear, and which eventually ran steeply down to a private sandy beach.

There were wrought iron eyebolts set in the wall and through these I ran a stout rope as a handrail. The world we had known had died and yet its plastic garbage still clogged the ocean and littered my beach. It took me three Sundays to clear the path, and two days of working dawn to dusk and well into the evening of the third day, to clear the beach. It was getting dark before I had completed a huge pile of rubbish and driftwood, which I set alight with a pint of petrol from the garage.

Not the most ecological thing to have done, but it was my farewell funeral pyre to all the consumer-driven short-sightedness of the old world. It burned until the incoming tide the following morning washed the charred remains away.

Josie's helper, Mrs Ruby Kirby, met me coming back with a large mug of tea which tasted just fantastic as it washed the taste of burnt plastic from my mouth. Not wishing to keep Mrs Kirby further I made myself an omelette and opened a tin of soup, which I ate before it was really hot enough. Falling asleep in the armchair afterwards it was dawn when I awoke stiff but rested. I did not know it, of course, but it was the last easy sleep I was to enjoy for a very long time. After a cup instant coffee and a wash under the kitchen tap, I changed into overalls and set about servicing the Norton. About eleven Susan came into the garage with a cup of tea and a piece of cake. I looked up. Running her fingers through my hair she said, "Errgh greasy, what will Mummy say, and it smells h h h- horrible!"

She was right of course. I did stink and needed a shower. Greasing the Bowden cables would have to wait. I drank the tea and ate the cake, disgusted at the state of my hands before heading back over to the house.

Josie met me at the kitchen door. "You have just enough time to make yourself sufficiently presentable to dine in polite company, or we shall leave you behind."

Without asking who or where, I scrambled in and out of the shower, put on clean clothes and clumped down the stairs where Josie, Susan, Alice and Polly were waiting for me.

"Here comes our beast of burden," someone said, and I caught on fairly quickly. We were to have a picnic. But not in the garden which would have been perfect, but on the beach. The last fifty yards of the path was down rather steep steps cut into the rock and whilst I had fitted a rope handrail I never imagined that I would need to use it whilst carrying a large wicker hamper full of china, cutlery and wine bottles. But I don't suppose that manhandling a carry cot had entered into Josie's calculations either.

We dined pretty well on cold chicken, green salad, potato salad, and hard-boiled eggs with junket dusted with spices and clotted cream to follow and somehow got through two bottles of Hock and two bottles of champagne between us. Will slept through it all without a sound. Susan asked if she might have a sip from Josie's champagne flute and drank it all, like lemonade. Then she got the giggles and started singing to the seagulls. Bending over she whispered something to Josie.

Josie sort of shrugged in a non-committal kind of way and Susan, biting her lower lip, threw off all her clothes and ran along the water's edge doing cartwheels and falling into the surf, which I thought hilarious. It was like watching a gigantic peeled prawn doing gymnastics. It dawned upon me that this was probably the first time she had ever been free to run and play on a beach. Josie and Alice were talking together with Polly, who shook her head. What were they hatching? To bury me in the sand perhaps. No. That would have been easier to take than what happened next. With mischief lighting up both pairs of eyes, they undressed and ran naked following in Susan's footprints. How alike they were I never realised. Except for Josie's red hair they might have been twins. They couldn't quite manage a cartwheel or a handstand and collapsed in a heap laughing. This was all a bit too much. If I would have expected hippy Polly to have run wild and free, I was mistaken for she had flushed bright red as perhaps I had.

With a curt, "Keep an eye on baby for me please, Polly, I have work to do." I left them to their fun and games and returned to my Norton.

A switch or something like it moved in my head in that moment and I was at a loss to understand it. I returned up the steep path and without bothering to change, went straight into the garage and knelt down to work and adjust the tension of the rear chain. Within seconds of starting I allowed the spanner to slip, tearing a flap of skin off my knuckles which allowed blood and black grease to ruin my new white cotton trousers.

It was not that I didn't find Alice attractive. No, not that, for after the recent delivery of our baby, Alice had the better figure of the two. Neither was it guilt in seeing her naked and within arm's reach most of the time in the house, lonely and estranged from her husband, a friend of mine, who – it turns out – had lost all interest in her charms since his whack on the head.

I left the spanner where it fell and returned to the house to wash my hands and find a bandage.

Josephine had walked into my life at just the right moment in many respects. The memory of my failed marriage to Sonia was slowly reversing into history, unlike my impossible relationship with Miranda Palmira, the debris of which had sunk deep roots into my subconscious and remained there ever present like the persistent ache of a failing molar beyond salvation.

Unable to find the disinfectant I poured a little household bleach into a bowl of hot water and quickly wished I hadn't. The raw flesh beneath the little flap of skin burned with red heat, but I kept my hand in the water.

What was this I asked myself, some sort of penance? No. Why should I even ask myself such a question?

There was, I realised, and not for the first time but the first time recently, a hole in in my interior life. A hole the shape, size and disposition of Miranda. A gaping chasm that Sonia was unwilling, or unable to fill in the least, although she was loving and kind enough to understand my torment, but not its real cause. She tried for as long as her hot temper would allow, and her patience remained unexhausted, and she then left to seek solace elsewhere leaving me to stew in my own juice. Her rejection of me and my problems injured my amour-propre no doubt but it was the disappearance of Miranda from the focus of my mind's eye which had driven me deeply into the consoling arms of a whisky bottle and to the brink of suicide.

With my hand throbbing beneath an ill-affixed bandage I flopped down into the big leather armchair and reached for the decanter that stood, temptation in three solid dimensions, on a small rosewood table.

I resisted for a moment, telling myself that this was some sort of test. I soon weakened and poured myself a large round Talisker; just enough peat in its spirited nature to confer character and no more.

Miranda Palmira still haunted me even after all these years. There remained a Miranda hiatus within me and with it pain which no amount of easy seductions could ever ameliorate.

I had no wish at this time to stir into flame old quiescent embers but the infernal mills of self-doubt, incomprehension and loathing when awakened and set in motion once again refused to be still.

Was there a deeply heartfelt Miranda lurking in me somewhere long before we had ever met? Was she perhaps the poor unsuspecting and unfortunate creature who in passing my way just happened to spring the pitfall? Alike enough to the psychic template to fill the need in me but unwilling to do so.

The blood had begun to seep through the bandage and a more creative man than I might have configured the devil's head in the pattern it created. I did not dwell on that for my glass was empty.

I poured myself another whisky, larger this time, knowing full well that the anodyne was but temporary. I gave myself a little credit, but not much, for not putting Richard Wagner on the turntable of the antique radiogram and winding up the volume to maximum.

When the sting of Sonia's departure was still recent and the acceptance that Miranda had closed both her heart and mind against me, I gave myself over to the Ring Cycle and encircled my drunken misery with the consolation that he alone must have known feelings such as these. The sadness and the destiny of a man who feels too much poured forth through his masterly work. The higher it lifted my mind to an awareness of the inevitably of suffering the steeper and more profound the descent into the pit of my depression which came with each new hangover. I was no stranger to this ground.

With the determination of an approaching tank, an idea, unbidden and unwelcome began to inch its way forward into my head, crushing and grinding as it came.

What if the need existed a-priori? Then co-opting Miranda or indeed anyone to fill that need was just wishful thinking. Like putting one's hand into a bucket of bolts of random sizes and working oneself up into a state that the one selected must fit the corresponding nut so preciously guarded. Just another fantasy to make the need retract back into its shell for a season. From this it must follow that what I thought was my love for her was unreal, a figment of my febrile imagination, a delusion. Nothing more. I see that now. If that was unreal what was real? Nothing.

But dear God, there is love in me, a pure gentle self-sacrificing love that must be of some value. But a key without a lock is valueless.

Love that could not be tarnished by events or degraded by circumstance. A love that needs must see its own reflection in the love of another if it is to flourish or indeed if it is to exist at all.

The stopper of the decanter slipped from my fingers and shattered upon the stone hearth.

Sonia and I had seldom used the "L" word and Josephine and I not at all. We liked each other a great deal and shared many moments of tenderness together and there was, without question, a bond between us. But was it love if it passed unexpressed? If it went without saying? Was there something, someone, that dwelt within her that was crying out for such a union of souls that I in my foolishness had believed existed between Miranda Palmira and myself?

Did Miranda intuitively understand that the love I spoke of to her was just so much smoke. Something to listen to for a season from a two-dimensional man with strangely idealistic ideas of love. Something worthless to be cast aside as soon as it became inconvenient and meaningless.

Then there was Susan who held the true monopoly on my emotions just then. Had I shot and killed her brutal stepfather in cold blood to protect her from further harm at his hands or protecting what I possessively now believed to belong to me? Were my feelings for her just something cooked up in my head in response to some subliminal atavistic need to protect one's offspring? But she was not my offspring. No relation at all. Just a poor mite that I had taken under my protection the way some people will adopt a kitten. Why did I not have the same feelings about Wilhelmina, who was my own flesh and blood? My little pink prawn, she was different. With my thoughts turned towards Susan's uninhibited gymnastics on the beach it was impossible not to see in the same second Alice and Josie as they skipped naked hand in hand towards the surf. With that image in my mind the whole dark carousel started up once again. I turned once more towards the scotch.

The decanter was empty. I rose to fetch another bottle from the pantry, but my legs refused to work. There remained a nearly full decanter of vintage port and that would have to do. As I made to tilt the long-necked decanter, it struck me as funny that there was still whisky in my glass.

What harm could it do to mix the two? No harm at all unless you think otherwise. Who did I think I was talking to? Idiot. I was on my own. Not a bad mixture that. Port and whisky. Whisky and port. What I needed now was a little Wagner. The Lohengrin or the Tannhauser overture for starters. Now if I can just stand up.

When I awoke, I was freezing cold sitting astride the Norton in the garage, but how I got there I had not the slightest recollection.

More sober than I had any right to be, I eased open the back door, walked through the kitchen, climbed the stairs, undressed on the landing and slipped quietly into bed beside Josie trying not to wake her. She was awake and it felt splendid to be beside her familiar warm body. If she had even noticed the mess downstairs and the shattered cut glass decanter stopper in the hearth she did not say but turned and kissed me warmly.

"Sorry darling if I embarrassed you down on the beach this afternoon. I don't know what came over me. Please forgive me. Tell me you are not ashamed of me. I don't think I could live without you now. It was such a silly thing to do I just wanted to feel like a child again".

True or not it made me feel a whole lot better and her silent tears were real enough. I forgave her – wordlessly. But I could sense that we had begun to drift apart from that afternoon onwards.

In very small ways the atmosphere in the house began to change. Susie began to ask embarrassing questions about love and sex. Josie, Alice and sometimes even Mrs Kirby who lived in now would be less than modestly dressed at the breakfast table. It began to feel as if it were not my house any more, but some sort of free and easy women's hostel. I started to spend more time away from home collecting works of art and locking them away in prison, and Josie spent an inordinate amount of time with the Albion sisterhood or whatever her support group was called.

Whenever we were alone together, we would make love but with less passion and less frequently.

CYBER BOMB

CHAPTER TWELVE

There was a gloomy atmosphere in Jack Wyndham's office when I arrived at the appointed hour for one of our regular meetings. Jack rose to meet me at his door.

"Come in Peter. Terrible news. Truly horrible. Young Anne Girling has been brutally assaulted, raped, her violin stolen, and it looks as if she may not survive. The perpetrator knows that we do not have the facility to test for DNA, or even a fingerprint expert."

"Who is looking into this?"

"One of your Royal Marines from Instow. Spent some time in the Military Police before he transferred to the Marines."

Much as I might wish to, there was little I could do to help capture the animal who had done this thing and recover the violin and said as much.

"Peter you have not attended a meeting of the full council yet, and I would very much like you to take a seat as our number one guardian of the nation's art treasures. Just like Herman Goering lifting anything you fancy, but on the side of the angels. Bring Josephine along too, as a spectator just for now. We always have a glass of wine after the close of business. Quite a little social gathering in fact. You must remember Parkinson's Law 80% of the work being done by 20% of the people. Come along and meet some of the 20%. Some of them you know of course, but it will be an excellent opportunity to meet some of the others. All very informal, no need to dress up."

He was quite correct about the dress code. There wasn't one. People turned up in what they wore at work and very few wore suits.

There were about thirty people in the council as a whole, mostly recent newcomers like, me unsure of what was expected of them.

About ten people formed an inner circle whose activities were considered vital.

Jack Wyndham, who was the chairman called for a minute's silence before opening the meeting so that everyone could have a moment of calm to get the subjects on their minds in order first.

As was customary when there were a lot of newcomers' present, the members stood up in turn and introduced themselves. These were:

Dr Aubrey Morgan, Chief Medical Officer; Chock Hutton who ran the wind turbines and the power station; Phil Berry, head of the education department; Corporal Harry Fielding who, as a professional soldier, had taken over the role of captain of our defences and ran the weapon awareness courses; John Kelleher, the IT expert who, with his assistant Albert Murry-Piper, now ran the radio station; David Westcliffe, our vet, who was unable to attend not having passed through quarantine yet; Mike Murphy, who ran the largest farm on the island, and Ken Fawcett, who kept the water and sewage plants operational.

The last person of any note was Claire Blackwater. Former deaconess, psychiatric social worker and now midwife and specialist in traditional herbal remedies. Above average height and build she gave every impression that she was not a person to be crossed. She reported that there were twelve newly confirmed pregnancies and seven new babies on the island. Five girls and two boys. This brings the total for the year to date to 150, which is slightly above the pre-emergency average. Her consultancy rooms are open to any woman who has any problems or would like to drop in just for a chat from 10 am onwards unless she gets called away. She went on to say that the artificial insemination clinic would be opening shortly and would appreciate it if there were any men in the audience willing to donate sperm and that she was looking to recruit three more helpers to be trained in Ai procedures. Anyone interested should call in tomorrow.

She sat down to a murmur of conversation from the public and some of the less involved councillors.

Jack Wyndham tapped the table with his gavel and called for order. Each of the other members rose in turn to give a brief update on their departmental activities, mostly lists of things.

"Before we bring this meeting to a close, I should first like to introduce you to our latest councillor, Mr Peter Marsh. Please stand up, Peter."

I did as bidden.

"As I have said many, many times in the past, our life here is not just a matter of producing as much food and as many children as possible, important as these are. We are the custodians of civilisation and it is our duty to protect and preserve as much of it as humanly possible. Works of art, certainly, but also books and music, sheet music scores, records and CDs, as well as the instruments and equipment that make such things possible.

"Peter Marsh here is collecting together as many works of fine art as he can lay hands upon and storing these in safe storage in the island's prisons, and all things considered I don't think that we can get any more secure than that do you?"

It was a rhetorical question and it raised a ripple of laughter. He continued.

"We had planned to lay on a small musical event in a couple of months but someone amongst us has assaulted our star performer who as we speak is fighting for her life in the infirmary. Not content in beating a small woman nearly to death he stole a very rare violin. Not a Stradivarius perhaps but only an expert could tell the difference. So if you can, keep your eyes open for this please.

"Were we not an island I would have sworn that it was not one of us that could have perpetrated such a vile, mean and cowardly thing. If you can't get in touch with me contact Mr Marsh or any councillor in a hurry. That's all. Please have a safe trip to your homes. Good night."

"Tell me, councillor, how do you like being a part of the government?" Josie asked as she slipped her arm through mine as we walked down to the car park.

"O Ho! Just you wait and see what I have planned in my forthcoming legislation. Steak and kidney pie three times a week, with spuds and fish and chips every other day with suet pudding and custard with every meal, and er..."

What I was about to say was something witty about unbridled sex but checked myself just in time. Had I not done so Josie would have started on about finding me a second wife, and I didn't want a second wife. Just a bit more carnal enthusiasm from the one I already had. What we had together was pretty good when she was in the mood, but that was not always when I was. Whenever my mind thought of such things I inevitable ended up thinking of Miranda Palmira and after years of practice I always managed to put her back in her box because if I did not I would end up drinking again. Instead, I thought of a large limewood carving I had seen on one of our scouting trips and wondered how we get it to the island without damage. But no such luck. Josie squeezed my hand.

"What do you think about that Claire Blackwater," she said quite obviously probing for a reaction.

"Oh I don't know. I only just met the woman tonight. Seems to have a certain natural authority. Was a man once upon a time I imagine and had the op to cut off her whatsit."

"I'll cut off your whatsit if you carry on like that. I think that she might be a good friend to have and I shall take Alice along to see her tomorrow."

"What for? Alice don't need a shrink. What Alice needs is for David to come home even if he is firing blanks."

"He might be firing blanks." Here she paused and drew breath. I almost knew what was coming, "But you are not. If you would, I wouldn't mind one bit. I know that you find her attractive. I knew it that day on the beach when you took yourself off a bit sharpish and got stinking drunk."

"Darling, it's not a question of me finding her attractive or you minding or not. It's just not my idea of, what's the word, fidelity I suppose. It is not something I could be comfortable with. What if it came between you two? What if it became between us? No, my dear, for lots of reasons like that, a relationship with Alice is not something I can live with, not now and not ever."

Everyone was fast asleep when we returned home. Josie opened a fresh tin of drinking chocolate and added a measure of rum into mine. She was forbidden on pain of death to ever pour malt whisky into anything except a glass. She put a recording of Chopin on the radiogram and through the hiss and crackle I was taken back to the Royal Festival Hall all those years ago when it was a pay-day treat for Sonia and me. Money was tight and we could only afford the cheap seats, but they were memorable days before the rot set in.

I am sure that I had only closed my eyes for a moment but when I opened them again Josie had already turned in and was fast asleep when I entered our room. It was still dark when I awoke. The bed beside me was still warm. As almost always in the morning I awoke feeling in need of my wife. I had dreamed that I was in a lifeboat with Sonia, Miranda, Josie and Alice, and they were all reaching out to me with the look of invitation in their eyes, but the boat was rapidly filling with water and I dare not stop bailing or we would drown. Well it was only a dream. Just then I felt Josie slide back into bed reaching for me in a way I need not describe and was unable to resist. A man knows his wife's body in every minute detail. The soft places, the firm places, and the moist places. This was Josie at her most amorous. But it was not her.

It was like her, so very much like her but the kisses were different and more needy. My curious fingers sought out confirmation, but it was too late to do anything except continue. Afterwards as we lay there in the warm afterglow no words passed between us. Josie had engineered this. The cocoa, the rum and the Chopin were all a part of her plan. How long had she been thinking of this or something very like it? It must never happen again.

Perhaps I dropped off back to sleep. When I stumbled into consciousness Josie was beside me again, her arms around me and her lips on my cheek.

"Now that wasn't too painful now was it my darling."

Not normally stuck for words. I was lost for words.

"I want you to be very grown up about this and not make a fuss. Not look all guilty at the meal table and not go all sulky and most of all not get all Wagnarian, and start drinking and carrying on about Miranda Palmira"

175

"What could you possibly know about Miranda?"

"Darling you can't remember because you were as high as a kite. The decanter broken; port spilled all over the place. One shoe in the fireplace, the other in the yard. We found you screaming, in tears and talking to the motorcycle about her. Whatever she did to you, or you to her and that poor girl Sonia I have no idea, but it is all over. You live in a different world now. You are a different person now. We all have to grow up sometime. I saw Alice smile this morning for the first time in ages. That at least should make you feel a better person and don't forget the pact you made with Professor Wyndham. The commitment to the future. Your household has now truly expanded, and you should be proud. I am. Alice is a wonderful girl and you have made her happy. Now stop moping about like a schoolboy, and get up and shower. Mrs Kirby will have the breakfast on the table any minute now."

I showered as instructed but did not stop for breakfast and quietly left the house. I felt that it would be better if I were away for a couple of days. When I returned everything would, I hoped, have returned to normal.

Roger Reynolds, one of the scavenger team, was pumping up one of the tyres on a Transit Luton and called out to me as I crossed the yard.

"Nice surprise waiting in your office, boss," he laughed.

I had asked him not to call me boss, none of the others did but I suppose that it was a deeply ingrained habit.

My two new assistants had arrived.

One of the assistants met me in the corridor carrying two cups of tea. Reynolds was quite right, this was a surprise. Tall, almost six feet tall, over half of which was composed of slim legs which even the clumsy hiking boots which she wore could not disparage. Her hair was long and blond, naturally so, I would surmise under the present circumstances. When she moved it was with the effortless languor of a young perambulating giraffe, head high, confident and daring the lion to do its worst. Men have sold out their country's secrets for less attractive women, but few for more. Certainly, this girl would not be without a husband and a family for long.

Balancing both cups in one hand she held out the other.

Such arms and hands with their long ring-less fingers and short clean nails were designed on a higher plane than this one, to be perfectly complimented by elbow length gloves and an evening dress perhaps.

"Giselle Morton. Everyone calls me Elle. I understand that we shall be working together."

I opened the door to my office. The other new assistant was standing looking out of the window and out to sea. She turned as we entered and smiled.

The next thing I remembered was being walked up and down outside between the stocky figures of Roger Reynolds and Mark Stevens.

"What happened?" I managed to say before it all came back to me.

"Easy boss, you had a bit of a turn that's all. I don't think it was a stroke or nuffink. Somefink you ate that didn't agree with you that's all. 'ere take a pull of this," he said and handed me a half empty, half bottle of whisky. It was foul stuff after the class of single malt I had become accustomed to over recent months, but it did the trick.

"Roger. Please convey my apologies to the girls in my office and tell them that I shall re-join them in half an hour or so. I must take a little walk to clear my head. Can I hang on to that bottle? I will replace it with a full one mind."

There was a time. A lifetime ago, when I strongly believed that every chance, happen-stance and encounter had a deeper meaning from that which was apparent from the surface. It was as though somethings were simply meant to be, and that even the not so pleasant events had a didactic purpose. Milestones on the road to a fuller understanding of the human condition and the evolution of the soul. Sonia was one such milestone and Miranda a lighthouse. Sadly, it was a lighthouse whose reassuring beam was not destined to be my salvation but reserved for others. The rocks upon which I floundered, I shall call extant reality, their dark presence knocked all such comforting delusions clean out of my head or so I believed for a very long time.

I walked about a mile in one direction then turned and retraced my steps. I cannot say that I saw my second new assistant for more than a moment or two before passing out, but it was enough to turn the clock back years. It was as though Miranda Palmira, wherever she might be now, in this world or the next, had lined up a doppelganger to dance upon the rotting bones of my sanity or to drive home the lessons I had previously failed to learn.

Short with close-cropped dark hair, a figure that no doubt she was never particularly proud of, deep soulful eyes and the sweetest little mouth set in a round face which was but a skilled caricature of an angel. I made a little bet with myself as I walked back to the office. I bet myself that her favourite composer was either Sibelius or Mahler and that she had a fondness for red shoes. I cursed myself for a bloody fool in the most vulgar and foul terms I could think of. Swore that I would never make the same mistake twice, that I should never have made once not in a million years. Nevertheless my heart which usually took its cadence from the tick-over of my Norton or the long case clock in our hall was beating like a road drill and nothing I could think of would restrain its impatient rush to self -destruction.

I finished the whisky and slid the bottle into the recycling bin before I entered the yard. I nodded to Roger Reynolds, and walked through to my office where Giselle introduced me to her friend.

I was right about the red shoes.

"Hello again Mr Marsh, allow me to introduce my friend Amanda."

For a moment I thought that I had actually fallen victim to the virus and that everything of recent memory was but the dreams of a man in a coma stuck in a fever ward some place covered in wires and tubes attached to a computer, but computers no longer worked. Did they? Or was that also a facet of the dream?

Amanda. Who but a man in a dream could have come up with a name such as Amanda, which sounded so like Miranda.

She held out a hand. I wanted to press it to my lips and swear that this celestial game which had held me in its maul for so long had at last run its course, but sense prevailed and I shook it gently.

"Toska," she said. "Amanda Toska."

This thing we call life had to be someone's idea of a joke.

Were Miranda and Amanda one and the same person? Did they exist independently or were they assembled on a quantum level from components that had lain dormant in my conscious mind since the first moment of waking?

How real are our emotions and feelings anyway? Like a blind man walking through rush hour traffic, we think that all is well because they belong to us, a guide to understanding our world, helping us to decipher the good from the bad and filling in the gaps between the hard stones of reason. They are our emotions, we say, because they belong to us when it might be equally true that we belong to them. How often is it said that we do not choose those we fall in love with. We see as clearly as sunshine the foolish love choices made by others but never our own. The crime, and I am sure it is a crime, is that emotions have the power to suspend the intellect.

The lover's paradox is that flaws can be spun and elevated to the status of virtue. Common sense ignored and prudence discarded.

By a supreme act of will I kept a distance between us over the following weeks, although she was constantly on my mind or never far from it.

I was quite at ease with Giselle Morton. She would join me on our scavenging missions out into the Hampshire countryside where there are many wealthy properties holding treasures well worth preserving. She had a great eye for quality and a feel for antiquities which might have earned her a sterling reputation and a salary to match in any of the well-known auction houses in London or New York.

For the time being at any rate I set Amanda to compiling a catalogue of the things we had saved to date. I could foresee that very soon our collection would outstrip the space available in Parkhurst and Albany combined and began to look at the other large buildings on the island.

From time to time I found myself thinking, "What will Patrick Tradescant make of this when I talk it over with him?"

Patrick was one of my oldest friends and a student, in a small way of business, of Carl Jung. But Patrick had left England for America in pursuit of his own holy grail just before the cyber bomb exploded, and for all I know was lost when the plane on which he was travelling dropped out of the sky, its controls frozen.

Although all modern aircraft have back-up systems they are also just as susceptible to the sort of complex computer virus that John Kelleher described to us on that first day. I hope that he made it over safely even though he was not built for brawling over a loaf of bread with gun toting New Yorkers.

I told myself that what I needed was a large shot of down to earth common sense, and for this I invited myself to Chock's house for supper; a visit which would also give me an opportunity to meet his numerous wives.

For reasons never discussed Josie never took to Chock.

His grease monkey image or his forthright manner might have had a lot to do with it. It was to be sure a class thing, not that such things would have mattered to either if there had been any empathy between them. He didn't care one way or the other except as far as it might affect our friendship. He only spoke of her in less than respectful terms once, when he referred to her as the great snow queen. I could see how from his perspective this might appear to be the case. Even with me she could be very imperious sometimes. The invitation to join Chock and his wives for supper was gently, but firmly declined. She had, it transpired, already agreed to spend a few days with Claire Blackwater and other women of The Albion Sorority at an isolated inland farmhouse. Quite a gathering I was led to believe. Members included Alice, Mrs Kirby, and numerous others; about twelve in all.

As I left the house to make my way to Chock's house she kissed me and said, "I hope that you won't mind

181

losing your assistants for a few days, but I have invited Giselle and Amanda to join us."

I grunted something in reply as I pulled up the collar of the big fur overcoat I now wore in cold weather, or at night. As the Norton pulled away from the house, I wondered what could possibly be cooking, what was seething and bubbling away beneath the outwardly calm surface of her mind? It perplexed me more than was proper and I nearly lost the machine on a sharp bend in the road.

His house was well set back from the highway, and mature azalea bushes lined the drive up to a large modern structure with nearly as much glass as masonry.

My arrival had been expected and his whole household were in the large hallway to greet me. Seven wives, an attractive housekeeper called Mrs Trent, and three children. Francis, the eldest and I supposed his number one wife, introduced me to everyone whose names I instantly forgot.

"Dinner is nearly ready. I hope that you like lamb stew and dumplings, it's my husband's favourite?"

I could have said that over the past few years I had eaten lamb until it came out of my ears and would rather eat carpet but said nothing.

As it turned out it was not too bad. Thin slices of lamb with most of the fat removed, marinated overnight in brandy and sweet spices followed by bread pudding made with apples in place of dried fruits with a rich cream sauce laced with Cointreau.

After supper he and I drifted into the snooker room and pushed the balls about with no great skill or enthusiasm before moving into the library where, with full glasses, we sank into matching Charles Eames Club chairs.

"Chock," I said. "Some of your wives look awfully young, little more than children. Do you think that it's right to be taking advantage like that?"

"Ha," he replied. "Yes, Peter, they are young, but it is not as lascivious as you, and others, might make it out to be. For a start the younger ones are wives in name only. That surprised you, didn't it?

"Yes, but even the others must all be under the age of consent. The tall skinny one can't be any older than my Susan, and I would shoot anyone who tried to drag her off to fill up a gap in his seraglio."

"Peter, you have it all wrong. None of these girls were dragged off, as you put it. On average one girl a week turns up on my doorstep asking to be taken in. They fully understand what is expected of a wife. They learn all about everything at school here.

"When we were at school, we learnt all about reproduction from the example set us by tadpoles and rabbits and were left to work it out for ourselves. Here at this point in time they get hands-on experience in the classroom or gymnasium. That's Greek by the way and it means to exercise naked."

He topped up my glass which was suddenly empty.

"You talk about the age of consent. Now that's a moveable date on the calendar if you like.

"In 1275 the Age of Consent was set at twelve by statute and was not raised until 1875 when it was raised to thirteen; two years later it was raised to sixteen where it had been ever since until the disaster overtook us. In the first French Constitution it was set at eleven, and in America it can be anything from twelve to eighteen. Its thirteen in Japan and in South Korea it's twenty. Meaning that you could have been arrested for sleeping with your wife had you found yourself in that country.

"All I am saying, Peter, is that sexual relations with the young are culturally determined and not absolute. Any girl wishing to enter into a domestic situation such as I have here must first be cleared by the doctor. Anybody harming a girl against her will is likely to find themselves abandoned in jeans and T-shirt some place in the New Forest on a winter's afternoon. Not only that but my housekeeper, Mrs Trent, would skin me alive if I harmed a hair on the head of any of her chicks and very likely I would wake up one morning with bits missing and no ready replacement. What I have built up here, what I have worked so hard for is a kind, happy and gentle environment for all who come under my protection."

He fell silent for a long moment before adding, "It may or may not be believed but I love them, all of them and I would die to keep them from harm."

He had obviously gone into his subject in some considerable depth and when viewed against the awfulness of the world outside of our perimeter and within the context of Professor Wyndham's plan, which we had all signed up to, to breed some new life back into a civilisation hanging on by its fingertips it was perhaps no great crime and who knows future generations might even find it commendable, but if not it was for them to decide.

"Every age has its taboos, Pete, some are more enduring than others."

"Really," I said not particularly interested and took another mouthful of brandy, but I can't say I tasted it.

"Solomon," he continued, "had 800 wives of all ages shapes and sizes."

The Chock of old would have seen that I had had enough and was within an ace of dropping off to sleep.

"By what I have read recently, God tolerated this behaviour but did not approve."

"No," I said but my eyelids were getting heavy. "I thought that you didn't believe in any of that sort of biblical stuff."

"I don't, Pete, but there is an object lesson in it for us. But it's too late now for the world we knew. You are old enough to remember that homosexuality was illegal. In a spirit of liberal toleration, it was decriminalised. Which is fair enough as far as it goes, but tolerance was interpreted as approval and you could not subsequently turn on the radio or TV without hearing some wet, whining creature spouting on about this or that. The BBC was the worst. Some sort of legacy from Lord Reith whose own personal morality was perhaps questionable. Do you know, I bet you don't, that sodomy still carries the death penalty in twelve countries, and is illegal in another seventy-four and is it any wonder? HIV-AIDs has carried off 35 million people worldwide. That's more than the total population of Australia, New Zealand and Norway with Malta and Luxemburg thrown in for good measure. The so-called gay plague makes Hitler's holocaust and Stalin's purges look like a bee sting at a picnic. Just think what we could achieve as a country with a fraction of that number, and here we are debating the age at which girls ought to become part of a family so that Jack Wyndham can save a little of our civilisation with a base line of 100,000."

By this time, I was drifting in and out of wakefulness and now can only recall snippets of his homily.

"Won't even get past the gate here."

"If they do the chances are, they will fail the medical and be turfed out."

185

"An unwholesome and unnatural practice by any standard."

"Bloody cheek to call their spineless mawkish sentimentality love."

"Even the bloody Prime Minister a few years back was proselytising on their behalf."

"The country was on the way down the sewer even before the cyber-attack. Still, might have been worse."

I had wanted to talk to him about my problems, but we had drunk the decanter dry and it no longer seemed the time and place to unburden myself. There was only a slim chance he would understand anyway, but he was my oldest friend. I rose to take my leave but stumbled. He stopped me dead in my tracks.

"Do you have a death wish or something, Pete? You have nearly a bottle of brandy on board plus the wine you drank at dinner, and you propose to ride home on a motorcycle. Can't you hear the rain pounding on the windows? It's bucketing down out there. You are sleeping here tonight and no arguments. You're half asleep already."

They put me up in a small cosy room smelling of lavender, and I was asleep as soon as my head hit the pillow.

I may have dreamt it, but during the night I felt the warm soft comforting presence of a small body beside me. It may have been Mrs Trent, a wife, or a child bride. I never moved to enquire and when I awoke in the morning she was gone.

After breakfast I rode to the office through intermittent rain showers where I sorted maps for a few hours and targeted a large country house for further investigation, briefed the crew and called it a day.

Susan greeted me at the door with a hug and Ruby our cook-housekeeper fried sliced potatoes and eggs for me and made a pot of pine needle and mint tea. There was still a substantial quantity of real tea to be had. At least one entire warehouse full of the stuff, but I wanted to see if I could get by without and set a family tradition at the same time.

One of the problems I faced at work, and these were the sort of problems I could usually handle, was that as our search radius increased so did the area of countryside we had to investigate and the number of properties containing material for our collection increased in proportion. This was brought home to me when we broke into Pyefort House, south of Winchester. Compact, modest by the standard of some English country houses, it was originally built in Tudor times and variously modified, reconstructed in the neoclassical style in the 18th century and at the time of that evolution had sat four square in excellent proportion to the surrounding parkland. However, sometime in the eighteen sixties someone had been wealthy enough, and ill-advised enough, to add extensive wings to the buildings east and west sides with a further smaller brick-built extension to the north.

The hall, the major rooms, and the staircase showed us that the masterly hand of Grindling Gibbons had been at work. Everywhere there were fine limewood carvings in the ornate style of the period. In my excitement, I squeezed Amanda's little hand which I ought never have done for she returned the squeeze firmly. She looked up at me with eyes which said, 'This is ours. Our own special place.' Which spun a cobweb of imaginings in my head for my mind had to wade through into the here and now, or I would have been rooted to the spot never wishing to leave.

After endless introspection and tormented soul searching, I still had no idea why I found Amanda and,

187

before her, Miranda so fascinatingly attractive. Her words, her gestures, like the one I have just described, her smiles and quaint demeanour of manners and dress ran like a silver ball in a pinball machine ringing bell after bell before escaping the flipper fingers and disappearing from sight until the next go around.

We wandered from room to room, her with her little notebook and me with my hands in my pockets, whilst the heavy mob who drove the van and did all the lifting wandered around the outbuildings or sat drinking tea brewed in a gillie kettle.

If I were ever to write my autobiography, I should have to call it, "Life in a cleft stick" which would cover just about every facet of my existence on this planet to date. There was no way that I would allow this building and its precious array of carvings to just sit here until nature reclaimed its own, rotting timber and reducing blown plasterwork to its basic dusty elements. Nor, given the resources available to our community, would I be able to remove all or any of the interior without damage.

Our workmen were, to be sure, a little disgruntled that we had made our way this far through overgrown byways. Moving fallen trees and skirting flooded areas to return empty handed and I was determined that we should not. We secured the building and moved off. There was, I seemed to recall, an industrial estate on the outskirts of Winchester a little way off the beaten track and decided to see what it had to offer. Most of the units were of no interest to us at all, containing cardboard packaging materials, computer hardware, or plastic garden furniture. The sort of things we were glad to leave behind in the ruins of the old consumer society. Amongst the other units we discovered children's clothing, wines and spirits, tinned speciality foodstuff from Poland, and the last unit contained industrial work-wear and protective clothing, so we took a good stock of these before heading home.

The road back was always easier than the road out for obvious reasons. We had had to clear the road on the way out but had a fairly straightforward route for our return.

I sat in the leading van with Jumbo Jones the driver and leafed through an edition of the National Trust Guide to houses of interest. It quickly dawned on me that the job of saving for posterity the country's treasures was far beyond the resources at our command even if I had a dozen vacant prisons at my disposal.

A vague plan was beginning to form in my mind, and I would have to give the matter more thought before running it past Jack Wyndham. There was no idea of how he would respond and even if he gave it a positive reception it still had to go before the council.

Being the lead vehicle and relatively lightly loaded we were pulling ahead of the others until there was perhaps half a mile between us.

Jumbo was not the greatest conversationalist, responding in monosyllables or grunts to any enquiry about his interests or his private life. There was a story there in his background somewhere and I was not particularly inclined to delve into it. He was a good worker and as strong as an ox. At least as strong as any two men anywhere but quite careful, gentle even when moving works of art.

He suddenly braked rather harshly and drew air in between clenched teeth. What he had seen in the road less than fifty yards ahead was a pack of some thirty dogs attacking a grey mare and her colt. It was an unfair contest. The colt had a dog tearing into a leg and went down as we looked. The mare was not giving in so easily. One dog lay writhing on the ground, its back broken. Another received the full force of a kick from a hind leg which sent it flying while a third went down pole-axed by a blow from a fore hoof. In a second, we were out of the cab, Jumbo with a shotgun in one hand and a crowbar in the other. I had a

189

pump action shotgun and let off three shots in rapid succession and had the satisfaction of seeing two dogs drop immediately and a third whelp in pain. I fumbled to reload while Jumbo lined up his target.

We were too close for any of the shots to miss now and he knocked over two with his first shot and blew a leg off a third with his second. By this time, I ought to have been reloaded but I fumbled and the cartridges slipped from my fingers and fell into the roadway. I reached into my jacket pocket for others, but too late for they were upon us. I kicked one squarely in the throat and Jumbo lay about him with his crowbar and I heard at least one blow find its mark on a canine skull. One large Alsatian-type dog leaped for my throat, but I knocked it aside with the barrel of my empty gun. Wearing my heavy motorcycle boots I hardly felt the bites of dogs that fastened themselves onto my legs. Jumbo screamed and fell over and they were on him. I kicked my way clear and as I did so the rest of the pack emerged from the undergrowth by the side of the road. I found the presence of mind to shovel three more rounds into my gun and blasted away at the dogs tearing into Jumbo's large frame. By some animal sixth sense they knew that three shots was all I had. They paused for just a fraction of a second before turning their attention to me. Flailing about with the empty gun I felt the barrel connect with at least one skull before I was overwhelmed. I threw up my arm to protect my face and a dog bit deeply into it. I had never known such pain, and with fear turning my guts to water I could feel the fetid breath of another in my face. My gun gone I punched out, but it made no impact. Suddenly I remembered the Bowie knife with its razor sharp twelve-inch blade which I carried in my boot. My hand was sticky with blood, my own. I lashed out, firstly slashing across its nose then brought the blade up into its chest. It collapsed instantly with a slight twitch. My troubles were not over. Another fiendish hound sank its teeth into my side. I thought I was about to die but rolled over pushing the body of the dead dog between us. It earned me just a moment's respite which was all I needed. The other vans in our convoy had caught up with us and with blaring horns bore down upon the melee. Screeching to a halt, there were soon half a dozen men with shotguns, axes and crowbars running to our aid. At an unspoken command, the dogs silently vanished into the undergrowth. Compared to Jumbo, I had escaped lightly. It was clear that he was not going to make it. Thanks to Jack's foresight everyone was given training in first aid, and as I was being patched up they tried to make Jumbo as comfortable as possible.

He took a few sips of cold tea from the Thermos which had been laced with spirits and called for me.

I had to lean right over his prostrate form to catch his words.

Even then his words were faint barely audible.

"Sorry, Pete. It all went wrong. I panicked. I didn't mean to harm the bitch. Do you think God will forgive—"

I had not seen it before, but there really is a shadow of death that passes across the face as the spirit leaves the body. I stood up and leaned back against the van.

"You OK, Boss?"

"Yeah, get me a drink will you. There is a bottle under the dashboard."

He brought it and I took a long swig. I never needed a drink so much in all my life.

"What did he say, Boss, any last words?"

"Nothing really, just gibberish. He wanted to know if God would forgive him for killing the dog. Was he a dog lover by any chance?"

"No idea. I don't think that he loved anyone or anything. Don't wish to speak ill of the dead but he was a miserable bugger most of the time with no time for anybody. Liked his drink though, but never shirked when there was work to be done."

Our conversation was cut short, though we had said all that could be said about Jumbo Jones, by Colin Barnes leading the mare towards us by a rope halter.

It was a magnificent dappled grey which would add greatly to our bloodline. It might have been imagination, in fact I am sure it was, but her eyes seemed full of sadness for her lost colt.

I called the men together.

"If someone will drive me to the Stock holding farm, David Westcliffe the vet in charge there will patch me up and send a loose-box back for the mare. It might be a good idea to find a quiet spot to bury Jumbo. Make it deep enough to keep the dogs off. Say a few words if you wish, I don't think that he was at all religious but do what you think best.

"I don't think that the hounds will be back, but keep your eyes open, keep your guns handy and loaded. Nobody to wander far away from the vans. See you all soon."

"Hello Peter, what have you been up to? You look like the dog's dinner?" said David as I nearly fell out of the van, my legs like jelly. Delayed shock I suppose.

Between the van and his office building I must have passed out for when I awoke it was full dark. I was in a bed smelling strongly of carbolic acid. A small girl with rosy cheeks sat reading by the side of the bed. She lay aside her book. It looked heavy and technical although I couldn't read the title.

"Good book?" I enquired.

"No, Mr Marsh. Not good but required reading. Mr Westcliffe is going to set a paper for me on veterinary practice sometime soon now. I really want to pass. I'll never know as much as Mr Westcliffe but—"

Hello, I said to myself. This one has a crush on the boss, or I am very mistaken? I went on to wonder if he had recovered from the blow on the head, he received at Windridge Farm, which had stolen his ardour.

"In one way, Mr Marsh, it was a good thing that you were dead to the world when you came in. We don't have any anti-toxin or rabies vaccine, so we deep cauterized the puncture wound with carbolic. Not a pleasant experience if you are awake."

"Did you get that from the book?" I asked, only half seriously.

"Standard practice, Mr Marsh. Sometimes we use permanganate of potash, but we haven't got any."

"Thank goodness that you didn't use something of which you don't have, not none of no how."

"Mr Marsh, I do believe you are trying to tease me," she laughed.

She had an interesting face if not attractive by most standards and the smile lit it up most satisfactorily.

"Is my driver still here?" I asked.

"No David, er Mr Westcliffe drove him back in the horse-box to collect the mare. He should be back shortly. He gave your man a note for your wife. Josie is it?"

I nodded. She silently disappeared, only to return minutes later with two tablets and a mug of hot milk.

"What's this?"

"Something to help you sleep. Now be a good boy, take your medicine and let me put out the light."

"Yes nurse."

When I awoke it was with feelings of nausea and dizziness. David was leaning over my bed holding up a thermometer to the light while his assistant hovered in the background.

"Well what shall we do with you old friend? If you were a horse, I should put you down. Temperature of 102, pulse racing like a Ferrari. All I can say at this time is that things will get worse before they get better, Peter."

"That's the good news. Now give me the bad news doc."

"You asked for it. If the fever doesn't break in three days, it's curtains for you old boy."

"Oh," I said. "Well I did ask, didn't I?"

"You did, but you ain't dead yet. We do have a few things on our side. One, you are a big strong healthy chap in the prime of life.

"Two, you are in a clean warm environment where you are in receipt of the best medical attention on hand. Three, we shall see that you get plenty of high energy food and drink and if that is not enough my capable little assistant Helen will say her prayers especially for you. That can't be bad can it? She never prays for me."

Helen, already rosy-cheeked, blushed. David, old boy, I remember thinking, you must be blind or incapable not to see that this little muffin has the hots for you. But if his fire has gone out what's to be done.

"So we just wait and see, is that it?"

"To a large extent, yes, but I have written to Dr Aubrey Morgan, who has Peggy Smith - the microbiologist – on the staff at the quarantine centre. They will have samples of your blood by now and may have some suggestions. Life without antibiotics is what it is all about from now on, Peter. As a last resort I have a witch's brew of stinging nettles and foxglove in alcohol."

"And you think that this jollup will work if all else fails?"

"Well I wouldn't bet my life on it."

"Just bet my life on it."

"Steady on, Peter. It's not an untried remedy you know. Nicki was bitten on the nose by an adder and we almost gave up hope, but Helen suggested this traditional infusion and Nicki was up and running about like a three-year-old in no time."

As it happened, I was spared this foul concoction and it was not until I was on the way home and standing by the main gate did I get to meet Nicki – a grey donkey.

CHAPTER THIRTEEN

I walked back into Jack's office feeling very much my own man once again. There is no feeling quite like it; the feeling of being just normal after a protracted illness or for that matter even a particularly bad hangover.

"Welcome back to the land of the living, Peter. For a while there we thought that we might be losing you. There is quite a lot I wish to fill you in on that's happened over the last week.

"Firstly, we managed to tap into one of the tall masts north of here belonging to the television people and up our signal strength at the same time. We kept quiet about that for a bit until we were sure who was out there, but kept up a twenty-four-hour listening watch. Only last night I exchanged signals with Sweden who are sending someone over in a fishing boat. At least I surmise it will be a fishing boat. Might be a battleship, but the Swedes are a peaceable people. Always an outside chance its Russians playing up, but we have to trust someone sometime. Let's hope for the best. Speaking of Russians, a most curious couple turned up at the main gate on the mainland claiming to be members of the Russian diplomatic service. All eyewash of course. Russians certainly. Diplomats, most improbable. They gave their names as Mr and Mrs Andropov, can you believe. She speaks quite good English, him almost none.

"She must have been quite a dish before this all started, but the years of living on her wits and his muscles

196

has left its mark on what was once a very pretty face. She moves like a dancer, he like a steamroller. John Kelleher, who you met on the induction day and who taught himself Russian as part of his job with GCHQ, has interviewed them, in English, not letting on that he speaks Russian. She did all the talking. Most entertaining by all accounts, but what John picked up when they spoke together filled in some of the gaps in our knowledge. They are not husband and wife, but were the mistress and minder respectively of ex-KGB officer and businessman Andrei Vostok who was well and truly taken to the cleaners by Jonah AKA Brian Phipps, the mad man who landed the world in this mess. I don't think that we can allow them to stay here, do you?"

"You are perfectly right of course, Jack, but you have just reminded me of the thoughts I was having before we were set upon by dogs.

"From the last place we visited I picked up a National Trust Guidebook. Very soon, Jack, our search area is going to include Petworth House which simply oozes with artefacts which need to be preserved. These things we cannot move without damaging them, and we do not have the facilities, space or skill to store them properly. Petworth is just one house, and there are dozens of others.

"My proposal is this. One thing I would ask, Jack, is that you take some time to think it over before you reply. Will you do that for me please?"

He nodded. "I can tell by your preamble, Peter, that you think that I will pour cold water on the idea from the off. I assure you that I will give whatever you say my very best consideration."

Reassured by his remark I set out my idea.

"What is our population now, 12.000 or thereabouts?"

197

"15,000 would be more exact, but a lot of the increase is down to the birth rate."

"And would you say that we were holding our own with respect to food production – animals, fish and crops?"

"Yes but I—"

"Allow me to continue, Jack." He nodded so I went on.

"The people who turn up out of the blue at our front door. What would you say was the percentage that didn't care for the system we have here, or were turned away for various reasons? Not counting the really bad eggs who would not be very welcome anywhere."

"About 2.5 % at a guess, Peter."

"That's 25 in every thousand, correct?"

"Yes, of course."

"Some of those will find life very hard going, and many may not survive at all on the mainland. Is that a fair assumption?"

"Yes, go on."

"My suggestion is that we install a few such people in each country house we would wish to preserve. We can let them have a few sheep or goats and a cow perhaps. A lorry load of firewood to see them through their first winter and some seed potatoes, corn and what have you. A starter pack in the home economics of survival.

"For their part of the compact and to ensure further deliveries of this and that from time to time they must live in the house and keep it secure, wind and weather tight. We could set them up with a two-way radio or even low-tec homing pigeons to contact us in an emergency. Being part dependent upon us they are less likely to throw in their lot with an insurgency should one happen to come along. We can still take away for extra safe keeping the silver, fine porcelain, and paintings. All things considered, Jack, I feel it would be an investment and a low-cost solution at that. Let me know what you think of the idea before the next council meeting and we can firm up on the logistics."

Just then the telephone rang, and he smiled, "Thank you, Ralph, I shall come right down. Peter Marsh is with me. I shall bring him along."

Ralph Eldridge ran the lifeboat, coastguard, and pilot boat from an office directly below Jack's. As we entered, he stood up and introduced us to Harry Wagstaff who skippered the pilot boat.

"Harry tell Jack what you just told me."

"Yes, skipper. We received a call about five o'clock this morning from a vessel heading up channel. They were not sure where they were exactly being about sixty miles out. We asked them to transmit at regular intervals so we could get a bearing. What we found nearly knocked our socks off. A whole flotilla of little ships, fourteen in all. There were only two to start with, but they picked up others on route. All from the islands off the Scottish coast. A coastal ferry from Skye, a couple of trawlers and small cargo ships which they call puffers. They came down, for the most part, hugging the coast. Not great navigators outside home waters I suppose.

"Some carried more people aboard than others but by my reckoning there are about 500. Mostly fishermen and crofters but a couple of much needed specialists. Two men who worked in the Tallisker distillery are sure to pay for their keep in no time. A dentist and his nurse. A police inspector from the mainland who got stranded on one of the islands. A weaver, two or three builders, a carpenter, a publican and a gamekeeper. We shall have a better idea when they have been booked into reception.

"At least they had the forethought not to come empty handed. Not the least of their cargo is quite a lot of vintage whisky. Some in barrels, some bottled and in cases. They should be dropping anchor off Hayling Island in a couple of hours' time."

"Thank you for that. A very concise report, Captain."

"Peter, can you get over there and bring Aubrey Morgan up to speed. Get him to call in Nurse Alison Barnes and the two girls under training as well. It's all hands to the pumps in a situation like this. In the meanwhile, I will alert all available medics to be on hand. Get the catering people into gear. Make sure that there is enough accommodation to get everyone ashore as quickly as possible. This is a first Peter, we've never had to deal with that sort of number in one go before. We must see that we have enough spare clothing and that sort of thing. Best thing for starters is to call a plenary session of the council for this evening. No time to lose. Now off you go."

I could tell by the excitement in Jack's voice that he was on edge, but he need not have worried, everything went like clockwork, then and afterwards. We found a dental practice for the dentist and a pub for the publican. Everyone else fitted in very quickly, although there must have been a lot that was new for them to get used to. When I returned home it was late. I showered in one of the empty bedrooms and crept into bed beside Josie and was asleep in moments, but not for long. Once again, I had been engineered into making love with Alice, but this time it was different. In the quiet time afterwards, we shared a single cigarette although neither of us had smoked in years.

Josie and I had been drifting apart ever since we arrived on the island although we still had every affection for each other whenever we were together. The intense energy I put into all of my projects had a lot to do with it, and the time spent away from home. Not to mention the fact that Amanda Toska was never too far from my thoughts even as I tried my best to stay away from her as much as possible.

I knew that Josie had inveigled Alice into my bed the first time and suspected that this was a repeat performance but no. This was on Alice's own initiative.

"Where is Josie tonight?" I asked Alice although I knew almost for certain what the reply would be.

"She is with Claire Blackwater."

"Did you not wish to go with her?" I asked. "I thought that you too were a paid-up member of The Albion Sorority."

"I am," she replied, "but our needs are different even if our feelings about things are much the same."

"Things. What sort of things?"

"Psycho, sexual, emotional and social. Claire has a way of making you reach down deeply into yourself and helps you to find the missing bits of the jigsaw puzzle and face up to your own demons.

"With me it was not so difficult but that's because I am not nearly as intelligent nor as complex as Josie. For years I was trying, without knowing it, to relive the life of my mother. Marry well, build a nice home, make the right sort of friends, move in the right circles. All things she wanted to do but never managed to. My father was dull, God bless him, and my mother was a snob.

"I was to be their life brought to its proper fruition. I was a prisoner inside my own head. There was just one chink of light. Only once did I rebel and felt guilty about it for years.

Did you ever hear Josie and I talk about Miss Clementine, a teacher at our school who took us for "deportment" as well as dance and drama? She was very smart and always immaculately turned out and as far as we were concerned the epitome of sophistication. Almost all the girls, Josie included, had a crush on her at some time or another. We would practice kissing after lights out, pretending that we were kissing her and that was as far as it went for most girls. But not me."

She leaned over me and dropped the cigarette into a flower vase where it hissed and went out.

"She had a flat, hers or one of her sisters, in Eastbourne, and she would pick me up in her red Triumph Spitfire sports car and we would go there, always on a Sunday afternoon and make love. It lasted a few months and we never met again, by mutual agreement I think, and my life moved on and into the mould cast for me by my mother, and here we are. You dear, Peter, are just another, and I hope final, piece of the jigsaw. Except for—"

"Except for a baby. Is that right?"

"Yes. You don't mind me using you like this do you?"

"No. why should I mind? I felt uneasy about wanting you and guilty as if even the thought was a betrayal of what I felt for Josie even though she said that she didn't mind. What are the pieces missing from her mind, I should like to know?"

"It is quite simple whilst being quite complex at the same time.

"Claire Blackwater is standing in for the experience she never had with someone like our Miss Clementine.

"Claire knows that Josie has no illusions about her feelings. Neither of them has any time for those silly young girls who take their infatuations to extremes. You know the sort; all hob nail boots and tattoos. My God, if they must pretend to be a man why not pick on someone with some style and not some underclass oik from a building site. That is not being honest with yourself, it's just play acting. I doubt if anyone with that sort of unhealthy obsession would ever get far beyond the gate at the reception area. Fancy a cup of tea?"

I lay there nursing my mind, for I didn't understand above half of this. What had any of this to do with me? If I understood anything it was that Josie had felt the need to go back into her early teenage years and relive the experience, she never had. On further reflection, I wondered if it was the same sort of thing which was behind Chock and his high school harem.

Alice returned with the teacups and slices of cake and I noticed for the first time that she was still naked. It came as a mild shock I have to admit as though I were a voyeur spying on my friend's wife, and I told her so.

"Part of your problem, and perhaps always has been, is that you are really a bit of an old stick-in-the-mud, Peter. Josie finds it a bit annoying, but I find it quite charming in a funny old-fashioned sort of way. A bit like Mr Pooter."

"Oh," I said.

"Don't look like that. There you go again. Every time you wear that expression, I shall call you Pooter."

To prove that she meant it she punched me playfully in the ribs.

"So, when will Josie fit all the bits together and put an end to this adventure? When she grows out of it, I suppose?"

"It's not an adventure, Peter. It's a voyage of self-discovery. You will know it's over when she shows you her classwork book."

That took me quite unawares.

"Classwork. What bloody classwork?"

"Claire believes that Josie has been experiencing an existential crisis which she describes as Cerebral Sapphic Syndrome.

"Something which she must come to terms with if her life is to have, for her, any meaning. Think of it as therapy."

"Let me get this straight. She has sex with this woman and writes about it afterwards as a sort of homework."

"Yes and no. The sex is just a part of these classes. There is much more to it than that. Some of the students work it out for themselves quicker than others. I did, and writing things down, memories, fears, dreams, ambitions, regrets and so forth sort of sets them in cement. Confines them to time and place whilst we move on, leaving all of that negative stuff behind. It is tremendously liberating and cathartic. You should try something like it but I cannot begin to suggest a guide who might be able to help you.

"It is obvious to me, as I am sure that it is to Josie, that you are having some sort of problem with Amanda. Would you like to tell me about it?"

"No, not really. It's all a bit too private."

"Ha! You talk about privacy, lying in the arms of a naked woman who has just tried to help you come to terms with the situation you find yourself in with your wife and now you want to shut yourself in and say it's private."

"Well if you put it like that."

It was about time I unburdened myself to someone and this was as opportune a moment as any. So I told her as succinctly as I could the ache which I still felt from the lacuna deep within me left by the disappearance from my mental panorama of Miranda Palmira, and how just when I began to feel that I had sublimated, if not forgotten, the whole episode, who should walk onto the scene but Amanda Toska. Identical in almost every diabolical dimension. From the page-boy fringe haircut down to the old-fashioned strap-over granny shoes. Red shoes at that. Why did they both feel it necessary to straighten my tie whenever we meet, or take my arm in a gesture of possession when walking down the street?

In our line of work, we collect a huge number of books. Hundreds, thousands perhaps. She kept one of these back for herself and when I saw it I nearly had a fit. It was the same book I had given to Miranda for her twenty-first birthday.

With my head resting upon her bare breast she stroked it lovingly and made soothing noises.

"I will bet that you feel that there is a plan in all this torment. That- there is a mind behind this pain, directing events and circumstances for some unclear didactic purpose and that you accuse yourself of stupidity for not being able to work it out. That you see a pattern but no logic and worse than that – no purpose. No loose thread to unravel to discover the mystery of it all at the end. How it must have hurt. How it still hurts. My poor, poor boy."

She drew a deep breath and, like a forensic detective, sifted through fact and supposition. After an endless pause she continued, slowly at first before returning to a normal conversational tone. "I will bet that reincarnation entered into your thought processes at some level."

She was right, but I dare not say a word. It all seemed so foolish a thing to have to acknowledge.

"Yes," she said, staring hard at the ceiling. "You told yourself that you and she had always been together through eons of time and many incarnations, bound together by a mystical bond of pain and torment, like Abelard and Heloise."

This was altogether cutting dangerously near the bone. Where was she trying to take me?

"And in the deep recesses of your mind's eye you saw yourself on some unavoidable quest for redemption. Wanting, needing and waiting for some incident or encounter to strike off your chains and expiate your soul offering a consummation of your unhappy heart and hers."

She snorted a laugh, which could have been cruel but wasn't.

"Just like Hendric Van der Zee, the Flying Dutchman, searching for Pandora through all the ages.

"Peter, Peter, Peter, dear Peter. In the stew of your emotions I can see many things. Profound, good things like resolve and constancy, love, faith, and a beautiful romantic melancholy, but viewed against the matrix of your real life, here on earth – it's pathetic.

"You torment yourself, that's fair enough, but that's not a licence to hurt those who love you. Oh yes, I know that you believe that you have no choice in the matter but it's not true, not really.

"I never knew her, but my heart really goes out to Sonia, and what you put that poor girl through with your boozing, Wagner and morbid introspection. Viewed objectively it was nothing but self-indulgent adolescent angst. You are too intelligent and imaginative for your own good, do you know that?"

I sat up sharply. I didn't need to listen to this, I had heard pretty much the same lyrics but with different music from Patric Tradescant. I opened my mouth to say something, but she pushed me back.

"Had I known you back then I would have brought you to heel, one way or another. Depressing was it? Well, perhaps it was my boy, but from where I stand it all sounds like the seismic aftershock of an over-romantic idealist brought down to earth with a crash and God help any bystanders caught up in the wreckage."

I could sense that she was about to get tough and wordlessly awaited the descabellar.

"You grew up too soon, many boys with your background do of course. You were a lugubrious cello before you became a violin."

It sounded silly at first hearing, but it dawned upon me that in this unusual metaphor she was right. I had grown up too quickly and had paid a penalty which might have been expected, keeping company with older people living in a world of antiques and old houses.

Jacqueline Du Pre closer to my heart than Bob Marley; Lorenzo Bernini closer than Anthony Gormley. Unbidden, the plaintive lamentations of the opening chords of Max Bruch's violin concerto seethed into my consciousness. With it came the memory that I had once heard it performed by Janine Jensen, Miranda Palmira by my side holding my hand like she meant it.

Strange to think of it now, but how alike in form and face were Janine Jensen and Alice But it was a transient and speculative observation which was quickly swamped by overwhelming sadness as I recalled the fate

207

of Anne Girling and the equally irreplaceable loss of the priceless Guarneri.

This was an Alice I had not even suspected existed. Thoughtful, understanding, and empathetic in a way I could never have imagined. I am not an emotional person, or so I often told myself, but I could not stop the tears which ran silently down my face and onto her bare breast.

We lay there for long moments without a word passing between us.

At length she said, "Sit up."

I didn't much like the tone in which she said it, fearing a telling off. I was not far wrong.

"Miranda Palmira is dead. She died in her icy mountain retreat of cold or hunger, or perhaps the virus claimed her. Probably died in the arms of some creature not fit to clean your boots. Either way it is of no consequence. She died the moment she flicked you off the surface of her life like a speck of ordure. Of less value to her than the beggars in the street to whom she might throw a few coins. To you she threw nothing but the mace of her indifference and the steel gauntlet of her silence. Had you earned her hatred it would have been a better return for your constancy of affection. Hatred, like love, requires energy but the exercise of silent indifference made no demand upon her at all. It's reception many times harder to bear and in the final analysis a thousand times crueller. How many times over the years have you thought of taking the easy way out? Millions of times I imagine, yet you are still here where you are needed. Where, as Jack Wyndham might put it, the future needs you more than she ever would."

Her words were like an ice bath. Needed but unwelcome.

"Do you accept that she is dead, Peter, and that the period of your bereavement has come to an end?"

Her reasoning was irrefutable, and I may have grunted agreement.

"Now you must prepare yourself for another shock or two. Do you have the strength to do it? Are you the man I believe you to be? The self-same man who faced up to that bastard Barney Mason and shot him dead in the gutter where he belonged."

"Yes," I replied but feeling that I could not face up to his like again. At least not in this moment but did not dare say so. A resolute grandmother with a damp dish cloth could have sent me packing with very little effort.

"You said something about further shocks to the system."

"Well for a start Amanda has no room in her life for a man. Not you, not any man. She and Giselle Morton are an item and have been for some considerable time. It is not a phase. Perhaps had it been when they were young, things might have developed differently. Had they shared a little tender passion at the right time, their lives might have reached a different balance. That is neither here nor there. They have made their commitment to a way of life and it would be improper and rather pointless were you to try to come between them. If I were to have read them right either would allow you to have sex with them. They like you and respect you and both wish to conceive. They would use you as I have just used you. But with a difference, I have known you a whole lot longer and, dare I say it, I have always been a little in love with you myself even though Josie and I sleep together from time to time. Surely you must have gleaned some idea from that day on the beach which upset you so much. I do not cavort naked before just anybody. I wanted you so much that day. Josie knew this and was a great comfort later whilst you were sitting aboard that

209

bloody motorcycle roaring drunk. Sometimes we need the love and comfort that only another woman can provide. It's the way we are.

"I make no excuses for her or myself. The love we shared, you and I just now, was wonderful and unless you plan to throw me out into the street I want to stay here with you and Josie for ever."

I pulled her towards me and kissed her as softly as I knew how.

It was all so new and very strange. Perhaps I felt less guilt this time. She snuggled in close and I wanted her again, but she pushed me away.

"I said that there were two home truths coming. You haven't heard the second yet."

I paused and drew breath.

"The only person you really love unconditionally is Susan, is it not true? The way you are going your real daughter is going to grow up without a father. As things stand there is no bond between you. I could easily believe that you have never cradled her in your arms, changed a nappy or sung her to sleep with a lullaby."

I had to admit that it was mostly true.

"You may or may not have noticed that Susan has grown up a lot lately."

"I should say I have. A regular little bean pole she has become, nearly as tall as me now. Bless her cotton socks."

"Peter, you are missing the point. Susan has turned into a young woman. She moves differently, talks differently, dresses differently, especially when Giselle is in the house. To cut to the chase Susan has an enormous crush on her.

When you are away on one of your expeditions, she stays with them."

"Well so what, lots of teenagers sleep over at their friends' houses."

"Peter open your eyes. They share a bed together. A ménage a trois if you prefer."

"But she is just a child, I shall have to put a stop to this."

"You will do no such thing. She is not a child any longer. Nature is filling up her bloodstream with hormones. What would you rather she did? Move in with your pal Chock and join his happy crew? I don't think so."

"As you say I love her. I want to protect her. There is so much sadness out there. I had hoped that one day she would settle down with a nice steady lad. Someone with prospects and a bit of get up and go. She is smart and kind and could take her pick and perhaps one day she still might."

"Just listen to yourself, Peter. You sound just like my father. Chain her to the kitchen sink why don't you. You ought to know that there is only one man of any interest to her and it is someone she can't have."

"And do you know who he is? I should like to have a strong word with him. A very, strong word. If he has touched her, I will break his bloody neck."

"Would you indeed. He's a killer. An adventurer. He climbs up roof-tops to fix things and rides a motorcycle. He gets drunk sometimes and comes home in a disgusting condition swearing and plays Wagner records in the middle of the night. Yet she won't hear a word said against him because her love for him is deep and beyond reason. She knows that he loves her too, and just for him she would move in with any Tom, Dick or Harry if he just asked it of her. Recognise him?"

The penny dropped.

"This is all a bit much for a bear with very little brain. I need a drink."

"Not at this time in the morning you don't. Go and shower while I cook breakfast. While you are eating it and thinking on what I said I will take my shower and together we can start to reclaim the bottom half of the vegetable garden."

How I was going to stop worrying about Susan's emotional life or how I could possibly adapt to two such freely loving women as Alice and Josie, I had no idea but like so many things in life that are radical, unacceptable deviations from the norm they soon become mundane as though things had always been ordered in such a way.

Having no better idea than patience I let things rest, hoping upon hope that one day I should come to terms with the situation in which I found myself.

CYBER BOMB

CHAPTER FOURTEEN

It was the savage death of a child and the grievous wounding of those who ran to her aid in what was supposed to be a relatively safe area that finally moved me into action against the packs of dogs which were becoming an ever growing menace.

The survivors of that attack reported that the dogs were getting smart. Whilst one group attacked and killed little Jane, another larger group formed a defensive ring around the killers to prevent interference.

About six miles inland, and away from the main road we found a large fallow field overgrown with weeds and wind-blown saplings and surrounded by tall hedges. About fifty men turned out to clear the field and to ensure that the hedgerows were sufficiently stout for our purpose. The single gate into the field was reinforced with barbed wire and chain-link fencing.

For several weeks the butchers, who were also slaughterhouse men, were instructed to retain all the offcuts and left overs of their trade, although there wasn't much, we found a use for just about everything, but they were instructed to keep what there was in the deep freeze.

Early one crisp sunny autumn morning our various convoys set out for their start positions.

There were seven cleared roads which led to our main entrance.

People who for one reason or another lived on the outside were told of the plan and advised to stay indoors and keep a strong-armed guard over their livestock.

At the agreed hour and position, the trucks were to turn around and head back towards the cleared field dropping bones, blood, and offcuts over the tailboard as they went.

Overlooking the gate to the field was a row of ten workers' cottages, and these we commandeered turning the first floors into a pillbox with two men armed with rifles at each window.

I had expected that a hundred dogs might have followed the trail of blood. As it turned out there were over a thousand in the field growling and snarling over the heap of bones in the centre, or roaming the perimeter for the sheep which they could smell and hear but not see, which were safe and under guard in an adjacent field.

I blew my whistle and the Ford van edged forward pushing the gate until it closed. For fifteen minutes all merry hell let loose.

To my right Andrew West, his hands still in bandages from trying to save his little girl Jane, was blazing away like a thing possessed, but not hitting much. To our left two Royal Marines were making excellent practice firing with cool deliberation and calling out each target to one another. "The big black one on the right, head shot."

"Result. Now watch this. The Alsatian getting into the pile of bones. Going, going, gone."

"Let's see if I can't get two with one shot."

214

He did too. Caught one high in the spine, with the bullet passing through to catch a dog standing to one side squarely in the throat.

It staggered about a bit before it fell.

I fired as calmly as I could, aiming where they were bunched up in groups. I cannot say how many I killed that day, but I fired and reloaded until I ran out of ammunition.

The boys positioned at the gate were having great fun blasting away at any dog in range. They would learn this day that the recoil of a twelve gauge will leave a blue reminder on their shoulder which they would not forget in a hurry.

When it was over, we moved with contagious, breathless lethargy as we bent to pick up the spent shell cases amid the pungent smell of burnt cordite. There was a stillness in the air to which the distant rumble of thunder only added an emphasis.

The slamming doors of the vans seemed louder than usual and fanciful as it may appear, disrespectful.

By this time tomorrow a million, million flies and bluebottles will have found this place. Carrion-eaters of every sort will congregate here in good fellowship, as on the battlefields of antiquity. There was plenty for all at the table we set this day.

The first heavy drops of rain sounded like a funereal drum on the roof of the van; a fitting punctuation to end the day's enterprise. We had well and truly paid them back for their assault on Chris Leather, Jumbo Jones and me, but there was no sweetness in the revenge.

In a year or two, or perhaps a decade, when we came to reclaim this land from the wilderness, nothing

215

shall remain except for a few bones to be ploughed under and then how today's red rain will let the harvest grow.

On the way home we saw smaller packs of dogs fighting over the trail of offal and bones we had left in the road and I made a mental note to run a rematch in a few months' time.

It was late by the time we had returned the Enfield service rifles to the armoury and helped Corporal Wingate clean and stack the weapons. In my office were several bottles of Jack Wyndham's Special Brew. I drank two before reading the handwritten label, which read 6.75 ABV which is about a potent as anyone could wish for in a beer and I was asleep on the office bench sofa in moments.

It was dawn when I surfaced with a surprisingly clear head but smelling of cordite and gun oil. I could smell blood too but convinced myself that it was imagination. Either way I needed a shower and a change of clothing. The Norton started first kick, as always, and I was home in minutes, cold and ravenously hungry.

The smell of frying bacon, sausages and mushrooms pounced upon me as I went through the front door. The shower and shave would have to wait. Josie and Alice were in the kitchen and with a conspiratorial exchange of glances which I didn't like by half, told me to take a seat at the dining table. This in itself was unusual; we normally ate a working day breakfast in the kitchen.

"Well what are you waiting for?" said Josie.

"And when you have finished eating, we have something to tell you," added Alice.

"Tell me now, is it something important? No. You must tell me now. I insist."

Not the best choice of words perhaps to use with either of them.

I dare say that I should pay for it later.

"My God you stink. Eat first and you can regale us with tales of the great safari later."

"*Ondoka haraka pace-pace. Kufanya kama nasema-Bwana.*"

I recognised it as Swahili although I didn't understand a word except Bwana, but everybody knows that.

I didn't know Alice spoke Swahili, but there was so much that I didn't know about either of them. Feeling like an unwashed schoolboy I wandered off to the dining room. I felt even more out of place seconds later. Seated round the table were Susan, Ruby Kirby our housekeeper, Amanda Toska and Giselle Morton, my two assistants. Amanda smiled as I entered with just the sort of smile which drove me crazy. The sort of smile which should have been reserved for a long-lost lover, which I wasn't, and knew that I never would be. Giselle grinned weakly and I knew that she too was a part of the conspiracy I had stumbled on in the kitchen.

She made a play of eating her bowl of home-made muesli, but she clearly had lost all interest in it. I felt that it was my appearance which had stolen her appetite.

Whatever it was they had to tell me they obviously felt that I would need a hearty breakfast. The words "full English" would not serve to describe it. Josie set it down gently. The plate was piled high with sausages, eggs, mushrooms, fried bread and tomatoes. There was toast in a silver toast rack, and an unopened jar of Oxford marmalade and English mustard. Bringing up the rear Alice brought in a pot of fresh coffee and a cream jug, also silver. The coffee was a rare treat which we reserved for Christmas and special visitors these days.

There was no way I could swallow a single mouthful in this atmosphere. I stood up and was told to sit down.

"You have to tell me what is going on. I haven't eaten for ages and I can't eat until you tell me. Now come on, this is getting beyond a joke. Tell me what's wrong."

Once again that conspiratorial exchange of glances, but this time they all shared it.

Josie stood up. "I hope that you can handle this but it's good that you are sitting down."

She paused and I found that I was holding my breath.

"I'm pregnant," she said at last.

I breathed a sigh of relief. I could live with that no bother.

"Me too," said Alice.

"So are we," said Amanda, "both of us."

"And that goes for me too," added Ruby.

I looked from face to face. Susan had begun to colour with embarrassment though she knew all about reproduction from her rather *avant garde* school lessons and her work with horses.

"Don't look so embarrassed, darling, soon now you shall have a whole lot of new brothers and sisters."

"Oh," she said drawing a deep breath. "Then they will be company for when I have my baby."

"Yes, darling, but that won't be for years yet. Will it Josie?"

Josie and Alice, Amanda and Giselle and Ruby gently shook their heads.

I was cross now and the blood lust was up. What bastard had been taking advantage of my little girl. I turned to Josie.

"Do you know about this? Who is he? I'll kill him."

"Oh yes, I know him very well."

"So, do I," said Alice. "Please don't kill him."

"He's the father of my baby too," said Ruby.

"And ours," added Giselle.

The eggs were congealing on my plate. Everything else was getting cold. Well this guy certainly got around. Susan was little more than a child and Ruby must be nearly forty. I meant to have it out with this monster. "OK who is he? He and I have to have one serious talk and soon."

"Oh, darling you should see your face and listen to yourself.

"Any minute you are going to hold your hand up to your forehead and point to the door and say, "Get out and never darken my door again" just like a Victorian father in a melodrama, or the painting *The Outcast* by Richard Redgrave. "Hudson fetch me my horse-whip, I shall thrash the bounder" Really darling. Do you really want to know who this cad is?"

"Yes, of course I bloody well do. Coming round here when my back is turned, creating havoc with my family. I shot a man once who dared to do that."

219

"So, you did and we are forever grateful. Aren't we girls?"

Clearly, she was enjoying tormenting me like this, they all were.

"It's you, you goose. These are to be all your children."

I slumped back in the chair.

"How, er, when, I never and I certainly never went—"

"When you were unconscious with the fever they asked for my permission to take some, er further samples and I agreed.

"You were milked my darling, twice a day, like a prize bull. Now isn't that flattering? Alice and I have no secrets, we had our quota delivered direct from the factory gates so to speak whilst the others had to go and collect theirs from Nurse Alison Barnes's fridge freezer. Don't worry. She is not going to run out any time soon. In fact, just from your donations alone she says that she could repopulate Belgium. Now wouldn't that be nice?"

"But Susan," I stuttered. "She is just a child, she can't, she mustn't."

"She wants to be close to you, her hero, and she wants a baby. Who else do you think she would let anywhere near her? Apart from you all men are carbon copies of her abusive stepfather, Barney Mason. She feels ready. Her body tells her she is ready. Dr Morgan gave her a thorough examination and passed her as fit and as her surrogate mother I gave my consent."

I am pleased when I think of how it turned out now, but then it was as if my world had turned upside down and as if I were suddenly a guest in my own home. A stray thought wandered into my head at that point. How soon would it be before women outnumbered men on the Council? They outnumbered men in the community already but were politically quiescent at the moment.

Sooner or later they would wish to take the reins of power unto themselves and how would that fit in with Jack Wyndham's plan to save civilisation? Perhaps we were in at the conception of the world's first matriarchal civilisation. I wonder how it will turn out.

A week or ten days later I was given something more pressing to worry about than the problem of widespread consanguinity a couple of decades hence.

The first of the carrier pigeons arrived. A gang of perhaps fifty men had stormed into the grounds of Trebrabon House murdering everyone in sight, shot the ducks and chickens at ridiculously close range and decapitated a swan. Finding no drink in the house they set it ablaze.

In my mind's eye I pictured the ornate staircase, hand blocked wallpaper and plaster moulding knowing that these things could never be replaced.

In council we were reasonably confident that as many of the houses we wished to preserve were located some distance away from main roads they had a half decent chance of escaping destruction. Even so we managed to get word out not to make smoke, keep their livestock close and prepare a safe laying up place deep in the woods to which they could retreat should the need arise and stay there until the storm had passed.

We had no real fears for our own survival. Everybody had received some training in the use of firearms although not everyone was a marksman of any competence, even the worst shot could chamber a round and, pointing a gun in the right direction, loose off a few shots.

A defence subcommittee was set up and detailed plans made to defend our mainland perimeter and our island.

CYBER BOMB

CHAPTER FIFTEEN

The equinox was upon us and the evenings becoming introspectively dark.

At home the talk was almost exclusively of childbirth and babies. In one way I was pleased of course and flattered but the thought of having so many children under my roof all screaming for food and drink at the same time or fractiously howling at the appearance of new teeth made me want to howl myself and seek out male company, old friends and new projects.

Pulling together enough people to form an orchestra was more difficult than I would have believed but we did it in the end. We also regularly hosted lectures by volunteer speakers which were well attended for the most part. Bee keeping, ceramics, brewing and metalwork were some subjects covered and I could easily understand why a group of isolated survivors would wish to learn about such things but not about the Congress of Whitby, quantum mechanics or ancient history.

It was during just such a talk by Jack Wyndham in which he expounded upon the curious concatenation of circumstances which resulted in the total collapse of civilisation in the Far East and the Mediterranean at the height of the late Bronze Age about 1177 BC. One by one he discounted drought, famine and internal unrest as the probable cause. He was about to come to the arrival of a mysterious group referred to in ancient writings as "The Sea

People". These it would appear were not empire builders or colonists but out and out destroyers and plunderers but who they were and where they came from and where they subsequently went remains an enigma as they left no visible evidence behind in the form of records and artefacts to mark their passing. I could not help but wonder what some far distant civilisation would make of our abrupt decline almost to the point of extinction.

Just then, with spine chilling prescience, Lance Corporal Bell tapped me on the shoulder.

"Excuse me sir. If I might have a word. It is important?"

"Yes OK," I replied wondering what was up. "Be right with you."

I collected my heavy coat and gloves and moving as quietly as possible followed him out into the foyer.

"OK Mr Bell what is so important that it needs to disturb my study of Minoan history?" I spoke with irony, but it was lost on him.

"Sorry sir but we've caught one you see, and the sergeant thought that you would want to be informed right away."

"Caught what? A killer shark, a dose of the clap or a rare butterfly?"

"No sir, a savage, a marauder. The enemy." This I had to see. We had been made aware, almost since the beginning, that there were gangs roaming the countryside, but we were confident that we could easily defend ourselves against a rabble. One Royal Marine was more than equal to a hundred undisciplined delinquents.

They might terrorise small settlements and set the Royal Pavilion in Brighton ablaze, but we would be a harder nut to crack. Or so we thought.

"Now calm down," I said, though he was pretty calm already, "and give me your report as we walk."

"We was patrolling just outside our outer perimeter, about five klicks or so having just dropped off some sacks of flour and crates of tinned goods to some of your funny fellows that you've got house sitting in Westleigh Court. Much too good a place like that for that sort of scum. What my Ellen would say if I was to say pack up darling, we are moving into a stately home. I bet she would have a fit but ..."

"Yes, very interesting but stick to the point please."

"Yes sir, sorry sir. At one-point Sargent Williams in the lead lorry pulls us over. Walks about a bit and says he can smell smoke. Well none of us could nor the civvies so we parks up and gets a brew on the go. We could all do with a cup of tea but when an old Jolly like the Sargent gets spooked you don't ask silly questions or hang about. We checked our guns and made ready to move off. To the civilians he says "Look, might be something or it might be nothing but set your lookouts, you know the drill, points of the compass and not too far out. Keep your shotguns handy but don't fire a shot unless you have to. No point in giving away your position for the sake of a pheasant or a rabbit. We don't know what's out there yet. Check your watches. If we are not back in two hours don't dawdle waiting for us but clear out quickly and report back to Mr Marsh. Got that? Two hours. Tell him that I had a creepy feeling and went to investigate. That's all. Don't embroider, just keep to the facts. Now carry on."

He drew a deep breath.

"We set off at a steady trot moving in extended order. After a couple of miles, we could smell burning too. What a

225

nose that man has. We thought he was making it up to start with, but somebody definitely had a fire going that's for sure. From about fifty yards ahead he signed for us to halt with a hand signal. He and I went forward alone, very cautiously, off the road where it was too obstructed or broken up. From a clump of trees on a small hill we looked down upon a roundabout where the road we were on joined a larger one. In the middle of the roundabout someone had built a large bonfire which had burnt itself out though it still smoked a bit when the breeze stirred up the ashes.

'The area was surrounded by litter. Beer cans, bottles, broken crates and other rubbish. Must have been one hell of a party sir with six bodies laid out, in amongst the grass and weeds all with horrible wounds. Crows, rooks or magpies were hopping about, I can't say which, I'm not good with birds except robins and jays of course and pigeons but ..."

"Yes, yes, get on with it please, never mind the bloody birds, this is important."

"Yes sir. ' Well, well, well,' he said handing me his non-standard binoculars. ' Picnics were never like this when your old sergeant was a boy. Quite dull by comparison, lukewarm tea from the thermos and sardine sarnies, with your auntie being travel sick.' I thought that he was rambling sir or talking to himself like, but the cunning old bugger was taking it all in every inch of the surrounding area, Every sight, every smell and every sound. I took a very close look at the bodies. One had his head right off. One was still alive or I'm no judge. He snatched the glasses from my hands."

"Bring up the others. I'm going down."

"Ain't procedure to go in alone," I said but all he said was "Just you sod off and fetch the others, at the double."

"The bloke was alive al-right but only just. Right old state he was in. A great flap of flesh hanging off his head

226

like an envelope. Broken leg and a gash a foot long on his chest. An amateur did that. If you want to kill a man you stab up, under the ribs see. Stab down and the knife just skids over his rib cage unless you're lucky and he ain't. Still we packed him up in field dressings and brought him back here and left Archer with him to see he behaves his self and don't run off."

"Not much danger of that with a broken leg."

"Not that exactly sir but the sarge thought that his gang might have followed us in and feel that he ought to be finished off like, case he told us something they might not want us to learn."

Well that was his story which ended as we pushed through the doors of the infirmary. The doctor when I found him was a new face to me but as people were turning up in ones and twos all the time that was not surprising.

The doctor; who looked about twelve and was called Alan, shook his head the way that they do whenever they have bad news to impart. Builders and garage mechanics have a similar system of non-verbal signals. Sighs and sucked teeth.

"Not long for this world and not much I can do for him. We set his leg and stitched up his scalp. I have closed up the knife wound on his chest, but it was very dirty, someone had smeared excrement in the wound if I am not mistaken. Blood poisoning almost certainly already and gangrene before long no doubt. Given the resources he would live but, and the council is very firm on this, our own folk first and last, with children at the top of the list. I don't have the supplies you see. Most of our antibiotics came in from Europe and we were so uptight about Brexit, hardly matters now. Not in the least."

I could see that he was turning over in his mind's eye everything that might have been. With that faraway look on his face he drifted off. I sent the marine off to scran and drew up a chair by the bedside. Over the next few hours, he drifted in and out of consciousness. Some of his ramblings were about a woman called Liz and the things he would do to her. All a bit earthy I suppose but not unexpected in the mind's eye of a man on the brink of death.

I dozed a little from time to time, I was ageing fast but awoke with a jolt when he screamed.

"Where's ma bling. They took it. King took it. I get even."

The bed rest and sleep or the rehydration and glucose, of which we had lots, brought him round and what he told me turned what was left of my hair grey.

His name was Derek, but his street name was Boot and until he fell out with a character called Ruben, was a member of a multi-cultural, multi ethnic gang calling itself The Spiders.

Ruben claimed to be Nigerian Royalty and liked to be addressed as O'King.

He was going to lead them to a land of milk and honey. He told them that it was God's will that he should do so. This was his way of keeping his followers quiet for there was considerable unrest as the pickings became ever thinner. He was going to take them to Hal-be-on and although there were factions that refused to believe such a place existed, he would refer them to their radio sets where they could hear Radio Hal-be-on for they selves.

A land of milk and honey. That was us and they had their sights on coming here to plunder rape and destroy. Well bloody good luck to them was my first thought. We had more than enough fire power to handle any undisciplined gang of thugs. What could be their numbers? Fifty or a hundred. Two hundred at the most armed with knives, machetes and a few guns picked up here and there. I wanted to get a better idea of their number.

I gave him a pack of Dunhill cigarettes and a cricket lighter as I asked gently and probed for information even suggesting that a bottle of vodka might be possible. It was hard to make out his words sometimes but what he told me was this.

About forty mechanicals and about the same number of motor scooters with perhaps a hundred on foot, making their way as best as they were able. This tallied with what I had imagined and felt pretty safe that we were more than a match for this rag-a-muffin army. I probed a little deeper.

I wanted to know more about what he called the mechanicals. I thought that they would be no more than recycled luxury cars loaded up with drunk and dope smoking layabouts. But that was before he told me, and the ice finally cracked and gave way beneath my innocent and optimistic feet.

A mechanical unit was a lorry or large van mounting one or more machine guns, and sometimes heavier armament and about ten men together with their women, ammunition, and rations. Rations which were running short in all the areas swept over by the gang. They were killing and eating all and anything they could catch. Dogs, wild sheep and birds of all sorts went into the pot even a badger was considered fair game.

A blue bottle landed on his face with a view perhaps to staking a promising provisional proprietorial claim to a maggot nursery of considerable potential but flying off was almost immediately and unprofitably distracted by a noisy quarrel with a windowpane.

It was a not dissimilar dispute, in its outcome at least, over a black cockerel that instigated the moribund patient's excommunication from the court of the king together with his supporters, motivated in their rebellion more by hunger than dogma. Just another scrawny chicken to them but to King Ruben it had other more significant mysterious nuances of meaning and foreboding. The dark gods in his dark heart cried out for retribution and sacrifice. Demands which must be met if the gods were to be propitiated in a manner sanctified by timeless custom. The ritualistic battle which followed did not last long and the bodies were left unburied on the roundabout. Although this place would henceforth be forever cursed it was insufficient to calm the king, for he too needed more blood, not to mention booty if he were to hold his tribe together. No doubt in rousing Churchillian tones, his ancestral robes billowing in the autumn breeze, he gave them yet again a taste of all that awaited the faithful in Hal-be-on just a little further down the road if only if they were patient and obedient to the signs sent by the spirits and followed him to victory.

The young doctor re-entered the room with a cup of tea. "Humm", he said as he let fall his patient's hand having felt for a pulse. "I will make a small bet with you Mr Marsh that he will be dead before you finish your tea," and on that engaging thought left for other more pressing duties. He was right though for I left the tea untouched. I had other things on my mind just then.

Seeing no purpose in prolonging the interview I rose to return to the island but before doing so I put through a call on the red telephone to our clerk – administrator to convene an emergency meeting of the full council without delay and accept no excuses.

I had no real military experience outside of the books I had read but it did not take a Wellington or a Montgomery to realize that we were vulnerable, at least on the mainland. I did not know what sort of General this King Ruben might make but my guess was that if he did not storm the main gate he would seek out some weak spot on the perimeter fence and burst through there. In the years before my arrival Jack and his friends had not been idle. In addition to clearing the area of cadavers they had strung a strong perimeter fence and put in place a very flexible plan for tactical defence of the mainland position. The perimeter itself was but lightly held for behind this were armed sections, a sort of mobile reserve which were able to quickly move in to contain any breach. Should this fail to succeed to contain matters there was a larger central reserve to call upon for assistance.

At the council meeting I gave an outline of the moves with which I proposed to counter the attack when it came. Apart for some details these were pretty much as had been anticipated. It was easy enough to shoot at the intruders from prepared positions overlooking the perimeter; we did not need to employ our trained marines for this. I suggested that the marines chose their own ground outside the wire where with their long-range Barratt rifles fitted with night vision scopes, they could take down their targets with impunity. At distances of about a mile or more they would not even hear the shot that killed them.

With a narrow-slit trench dug about ten-foot-wide inside the main gate and covered over with thin sheets of plywood we were as ready as we would ever be. Any vehicle trying to force its way through would be brought to a crashing halt as its front wheels dropped into the trench and come directly under the fire of the machine gun concealed in the Mister Whippy ice cream van.

Before we broke up and went to make our individual arrangements Jack Wyndham caused considerable unrest and heated debate by stating that there were to be no prisoners taken.

His logic was, as usual, flawless even if some people thought this to be barbaric and cruel in the extreme.

Holding up his hands for silence he explained his position.

"Ladies and gentlemen. Please be very clear about this. We are not in a position to hold in secure accommodation in quarantine an unknown number of men who would have to be fed and guarded twenty-f o u r hours a day for an unlimited period. Even if only a few escaped, their capacity for mayhem would be considerable and perhaps totally ruinous. We have no valid method of sorting out the evil element from those who were just drafted into this malevolent army by cold, hunger or other circumstances.

"They all have had their choices and have run wild for a season. This was the outcome of those choices and for them the bitter end of the road. Should we in the name of humanism, just send them packing we would never know when they might return, reformed and rearmed. As it is, we live on a knife's edge. All of our tomorrows hang in the balance. Our margin of survival could be taken from us at any time by any number of events, but this was one event we can have done with here and now, once and for all. Killing a young man who is perhaps already wounded is a hard and unpleasant thing to have to contemplate but we have no choice in the matter. It is harsh but far better to cut out this cancer now than have it fester at the very root of our community, our civilisation and our future."

He was right of course, he generally was, but I wanted to further the debate by saying - even a woman, but the devil held my tongue. I was not sure that I could shoot a woman myself but as it turned out I never had to.

Without doubt some of the women were little better than slaves dragged out of their hiding places and taken along with the group, but Jack was adamant.

I reasoned slightly differently. Any girl who had the fortune to escape from the fire-storm which awaited them might well find sanctuary with the outcasts in some grand house to make of that situation what they will. There they would at the very least be fed and free from further molestation.

With observers, one marine and two civilians positioned on all the approach routes and equipped with a sniper rifle and an off-road motorcycle to relay intelligence we were ready.

The first shot to be fired at nearly a mile arrived before any sound and punched a neat hole in the radiator of the leading lorry which erupted in a blizzard of steam and hot water. It was pushed off the road and another vehicle took its place but fifty yards later its front near side tyre was hit by another high velocity round.

Corporal Swinton chuckled to himself in the quiet way that special forces operators do.

"Now what else Bill, eh?"

A large man pushed aside the other drivers who had stepped down to see what was going on made his way to the head of the column.

"How about giving him the good news corp?" He said having picked up some military by-words suggesting that the corporal ought to shoot the man in his sights.

"Nah, I've a better idea, evil bugger that I am, watch this. Now keep your eyes on the jerry can strapped to the wing of that lorry. Got it?"

He gently squeezed the trigger and a second or two later a ragged hole appeared in the can spraying petrol in all directions, much of it over the large man standing in front.

"Now if this were the movies that can would have exploded in a ball of flame but it doesn't happen in real life."

He worked another round into the breach.

"If some clot down there starts shooting the whole lot will go up."

Before he could fire again the petrol mixed with air exploded.

"Oh dear me, some naughty boy been playing with matches. Probably lit a fag to pass the time."

With his next five rounds five men died and never heard the shot which killed them.

"They are all under cover now and more difficult to hit. I will stay here until I run out of ammunition. You hop it back and report to Mr Marsh.

"Tell him that they will pass on this road and will sweep around and go in via these two routes. I have marked them on the map for you. Don't lose it. I will cut through these woods over there and block the road by Fords Farm right on the bend by the humpback bridge. From there they will have to reverse back for about half a mile on twisty narrow country roads.

"Should take them a month of Sundays. One of those monkeys is sure to drop an axle into a ditch, bring a wall down or hit a tree. Now off you go. If I can't get back safely, I will go to ground ap LUP Alpha or Echo until I can do so."

I received this report whilst in the armoury as the marine on duty there dished out ammunition. I thanked him and went to check on the perimeter defences for the tenth time and was fairly satisfied that even if they should force a passage, we had enough fire-power in secondary supporting positions to halt any assault. Everything depended on what sort of general this Ruben turned out to be. Although I knew that one should never underestimate one's opponent; that is exactly what I did.

For the next three days nothing happened and the only report from our patrols was that the savages were drifting north and taking their time about it. Even so we remained on high alert with trip wires connected to hand grenades set every evening about a mile down the road and taken down at dawn.

The attack when it came was at lunch time. Groups of twenty or so attacked the perimeter fence at either end with heavy duty wire cutters and a lot of shooting and yelling. It was an expensive feint for they were slaughtered. When the shooting died down a lorry with its radiator protected with logs and loaded with bricks crashed through the main gate

followed by others packed with well-armed men. The brick lorry came to an abrupt halt as its front wheels dropped into the trench we had prepared and was hidden from sight by a few sheets of black painted plywood which instantly gave way The load of bricks shifted with the sudden stop and crushed the cab of the lorry and the men inside. Three men died immediately but one continued to scream and moan until at last one of his own comrades shot him in the head at close range. An act of mercy for which he was no doubt eternally thankful.

The fire fight lasted for less than half an hour. At a rough count we had killed about one hundred and fifty at a cost of none of our own. Our only casualty being Ranjit who did good business selling curried dishes from a small eating house on the waterfront. He had tried to get a better shot by holding an automatic pistol with both hands as he had seen detectives do on television. In his excitement he held it wrongly and when fired the slide recoiled and smashed the top knuckle of his thumb.

Very slowly my brain began to work on the things I had just seen and what I knew of Ruben's army. This attack represented but a fraction of the forces under his command. Would there be a follow-on assault whilst we were disorganized and congratulating ourselves on the splendid show we had just put up.

Whilst I tried to work out what might be the next move a breathless messenger arrived on a bicycle.

"The red phone, the red phone, the red phone," he gasped.

I wanted to slap him to calm him down and get his report in clear and unhurried language. Unable to do that I shook him a couple of times by his lapels.

"Boats, hundreds of en, heading for the island. Thousands of men with guns."

I knew that there were not thousands of men but even so. Ruben was a better general than I thought. Not only did he launch a feint attack on the main gate but even engineered feint attacks to cover that assault to draw our forces away from the island, the real target.

Neither I nor anybody else had imagined an amphibious assault from the sea.

My mind must have been swimming in cement for it was some seconds before it dawned upon me like a thunderbolt that my home and family were on that island. My house full of pregnant women and girls near their time. My god, household helpers and the nurses and the senior midwife.

Everything I loved or valued was to be at the mercy of these criminals.

For the first time in all that had happened and all the things I had witnessed I felt frozen in panic and fear. If you have never known real fear you can never understand but if you have, you will know how hard it is to stop from soiling oneself. I didn't but it was a close call.

It took but a few moments to give orders to make good the defences and to rally a few Royal Marines to my side. One was to come with me the others were to get as many armed men as possible over to the island. I might have said shoot first and worry about it afterwards but that would have been to waste time. Everyone knew that we had but this one last throw of the dice to save the precious remnants of our world so carefully garnered here over the past years.

It would in truth be better to die here and now than try to survive in the world which Ruben and his like would leave behind if they were triumphant.

We chose a cabin cruiser with large twin outboard motors which thankfully started at first attempt. We never checked the level of fuel in the tanks. If there were sufficient to get us there it would be enough.

At full throttle with the tide against us it seemed to take forever to cross the Solent. The harbour was full of small craft, mostly just abandoned to float where they will. It later turned out that with typical clear headedness Jack Wyndham had organized an effective improvised defence centred upon Chock and his gang of engineers and mechanics. With a solitary machine gun and various small arms, they effectively took the impetus out of the main assault.

Turning away from the harbour we made our way round to run aground on what I had come to call my private beach. Once again, my stomach clenched into an unrelenting ball when I saw that two large power boats had arrived there before us. I was over the side before the engines had been cut and landed up to my waist in cold water. Half running half stumbling I made my way up the cliff path, unavoidably thinking of our first picnic there and everything which followed. There were tears in my eyes I am not ashamed to say. If this scum had harmed anyone, they would die most horribly for it or I should die in the attempt. In the top garden three of the attackers lay dead half on the grass and half in the dirt of the flower beds.

With a gun in each hand I ran through the front door, Private Carpenter close at my heels. He fired, so close to my head my ears rang and a stranger, his hands full of roast chicken paused for a second too long before reaching for his pistol. The blood from the wound in his neck sprayed over the chicken. Without a doubt the seagulls who would eat it later when it was thrown out into the yard would neither know nor care. Private Carpenter sidled over to the kitchen door kicking the corpse in passing in time to see two figures making a hurried exit. He took a snapshot at one which missed but hit a tin of baked beans which he was carrying. It exploded like a histrionic and petulant rose sending outwards dripping crimson shards of tin, one of which caught him in the side of the head tearing an eye from its socket. He dropped his other booty and staggered out into the garden followed by Private Carpenter shooting from the hip. In that moment I heard the unmistakable sound of a pump action shotgun chambering a round. I turned to see two men. One dressed in ornate flowing tribal robes holding a pistol in one hand and an African fly whisk in the other.

"Shall I kill him O' King or would you like to do it?"

So, this was the dreaded King Ruben. A gifted general he might be but in the final analysis he was just another cruel dictator seeped in blood and destruction.

Just then there came a scream from upstairs quickly muffled.

"You kill him or have fun with him if you wish it is of no consequence.

"I have other more interesting things to do upstairs. These are his women you may be sure my friend. Better not kill him yet until he has seen what a king may do. Bind him."

From his belt he pulled a length of cord. Where on earth had Private Carpenter got to?

In the very second that he moved towards me a shot rang out and the hand of King Ruben that held the fly whisk disappeared in a froth of blood followed a split second later by another shot which caught him full square in the face.

That was all the distraction I needed for I turned on my would-be jailer and hit him in the throat with my rifle. Before I had a chance to chamber a round, he twitched and lay very still. I must have hit a nerve, or a pressure point or something. Whatever, I put a round through his temple at short range to be certain.

I was about to breathe a sigh of relief when the shotgun which claimed the life of King Ruben fell from small hands and clattered down the staircase. At the half landing stood Susan one hand at her swollen tummy.

"Hello Daddy. I enjoyed that. He reminded me of Barney Mason. I think that perhaps I should go and lay down now. All this excitement. Gun shots and worry. My waters have broken. Help me into bed please.

"And when you have done that send Zhara in to see me. Oh yes Mummy has something to show you."

What sounded like a full clip of ammunition and a couple of single shots rang out from outside in the garden.

"That's the lot sir, well round here at any rate. There's still some shooting going on somewhere, but I can't say where exactly but it doesn't sound like much. Mopping up most probably."

With Susan resting on top of her bed I kissed her lightly on the forehead then as the nurse Zhara entered I made my way along the corridor to my room.

Alice sat in a low upholstered chair with a baby at her breast and Josie sat up in bed with a baby cradled in each arm.

"Hallo darling, had a busy day at the office? I've been pretty busy myself. Would you like to meet your boys?"

I did not need the use of words to answer. My mouth was too dry in any case. I just beamed.

"I thought that you would like to call this one Bill and this little one Jack. How would that suit you?"

Finding my tongue, I replied "It suits me very well. Yes, very well indeed. Turning to Alice I ran a gentle finger over her baby's head.

"And what are we going to call this little fellow?"

This was the moment she had spent so many frustrating years looking forward to, her face bloomed like a peach. Peaches and cream indeed with pure happiness.

"If it had been a little fellow, I thought about Ruben or Rex something like that, but you don't like those names do you?"

I do now, I thought to myself with the self-proclaimed King Ruben stretched out on the hall floor never to rise again shortly to be dumped well offshore with the rest of his evil gang.

"But as this one is a little girl, I thought that we might call her Miranda".

I gagged a little with surprise, but she knew everything of course. I had no secrets any-more, not in this house at least.

Her eyes met mine. She smiled a secret smile of conspiracy which lit up her whole face. She reached out a free hand to Josie.

"So that whenever you think of her or hear the name Miranda spoken it might be with visions of the tremendous happiness for the future which we all will share together and not endlessly dark sad memories, regrets and self-recriminations that exist only in the distant past. Imaginings, things long since dead and gone. Ghosts that no longer have it in their power to distress and torment us. Don't you agree?"

I agreed.

CYBER BOMB

POSTSCRIPT

It has now been fifteen years since the world staggered blindly into the Silicon Valley of death and here on the Isle of Wight civilisation is hanging on by the skin of its teeth.

Jack Wyndham, whose foresightedness gave us one last throw of the dice, died peacefully at his home on his 83rd birthday naming me as his successor as president of the council although this has yet to be ratified by the full assembly in plenary session. The population of the island now numbers thirty-three thousand with perhaps another thousand or so living on the mainland. Undesirable heretics Jack would have called them, all those who refused to buy into our agreed plan for the future and those whose chosen lifestyle preclude them from taking part. Some of these outcasts are living in our historic buildings cleaning out the gutters and cutting the grass in return for enough supplies from our farms to keep body and soul together. If they want any more, they must contrive to secure it by their own efforts, and to be honest quite a few do.

Although I am hard pressed to remember all their names I find that I am the father to twenty-seven children whose mothers I know and perhaps many more as a result of the artificial insemination programme. It is the strangest feeling to move around the island and see in fresh young faces features which remind me of my parents' generation. That boy there I might say to myself, spitting image of Uncle Jeff when he was a boy or Aunt Kitty who stood beside him in the same old photograph.

Three years ago, the Council began charging, in gold artefacts for the more exotic items of plunder. Brandy, cigars, designer clothes and the like. This did not present a problem for most people as gold wedding rings might have been picked up at any time whilst we were removing the island's cadavers, and later, as the area in which we scavenged increased these had been used as informal tokens of barter for some time. A year later we began to mint our own gold coinage. With milled edges and officially called a pound, they were generally known as a Jack from the head of Jack Wyndham on one side and bearing the words. SERVICE-SACRIFICE–SURVIVAL. The reverse showed an outline map of the island, with the words

"NEW ALBION Civilisation shall prevail".

I had expected quite a debate about there being Jack's head depicted but there was none. On the reverse there was quite a bit of competition for the inscription. When it was put to a vote I proposed "VECTIS EX OVUM PHOENIX" but this received very few votes.

"ET SI RECUPERET" about the same and "JOHN 12 – 24" none at all, which was, I felt a lost opportunity to link the past with the future. The reasoning behind the adoption of a gold standard currency was that we had to have an adjudicator to sort out some of the bargains between the trades people and farmers. Such transactions are fairly easy to sort out if it's a question of so many eggs for so much shellfish, but what is a tooth extraction worth, or a pair of special boots? Much of what was done or provided was mostly in the free and easy spirit which prevailed in the beginning. When one has been spared from an almighty cataclysm one is less inclined to be hard nosed about the mundane business of living. The gold coinage not only made transactions more uniform and regular but also sent the message that things were at last getting back to normal and the weekly market became something of an event. The more adventitious yachtsmen had been putting into European fishing ports for some time, but it was not until we found that the Belgians had huge stocks of coal that we needed to offer them something more portable than sheep in exchange. Once a year we would import a shipload of coal and usually a few migrants as well. In this way we acquired a confectioner, an optician and a gunsmith. Jack's dream of one hundred thousand in one hundred years looks more than possible now.

Our radio station now transmits on two frequencies at two power levels. One at fairly modest power for local consumption broadcasts, local news, popular music from the decades before the crash and helpful talks on everything from the best way to raise runner beans to serialised classical novels. The more powerful transmitter can, I am told, be picked up in New York or Rome.

This transmits mostly classical music, it being reckoned to be more civilised, international, and non-threatening.

In the event, however, that there are groups out there with territorial ambitions, we have two hundred men with experience of life in the armed forces who meet and exercise regularly and almost the entire population have received some training in the care and use of weapons. If an enemy should come we are ready to meet with them, but I hope more than anything that they never do. We have seen enough death and despair to last a hundred lifetimes.

One unexpected bonus resulting from our international radio broadcast was the arrival of a full-blown sailing schooner from Norway with a cargo of a complete, if reduced in numbers, orchestra. We have at least some excellent musicians of our own to fill the gaps. Our own idea to put on live concerts had faded with the murder of Annie Girling and the loss of her priceless Guarneri violin.

After the Norwegians arrived an island-wide search was organised to find the missing instrument. It was found amongst the possessions of Jumbo Jones who had been ripped to pieces by dogs. I now understood his final words of, I hesitate to call it contrition, about killing the bitch.

We are now totally self-sufficient in beef, lamb, poultry, dairy products, wheat, barley and vegetables of all kinds. We brew our own beer and are experimenting with distilling spirit though from my own experience I should not like to call it whisky.

Jack Wyndham had set himself, and us, a target of being able to stop the slide back into ignorance and savagery by adopting the lifestyle of England at or about the year 1900. We are not there yet but as families sit down to their New Year's dinner and children open their festive gifts, mostly home-made, before roaring coal fires we have every reason to feel that the future is considerably less than bleak.

THE END

CYBER BOMB

EPILOGUE

Unable to substantiate any charges against Andrei Vostok, Galina and Zoran were released at the same time, Andrei Vostok swearing in the basest Russian that he would find and extract the cruellest revenge upon the body of Brian Phipps. Inspector Cummings saw him off the premises via the heavily fortified front door and in the mocking sardonic tone which CID officers practise so frequently said, "What are you going to do now Andrei? Your money all gone. Your American Express, Diners and all other cards useless. You are in deep shit my friend with not even a pot to piss in and it couldn't happen to a nicer chap. Now on your way sunshine."

Turning, and with a wicked and totally false smile on his face, he came back with, "I started with nothing; I might have nothing now and shall start again. I still have a network of loyal and powerful friends." He turned his head as if to confirm the fact that his closest associates were standing by him, but Galina and Zoran were nowhere to be seen. They had slipped out into the early evening rush hour crowds and he was never to see either of them again.

It started to rain as he left the Paddington Road Police Station. He still had just enough money in his wallet for a taxi home but there was not a taxi to be seen.

It was a long walk to his West Kensington flat and by the time he arrived there he felt that every pore in his body was clogged with grime and traffic fumes. Only the thought of his welcoming apartment, a hot shower, and a glass of champagne from the fridge kept him going. Unused to walking, he soon developed blisters and he hobbled the last few hundred yards like a crippled geriatric.

Galina and Zoran will come crawling back he thought, and then he would punish them, but he was never to get the chance, they had gone for good. Brian Phipps he would run through a bacon slicer. First one hand and then the other. There were any number of ways Brian Phipps would die, but like a contrite Galina and a pleading and humble Zoran, this too was a pleasure he would have to forego.

The front door to his apartment building was protected by a state-of-the-art computer-controlled entry system. Within its memory were dozens of thumb-prints and retinal scans, but amnesia had struck, and it refused to recognise his and remained mute and inoperative. A neighbour from an apartment on a floor below his left the building in a panic and he slipped in before the door closed. The lift too was less than cooperative, and he began to climb the ten flights of stairs to his own door.

Before he had taken possession of the property he had Messrs Kemp and Brasted, Security Consultants to royalty, replace the standard door with one of tempered steel laminated with Kevlar into a highly resistant barrier with just a veneer of limed oak for the look of the thing so that it looked just like any other door in the building. The frame too was of an equally impressive specification and the electronic lock was a direct copy of those used in the most secure offices in Lubyanka.

It was all too perfect.

Nothing but a thermic lance could reunite him with his shower and refrigerated champagne. Not to mention his wall safe with his last line of defence consisting of several thousand pounds, 500 gold rubles and a customised Yargin-Pya automatic pistol.

Disconsolate he left the building and walked into a damp and darkening evening.

Life out on the street was hard even for those streetwise people inured to its rigors. His credit cards worthless, cash machines were deaf to his entreaties. He ate his last civilised meal, leaving the restaurant quickly and without paying. Turkish restaurateurs are not so easily swindled, and he was chased for half a mile before the Balcan brothers caught up with him.

KGB officers, even ex-KGB officers, are no pushover when it comes to a rough house, but he was exhausted, his feet hurt, he was full of food and wine and every punch to the stomach hurt more than the last. Within minutes, that felt like hours he was bruised and filthy laying in the gutter, his Armani suit torn and marked with his own blood from a split lip which continued to dribble down his shirt front. He might have speculated in that moment that his restaurant dining days were well and truly over, but his mind did not take that direction.

His next attempt to provide for the necessities of life, such as a roof over his head, was to mug an elderly, grey haired gentleman in a side street. Had it been just any OAP he might have been in luck, but the tide of his fortune was not running with him that night for his victim was none other than Dynamite Freddy Wells, British light heavyweight champion boxer back in the day.

It was fully dark and very cold when he came around, his head spinning and at least one tooth felt as if it might drop out at any moment.

Rabin. Yes. Morris Rabin would help him to sort himself out. He had no idea where he lived but would visit his office first thing in the morning.

It began to rain harder. He sheltered from time to time in doorways and under awnings, but there was nothing for it but to press on. There was a hostel of sorts behind a church in Piccadilly; he would go there first. At the very least he would be offered a cup of tea and perhaps get the chance to have a wash and smarten himself up a bit. Unfortunately, it was shut.

The staff and helpers who usually helped out there had been unable to get in to work and those that did quickly found that there was no power to the building and the stock of food had quickly been exhausted, and with the computer down unable to re-order more.

He stood for over two hours at the doorway to Morris Rabin's office and slept there the following night, but he too was absent; at home and trying to breathe some life into his computer.

After just three days of living rough his lightweight Italian shoes had begun to disintegrate. Bareheaded and carrying one shoe he headed for the Thames Embankment where once, ages ago, he had seen a Salvation Army van serving tea and sandwiches to vagrants. His last meal had been, how long ago? It felt like forever. There was no Salvation Army van in evidence. The few people who were about, unusually few as it happens, gave him a wide berth as he stumbled along muttering and swearing in both English and Russian. How quickly the sun set at this time of year.

Cold and unable to sleep he stole a nearly full bottle of rough cider from a sleeping vagrant which he drank immediately, returning the empty bottle from whence it came.

For a full fifteen minutes it lifted his spirits and with it his lust for revenge, but the feeling was only temporary. Exhausted beyond his imagining he leaned back against a parking meter and slid noiselessly to the ground. He thought of his mother and his early life before they sent him to school, joining the army and the passing out parade.

How smart he had looked in uniform. How glowing the reports of his superiors.

With the utmost gratitude for the warmth and peace it provided he closed his eyes and embraced oblivion. Shortly thereafter, with the chimes of Big Ben striking twelve in the distance, with a good grace and complete resignation he surrendered to oblivion's sister who is death.

From the roof of the disused telephone exchange which he chose to call his wolf's lair, Brian Phipps looked out west across the Thames towards London. It had been a long, hard winter. They should be ready for him now. He could pick and choose, take this girl or that. Slap that one. Kiss another. Crush anyone who stood in his way. He had no way of knowing how the concatenation of food shortages, power failure, Corona virus and a crippling cruel winter, followed by a plague of rats and dogs had reduced the population of one of the largest cities in the world to almost zero.

There would be precious few girls to choose from.

While the world starved, froze, suffered and died, he had not been idle. Eight, and sometimes ten, hours a day he pumped iron, cycled on one machine and jogged on another. On a wall he charted his progress. He consumed anabolic steroids and ate protein rich preserved foods such as whey powder with every large meal. Vitamins and minerals were a staple. Nor did he ever forget to take a high fibre supplement, for he was obsessed with his bowel movements. It was with mounting excitement he stepped out through the rear door into the world.

He was well prepared. He carried a fully charged emergency start battery, heavy but he would only need to use it the once. In a case over his shoulder his laptop with which he could unscramble any computer infected by his very own virus. Armed with a home-made electric cattle prod he could deliver a stunning 50,000 volts to anyone, man or beast, who might wish to interfere with his plans to rule the world. In his pocket another home-made device which could produce high volume, high frequency sound adjustable across the range of 7 to 38 Khz enough to dissuade anything from a mouse to a lion. With a Gurkha kukri in his belt he felt that he was more than equal to anything the world, now on its knees, might send his way.

From the car park of the luxury Double Tree Hilton Hotel he opened and started a large new expensive sports utility vehicle.

He drove away with some confidence into the centre of Dartford where to his utter amazement he saw dogs, hundreds of them, either lazing in the road indifferent to the blare of his horn or milling about the streets. Some were fighting, some were ripping apart smaller dogs that had fallen victim to their hunger. He was not worried; he had his electronic weapons.

Just then a soft, slightly American female voice broke the silence inside the vehicle. "Phone charging."

It took him several seconds to realise what was going on.

He had reset the car's on board computers, but the phone in the glove box was still infected. Perhaps it had been switched off for some time before it had become voided by the virus, meaning it was still infected and once it had sufficient power in its battery would infect every other computer device within the range of its transmitter. Brian Phipps realised this and began a panic search for the mobile phone. He found it a second too late. The engine cut out instantly and his laptop made the strangest noise, which a more imaginative man than he might have described as a death rattle.

Here then was his problem. He could not restart the engine of this vehicle. The jump start battery pack he had left behind in the hotel car park. His cattle prod would without question stop any dog in its tracks, but there were hundreds of then. He could not shock them all at once and the batteries in the handle would not last for ever, he had no idea how long, but not long. The sound generator would clear a path through the pack, but for how long and where could he go, on foot? He might just make it back to his stronghold at a run but if he did, then what? His laptop had all the answers and now it was corrupted. Seeing him moving about inside the vehicle, some larger dogs scratched at the windows with their forepaws. He cracked the window down a fraction and gave them a burst from the sound generator. It worked, but he felt the power of it also and stopped.

The larger the animal the more power was needed to act as a deterrent. At these power levels the batteries would last not hours, but minutes. Suddenly he remembered his bowels and became agitated as well he might. An hour later he was sweating and afraid. Outside a horrendous death awaited; inside the vehicle a slower but no less certain one. He had conspired to control the world but in the final analysis he could not even control his bowels, and thus four days later the master of the world passed from this world surrounded by his enemies in a mausoleum of rusting steel .

Printed in Great Britain
by Amazon

63363481R00151